continued . . .

Cooking Up Murder

"Charming . . . A blissful who-done-it that is filled with some very funny scenes and characters who care about each other."   —*Midwest Book Review*

"The writing is spellbinding. The blend of mystery, humor, and romance keeps the reader hooked to the pages. The characters are entertaining, and it is not surprising that I find myself eager to read more about this duo. The addition of recipes in the back of the book only adds to its charm. Culinary-mystery fans will need to add this book to their reading piles."   —*Roundtable Reviews*

"A fun, quick read. A new twist on the favorite culinary mysteries."   —*The Mystery Reader*

"Light and breezy, touched with humor and a bit of romance. The protagonists are spunky and adventurous, and readers will be cheering for this delectable duo to crack the case."   —*Romantic Times*

Dying
for
Dinner

MIRANDA BLISS

BERKLEY PRIME CRIME, NEW YORK

THE BERKLEY PUBLISHING GROUP
Published by the Penguin Group
Penguin Group (USA) Inc.
375 Hudson Street, New York, New York 10014, USA
Penguin Group (Canada), 90 Eglinton Avenue East, Suite 700, Toronto, Ontario M4P 2Y3, Canada
(a division of Pearson Penguin Canada Inc.)
Penguin Books Ltd., 80 Strand, London WC2R 0RL, England
Penguin Group Ireland, 25 St. Stephen's Green, Dublin 2, Ireland (a division of Penguin Books Ltd.)
Penguin Group (Australia), 250 Camberwell Road, Camberwell, Victoria 3124, Australia
(a division of Pearson Australia Group Pty. Ltd.)
Penguin Books India Pvt. Ltd., 11 Community Centre, Panchsheel Park, New Delhi—110 017, India
Penguin Group (NZ), 67 Apollo Drive, Rosedale, North Shore 0632, New Zealand
(a division of Pearson New Zealand Ltd.)
Penguin Books (South Africa) (Pty.) Ltd., 24 Sturdee Avenue, Rosebank, Johannesburg 2196,
South Africa

Penguin Books Ltd., Registered Offices: 80 Strand, London WC2R 0RL, England

This is a work of fiction. Names, characters, places, and incidents either are the product of the author's imagination or are used fictitiously, and any resemblance to actual persons, living or dead, business establishments, events, or locales is entirely coincidental. The publisher does not have any control over and does not assume any responsibility for author or third-party websites or their content.

PUBLISHER'S NOTE: The recipes contained in this book are to be followed exactly as written. The publisher is not responsible for your specific health or allergy needs that may require medical supervision. The publisher is not responsible for any adverse reactions to the recipes contained in this book.

DYING FOR DINNER

A Berkley Prime Crime Book / published by arrangement with the author

PRINTING HISTORY
Berkley Prime Crime mass-market edition / December 2008

Copyright © 2008 by Penguin Group (USA) Inc.
Cover illustration by Stephanie Power.
Cover design by Rita Frangie.
Interior text design by Kristin del Rosario.

ISBN: 978-0-425-22610-0

BERKLEY® PRIME CRIME
Berkley Prime Crime Books are published by The Berkley Publishing Group,
a division of Penguin Group (USA) Inc.,
375 Hudson Street, New York, New York 10014.
BERKLEY PRIME CRIME and the BERKLEY PRIME CRIME design are trademarks of Penguin Group (USA) Inc.

PRINTED IN THE UNITED STATES OF AMERICA

10 9 8 7 6 5 4 3 2 1

It's payback time!

And I would like to thank my wonderful fellow brainstormers:

Diane
Emilie
Jasmine
Karen

for helping me think my way through this book.

One

❖

"TODAY IS THE FIRST DAY OF THE REST OF MY LIFE."
Brave words, yes? I actually might have believed them if as I was speaking, my voice didn't waver and my knees didn't knock together like castanets in a flamenco frenzy.

In an effort to calm myself, I took a deep breath and a long look around. Now that I'd finished checking in our latest batch of cooking students and they'd headed into the kitchen for week number one of Cool Gadgets = Hot Dinners, I was alone in Bellywasher's. It was a Monday night, the restaurant was closed, and, always on the lookout for ways to control skyrocketing costs, I'd turned out every light but the one over the bar. The quiet didn't bother me. Neither did the dark, or the play of shadows against the walls with their painted border of thistles. My gaze glanced over pictures of Scotland, Grandpa Bannerman's walking stick (hung in a place of honor), a kilt, and an autographed photo of Mel Gibson, his face painted blue. The familiarity of the place and the funky, eclectic objects that filled it warmed me through and through. For the first time since I'd walked into the pub, I managed a smile.

Day or night, dark or light, I could never be uncomfortable in Bellywasher's.

I know, I know . . . this seems especially crazy. Logic dictates that the food service business and I cannot peacefully coexist.

I don't cook, see. I don't even like to cook. In point of fact, I am not only the world's worst cook, I am dangerous near a stove. Or an oven. Or a chopping table. Or any other piece of equipment, any appliance or gadget, or any heat source that has anything to do with preparing a meal.

Still, facts are facts and here's one that's indisputable: Bellywasher's holds a special place in my heart.

For one thing, it's owned by Jim MacDonald, and Jim is not only a born pub keeper, a wonderful and creative chef, a great guy, and a honey of a hunk, he's *my* honey, too. Over the last few months, we've gotten closer than ever, and believe me, I know I am one lucky girl. Jim likes me. He more than likes me. Jim believes in my abilities, my level head, and my sound judgment enough to allow me to manage the day-to-day business of his restaurant. He values my opinions; he trusts my decisions. Jim laughs at my jokes, and even though I'd heard it from so many guys over the years that I'd come to realize it was code for *Let's just be friends, why don't we?* Jim has never once in the year I've known him called me *cute*.

Even though I have never been and will never be a flashy dresser, Jim always compliments my choice of clothing. He never forgets to tell me my hair looks nice, even when it is at its curly, unruly worst. He tells me I'm pretty, and he lets me know that he thinks I'm smart, and believe me, for a woman who's gone through what I went through with Peter, my ex, this is a whole, new, wonderful world.

Jim is so terrific, he doesn't even complain (at least not too much) when I investigate a murder or two.

Oh, yeah, he's a sweetie, all right, and since Belly-washer's means the world to him, it means just as much to me, too. Our customers are important to both of us. So are our employees, and our place in the community of businesses along King Street in Old Town Alexandria, Virginia. I know I am part of something wonderful, and I am grateful for every bit of it, even things like the photograph just over my left shoulder, the one that is supposed to show the Loch Ness Monster. Call me cynical, but unlike the customers who marvel at the gray and grainy picture and swear they can see Nessie as plain as day, I'm not so sure. To me, the photo is just a jumble of blurred images. It looks like whoever was holding the camera had aimed it toward the loch just as he or she sneezed. Or maybe the person was just so jazzed about being in the Highlands and maybe actually catching sight of the beast, he or she was having a fit of nerves.

Just like I was at that very moment.

So much for keeping my mind occupied and steadying my jitters. The moment I let down my guard, my doubts closed in on me. My stomach tied into familiar knots. The rat-a-tat of my heart thumping against my ribs started up in full force, and I gulped down my misgivings.

"Today *is* the first day of the rest of your life, Annie," I told myself again, just so I didn't forget. "Make the most of it. Enjoy. Learn all you can. And stop being such a wuss. You did what you had to do. More importantly, you did what you wanted to do. Nobody made you. You did—"

"There's the lady of leisure!" Eve DeCateur was no stranger to Bellywasher's, either. Eve is our hostess. She's also my best friend. I'd locked the front door (what

security-conscious business manager wouldn't?), but Eve
had her own key, and she breezed into the restaurant and
called out her greeting right before she set her Kate Spade
bag on the bar and put one arm around me for a quick
hug.

"You are not looking as happy as you should be today." Eve's hugs were like everything else about Eve—
fast and furious. Almost before she had loosened her
hold on me, she was leaning forward for a better look.
"Annie, you're not having regrets, are you?"

I could lie to myself. I could even lie to Jim when it
was for his own good. I could never lie to the woman
who'd been my best buddy since forever.

I tried anyway.

"Regrets?" I'd learned a lot from Eve in all those
years. Like I'd seen her do a million times in a million
different situations, I tossed my head and laughed.
"Why would I be feeling any regrets? Today is the first
day—"

"Of the rest of your life. Yeah, I know." She didn't
sound convinced. Which pretty much meant I wasn't fool-
ing her. She stepped back, her weight against one foot and
the bright yellow stiletto that encased it, her hands on her
hips and the short, short black skirt that looked just right
with her buttery yellow blouse. Her head tipped, she narrowed her brilliant blue eyes and looked into my ordinary
brown ones, her Southern accent suddenly as thick as the
humid summer air outside.

"Why, Annie Capshaw, I do believe you're trying to
pull the wool over my eyes."

My shoulders drooped. "I was. I did. I thought—"

"That if you fooled me, you might also fool yourself."

I hate it when Eve is insightful. Not that a best friend
doesn't appreciate honesty from another best friend, but
Eve and insightful . . . those two words don't exactly
belong in the same sentence. Eve is kindhearted, sure.

She's funny and unselfish. She's as good as anyone I've ever met, and twice as supportive. If I could pick anyone—anyone at all—to help me out with my investigations, believe me, it would be Eve. That's how much of a team player she is. What she's not, usually, is insightful, and when she is, I know she's always right on the money.

I shifted uncomfortably from foot to foot, and my sneakers squeaked against the hardwood floor.

"It's that obvious, huh?" I asked.

"Pooh!" When she tossed her head, it was far more dramatic than when I'd done it. Of course, she made that little hand gesture to go along with it, the one that was dismissive and spectacular all at the same time and just happened to show off her perfect manicure and her slender, elegant fingers. "It doesn't take a genius to figure out what's going on with you, honey. Even before I took one little look at you, I knew you'd be a basket case today. Of course you are. Who wouldn't be?"

"You. You wouldn't be."

Another toss of the head, and Eve's blonde hair gleamed in the glow of the overhead light. "I am not nearly as dependable and responsible as you. Never have been, never will be. My goodness, Annie, do I have to remind you? I've had more jobs in my lifetime than I can count on both hands. And you—"

"I've been a teller at Pioneer Savings and Loan since I got out of high school. Until . . ." I couldn't help it, I gulped. "Until today."

"That's the spirit!" There was no spirit at all in my words, but Eve didn't let that stop her. She clapped me on the back. "That's old news, honey. This is where your future begins." She made a broad gesture toward the darkened restaurant. "Think of how much easier your life is going to be now that you've quit your job at the bank. No more working all day there, then rushing over here for the evening so you can take care of everything that needs to be taken care of."

"That's right." It was one of the things I'd been reminding myself about since the day I gave notice at Pioneer and, hearing it spoken out loud, some of the weight lifted from my shoulders.

"No more working yourself to a frazzle. Now you can focus on the restaurant and your head won't be filled with all that boring banking business."

"Right again." I nodded. Sure, it was the same ol' rah-rah speech Eve had been giving me since the day I announced I was thinking about quitting my job at the bank so I could devote myself full time to Bellywasher's, but I never tired of hearing it. And more importantly, I needed to hear it. Especially at times like this when my resolve was wavering and I was questioning what I'd done. It was, of course, exactly why Eve was saying it.

"The bank was boring," she said. She was reading my mind. "The bank was dull."

Truer words were never spoken.

"Now you can concentrate on other things. Like murder investigations."

I'd been so busy finally feeling good about my decision and everything it meant, I never saw that coming. Eve's words hit me somewhere between my stomach and my heart and automatically, I balled my hands into fists and pressed them there. Like that would actually help.

"Oh, no," I said, but even before the rest of my objection could form on my lips, Eve stopped me.

"Don't kid yourself, honey. You're good at being a detective."

I was.

Some of the tension inside me uncurled.

"You're smart and you're clever and, so far, you haven't got yourself killed."

This was supposed to make me feel better?

That knot of stress wound tight again.

"Come on, Annie. Admit it. You like the excitement of investigating."

I did. This was one thing I could never lie about, so I didn't even try.

"It's just that I don't want anyone else to die." This was the honest-to-gosh truth, and though I realized with a start that I'd been thinking about it for months, I'd never actually put it into words. "If I have to investigate, it means someone near and dear to us is in trouble. Like you were last winter when you were a suspect."

"Pish-tush." Eve is the only woman I know who can actually say this and not sound ridiculous. She pouted. "I'm not going to get accused of murdering anyone ever again. You don't have to worry about that."

"Good." I drew in a long breath and let it out slowly. "I do like investigating," I said. "I like stretching my mind and my skills. I like solving the puzzle. But even that . . ." Another long breath. This one couldn't still the butterflies that fluttered through my stomach. "I don't want to get that close to murder. Not ever again."

"Agreed." Eve grinned. "I'll tell you what, then. You just forget I ever mentioned murders and investigations. Think about all the other things you'll be able to concentrate on now that you've quit your job at the bank. Not just Bellywasher's." Her eyes lit. "Think about Jim."

A smile blossomed across my expression. Eve always knew how to get to the heart of the matter.

"You're right." The pep talk bolstered my spirits and, feeling better, I turned to go into the kitchen. "I've been through all the doubts and all the worries. A hundred times."

"Oh, honey, more like a million." Laughing, she fell into step beside me. "But don't worry, nobody holds that against you. You're not the type who looks before she leaps. We all understand that. We knew once push came to shove, and you actually gave notice and quit, you'd be a little—"

"Obsessive?" I was afraid if I didn't supply the word, she might pick one that was more to the point—and more bruising.

"I was going to say crazy out of your mind." She laughed. "But yeah, I guess obsessive about covers it. If you weren't, if you didn't worry about walking away from that nice, steady paycheck and that benefits package and that big ol' pension plan—"

"Stop!" I clamped a hand on her arm. "There's no use going over it again. I looked. I leapt. Or is it leaped? Either way, that's the past and what's done is done. It felt weird not going into the bank today. It's going to feel weirder tomorrow coming here first thing in the morning. But I'm done agonizing over the decision. I know I did the right thing."

"Absolutely!"

"I'll just go into the kitchen and tell Jim I'm done checking the students in, see if he needs anything, and straighten my office. That way when I come in tomorrow morning for my first full day on the job, everything will be ready."

"You go, girl!" Eve said and ducked into the ladies' room, no doubt to make sure her makeup was perfect and her lipstick just right before she popped into the kitchen to meet our newest crop of students, even though her makeup was always perfect and her lipstick was never anything but just right.

Cheered, I didn't wait for her. I stepped into the kitchen of Bellywasher's feeling as self-assured and as confident as anyone could upon entering the scene of so many culinary disasters. Not on Jim's part, of course. Jim is a consummate cook, and his assistants, Marc and Damien, were learning quickly. My own efforts in the kitchen left a little more to be desired, and just so Jim didn't forget, I made sure I kept my distance and stayed near the door. He was up at the front of the room near the rolling cart he kept there for cooking demonstrations. He looked my way, and I waved.

"You've met Annie." Jim said this to the dozen students gathered around him, their crisp white aprons over their street clothes, their expressions eager. "Last time we held a cooking class here at Bellywasher's, she was my assistant."

I didn't need the reminder, and had Jim been thinking clearly and not caught up in the heady excitement of a new class and the aromas of chopped garlic and fresh herbs that permeated the kitchen, he would have known that. Of course, I couldn't hold it against him. Not when he smiled at me and that little dimple showed in his left cheek.

"I won't be calling on her to help this time," he told his students, and I let go a breath I hadn't even realized I'd been holding. "That's because we have something new and different planned this time around."

Of course I knew exactly what Jim was talking about. After all, I'd helped him plan the class. That didn't make me any less eager to stand there and listen to his opening speech. For one thing, Jim's got that wonderful Scottish accent that I never tire of hearing. For another . . . well, I never get tired of watching Jim, either, and while he talked, I stepped back and simply enjoyed the way the light gleamed against his mahogany hair and sparked in his hazel eyes when—now and again— he glanced my way.

"I've got a new assistant this time around," Jim said, at the same time glancing toward the swinging door that led back into the restaurant. "Some of you may have heard of him. He's Monsieur Jacques Lavoie."

"You mean the chef who owns that fabulous gourmet

cooking shop over in Arlington?" A man up front spoke these words with as much reverence as if he'd been told that Julia Child had risen from the dead and was going to be sitting in on the class. I shouldn't have been surprised. Jim's classes were popular, and he'd already gained attention from the local cooking crowd for his insistence on proper cooking procedures and his emphasis on fresh ingredients and innovative recipes. The people who signed up for Bellywasher's Cooking Academy were cookaholics, and anyone who knew anything about food also knew that in Washington, D.C., Arlington, and beyond, Jacques Lavoie was a legend.

Monsieur Lavoie was the proprietor of Très Bonne Cuisine, the gourmet shop where I'd taken my first cooking class, where I'd met Jim, and (not incidentally) where I'd first come across a murder and learned that though I might not be much of a cook, I have a better-than-average talent for detecting. In addition to being a larger-than-life figure, a vocal opponent of fast food and shoddy cooking technique, and the face on the label of Vavoom! the pricey, addictive seasoning he sold at his shop, Monsieur is a regular at Bellywasher's, sometimes stopping by to help out on nights we're slammed, other times dropping in for a glass of wine or a quick meal. For this series of classes, I knew that Jim had arranged for Monsieur to provide the kitchen gadgets he'd feature and teach the students how to use each week. Like Jim, I'd been expecting Monsieur to arrive, but I'd been so busy checking the students in, and so focused on my own oh-no-what's-going-to-happen-now-that-I've-quit-my-job insecurities, it hadn't registered that Monsieur had yet to make an appearance.

When Jim looked my way with a question in his eyes, I simply shrugged.

"And isn't that just like a Frenchman!" Jim said this

with so much good humor, everyone laughed. "We're de-
pending on Monsieur Lavoie to help us out this evening,
but no worries. We've got some prep work to do before
we start with the cooking, so if you'll all adjourn to your
stations . . ." With a sweep of his arm, he directed his students to their proper places. A pair of students was as-
signed to each area: the grill and industrial stove behind
Jim, the salad table, prep and side dishes, desserts, pre-
sentation, and drinks. It was the same setup he'd used in
the last class he'd taught and it had worked well. Aside
from the fact that one of the students in the class was
murdered and another was the murderer, of course.

While everyone was busy getting settled, Jim crooked
a finger to call me over. I approached the stove carefully,
and when it didn't flare up, blow up, or break down, I
breathed a sigh of relief.

"What's up with Jacques?" he asked. "He was supposed to be here by now."

I could only answer the way I had before. I shrugged.

"You haven't heard from him?" Jim might be cool,
calm, and collected in front of the class, but he was also a
stickler for perfection—especially in the kitchen. With
his back to his students, I saw the way his eyes glimmered
with annoyance. When his accent thickened, I knew we
were in trouble. "Where can the man be? He's supposed
to show them the proper roasting pans. He's supposed to
bring a mandoline from the shop and demonstrate how to
slice the honey-roasted ham we're making. He said he'd
be by with the ice cream maker we're to use for the
dessert. What's wrong with the man? Is he daft? How can
we have cool tools and hot meals without the tools to
make the hot meals?"

Have I mentioned that I'm the soul of logic and reason?

Maybe it goes without saying since I'm the business

manager of the place. Like any business manager, I
looked beyond the problem and directly for a way to
fix it.

"You've got roasting pans," I told Jim. "You can use
those."

"Aye, we can. Only Jacques was supposed to bring a
whole slew of them. You know, stainless steel in different gauges and a slow cooker just to show that there are
other ways of doing things. We agreed it was a good
way to introduce something new into the classes and
a great way for him to advertise his business. And
besides—"

"But the roasting pans you have will work fine." I
stuck to the topic and refused to get sucked in by the
emotions and, just as I expected, Jim caved.

"Aye." Some of the stiffness went out of his shoulders. "You're right, of course, Annie. As always. We'll
make do. If the mandoline doesn't arrive—"

"Monsieur's bringing a musical instrument?"

This was a legitimate question, so Jim shouldn't have
rolled his eyes. He went right on as if I hadn't said anything at all. "Then I can show them proper knife work
instead. And if the ice cream maker isn't here—"

"I can run out and pick up a couple half gallons of
chocolate chocolate chip."

I was going for funny. Jim knew it and smiled. He
gave me a peck on the cheek.

"As always, you're the one who keeps things here on
an even keel. Thank you. Only . . ." Once again, his gaze
strayed to the doors that led into the restaurant. "He said
he'd be here, and it's not like him to be late. Or to forget
completely. You don't suppose—"

"Anything's wrong? Of course not." It was a cavalier
statement and Jim knew it, but that wasn't about to stop
me. I wasn't going to let my imagination get out of
hand. "Monsieur is healthy and active and everybody

loves him," I reminded Jim. "Nothing's happened to him. Nothing's wrong. He's probably stuck in traffic. I'll tell you what . . ." I moved toward the door. "I'll call the shop and ask his assistant, Greg, what time he left. Then we'll know if we need that chocolate chocolate chip or not."

"That's my girl." Jim gave me a wink before he turned back to his class.

And I walked back into the restaurant and grabbed the phone just as Eve was coming out of the ladies' room.

"Calling Très Bonne Cuisine," I told her, the receiver to my ear but my hand over the mouthpiece so I wouldn't confuse Greg when he answered.

Only he didn't.

Answer the phone, that is.

I checked the clock that hung over the bar. Being a Monday, I knew the shop was open until nine and it was just a bit past seven. I hung up, then dialed again.

There was still no answer.

"That's weird," I said, and I didn't have to explain. Eve knew exactly what I was talking about. She reached into her purse, pulled out her cell phone, hit a button, and handed the phone to me.

"Monsieur's cell," she said while I listened to the ringing on the other end. "I have his number programmed in. I'll bet he's stuck in traffic."

"That's what I told Jim. Only if he is held up somewhere, you'd think he'd call and let us know. And you'd think Greg would answer at the shop. Unless he's tied up with a customer." I waited until Monsieur's message came on, left a brief one that said something like, "Just hoping everything is OK and that you haven't forgotten," and handed the phone back to Eve.

"That's weird."

"You said that already."

"But it is." I drummed my fingers against the bar.

"Monsieur is always anxious to promote his shop, and this is a great way for him to do it. Besides, he wouldn't blow Jim off. They're friends."

"And you're worried."

I looked to Eve for reassurance. "Think I need to be?"

"I think we'd better find out what happened, or you're not going to sleep tonight and then your first full day here is going to be miserable and you're going to say it's because you never should have quit your job at the bank and then you're going to get all crazy and obsessive about that again and I'll never have any peace."

I am not that much of a drama queen, but I didn't bother to remind Eve of that. I was too busy grabbing my purse from my office, sticking my head into the kitchen to tell Jim I'd call him when I found out what was going on, and heading for the door.

According to those online mapping programs, it's a little more than eight miles from Alexandria to Arlington, and it should take the average driver somewhere around fifteen minutes to get there.

Eve is not anyone's average driver. She's got a heavy foot on the accelerator, little tolerance for other drivers who get in her way, and is subjective about what, exactly, constitutes a red light that is red enough to make her stop.

But traffic in the D.C. area is nothing if not brutal, and it took us nearly a half hour to make the trip to Très Bonne Cuisine.

By the time we got there, there were already four police cars in front of the place, their lights swirling.

Two

✦

TRÈS BONNE CUISINE IS ONE OF THOSE FANCY- schmancy cooking shops where logic (and my own, sad history with the culinary arts) dictates that I should have felt like a fish out of water.

All that expanse of polished hardwood floors.

All that gleaming chrome, the sleek cabinetry, the granite countertops.

All that pricey cookware. And the knives that came in more sizes and for more specific purposes than I ever knew existed. And then there were the linens, so perfectly coordinated and so prettily displayed, they literally took my breath away. Especially when I took a gander at the price tags.

And yet even a kitchenphobe like me had never felt unwelcome or uncomfortable in Monsieur Lavoie's shop.

At least not until that night, when I wound my way through the press of people gathered on the sidewalk as if I had every right to be there, stepped into the store, and saw the pool of blood on the floor in front of the cash register counter.

And the body lying facedown in it.

My stomach clenched and though I don't know how I found the breath to make so much as a sound, I guess I must have let go a gasp of horror.

That would explain why the cop standing nearest to the door turned away from the crime scene and gave me a dirty look.

"No reporters." He grabbed my arm, all set to escort me back out the door.

"I'm not—"

"No gawkers, either."

"But I—" I might have been better able to state my case and my intentions (such as they were) if I wasn't so transfixed by that body. From where I was standing I could see that it was a man and that he was clothed in crisply pressed khakis and a blue oxford-type shirt.

The same clothes Monsieur always wore at the shop.

"Get going, lady." The officer's voice snapped me out of my daze. "Or you're going to leave here in the back of a squad car."

"I can't. I—" Who would have thought that I'd ever see Tyler Cooper as a savior! Yet when he appeared out of nowhere, walking up an aisle from the back of the store like he belonged there (which I guess he did, seeing that he's an Arlington homicide detective), that was exactly my reaction.

"Tyler!" I raised my voice and a hand so that he couldn't fail to notice me. "Tyler, I need to talk to you."

I knew exactly when he caught sight of me. That would be when a dusky flush darkened his cheeks. As if praying for strength, he closed his eyes for a moment, but when he opened them again, he signaled for the uniformed cop to let me go.

"What happened here?"

Was that my voice? It was choked and breathy. I am anything but clingy yet I somehow found myself with my hand on Tyler's arm, holding on for dear life. "Tyler, what happened? When did it happen? Do you know who did it? Is Jacques Lavoie—" I could barely get the words past the sour taste in my mouth. "Is he—"

"Dead?" Leave it to Tyler not to beat around the bush. He put a hand on my shoulder and turned me around to face the body just as the cop looking over the crime scene turned the victim onto his back.

"He's dead," Tyler said. "But it's not Jacques Lavoie."

"Greg!" I looked at the face of the retired teacher who loved to cook as much as he loved helping Monsieur with the everyday tasks of running the shop. Relief swept through me and instantly I felt guilty. Greg had worked at the store for nearly six months and in that time, I'd come to know him. He was a nice man, single, and he never made me feel stupid or inadequate when I walked into the shop on some mission or another from Jim. He was soft-spoken and helpful and though he could be prickly with customers who came in and acted as if their knowledge of food and wine made them superior to the rest of the human race, he'd always been kind to me.

"It isn't Monsieur. It's Greg. Poor Greg!" My vision blurred and I blinked, and tears streamed down my cheeks. I wiped them away with one hand. "What happened?"

"How about if I ask the questions?" I doubt if Tyler was being kind. Tyler didn't have a warm and fuzzy bone in his body. I think he was just trying to make sure we stayed out of the way of the folks swarming over the crime scene. That's why he turned me around the other way and, one hand on the small of my back, marched me down the nearest aisle. He finally stopped at a place where we were surrounded by a display of jars of Vavoom! on one side, and shelves of enameled cookware in brilliant primary colors on the other. "You want to tell me what the hell you're doing here?"

I tried. A couple of times. It was hard to get anything like a coherent sentence out of my mouth.

Because he's the ultimate hard-nosed cop, I knew that would never satisfy Tyler. Like Jim is in the kitchen, Tyler is a stickler for procedure. I know (at least I suppose) that since he's alive, he has a heart, but I am just as sure that it's as cold as ice and as impenetrable as a brick.

I know this for a fact, too. Tyler, see, just happens to be one of Eve's former fiancés.

Let me explain.

Eve has been engaged any number of times. And, since I guess the time she was engaged to the man who was a murderer and tried to kill us both doesn't count, she's broken off every one of those engagements.

Every one but the one to Tyler.

He's the one who called off that wedding, and, Tyler being Tyler, he didn't try to soften the blow. He told Eve point-blank that there was no way he could marry her because she just wasn't smart enough.

Ouch!

Point of fact, it was Eve's reaction to Tyler's attitude that sent us off in search of our first killer. After all, Eve reasoned as only Eve can, if she could prove to Tyler that she was smart enough to solve a murder, maybe he'd see that she wasn't the airhead he thought she was.

Since that time, we'd solved that murder and a couple of others besides, but that hardly changed a thing. As far as Tyler was concerned, Eve was nothing more than an unfortunate footnote in his past. We'd heard through the local grapevine that Tyler was engaged to another cop named Kaitlin Sands. If memory served me correctly, the day of their nuptials was fast approaching.

What did I think about the whole Tyler/Eve situation? Honestly, I thought that the day Tyler and Kaitlin tied the knot should (theoretically) be the happiest of

Eve's life. Once Tyler was married, she could officially stop thinking of him as available. He'd be out of her life and her heart, once and for all.

Eve, of course, had a different take on the subject. For her, Tyler Cooper was like a severe case of poison ivy.

So far, she hadn't found anything—or anyone—that could ease the itch.

But I digress.

Tyler was waiting for some kind of explanation from me, and I knew if he didn't get it—fast—I'd be out the door before I found out what had happened to Greg and who was responsible.

"Monsieur Lavoie was supposed to stop at Belly-washer's tonight," I told Tyler, my words choked by the painful ball of emotion lodged in my throat. "He didn't show. I came here . . ." I heard one of the cops working the crime scene call another man over to look at something, but I refused to turn around to see what they were up to. One more look at all that blood and I wasn't sure I could continue. "No one answered the phone when I called, so I tried Monsieur's cell. He didn't answer that, either, so I came over here to see what was wrong."

"Is Eve with you?"

It wasn't a question I expected and my head snapped up. I was just in time to see the wave of regret that clouded Tyler's expression and I knew he'd slipped up; he hadn't meant to ask about Eve. It was an uncharacteristic moment of weakness, and Tyler wasn't happy about it. Heaven forbid anyone should ever think he's human!

"She's parking the car," I told him, but if I expected him to surrender to his curiosity and ask another personal question, I knew I was mistaken. I stuck to the matter at hand, partly because I knew he'd appreciate it and, thus, be more forthcoming. Mostly because I was concerned, not to mention curious. "I came here because I was worried about Monsieur Lavoie."

"You mean this guy?" Tyler took a bottle of Vavoom! from the shelf. There was a black-and-white caricature of the Frenchman on the label that emphasized his round-as-apple cheeks, his sparkling eyes, and a smile as long as a baguette.

"That's him," I said, and, being careful to keep my back to the crime scene, I peered down the nearest aisle. "He's not here? Not anywhere? Are you sure?"

Tyler concentrated on the Vavoom! bottle. "You use this stuff?" he asked.

It was another question I wasn't expecting, and for the second time in as many minutes, I felt as if the polished-to-perfection hardwood floor had been pulled out from under my feet. I looked at the dozens of Vavoom! jars on display. "I . . . I used to."

"People say it's really good. Why don't you use it anymore?"

"Take a look at the price tag." It was a simpler answer than the truth, which was that in the course of my first investigation, I'd learned that Vavoom! wasn't the won-derful, magical seasoning everyone thought it was—Monsieur bought seasoned salt in bulk and repackaged it as Vavoom! Though it wasn't technically honest, I didn't imagine what he was doing was technically ille-gal, either, which was why I'd never divulged his secret to anyone. Besides, what was that old saying about a sucker being born every minute? If folks wanted to plunk down way too much of their hard-earned money for the stuff, that was their business. The fact that Jacques Lavoie promoted Vavoom! like gangbusters and used his own personal charm and the force of his very Gallic personal-ity to convince them to spend that money was Mon-sieur's. If nothing else, he deserved points for being a marketing genius.

"So you were worried about him." I drew my gaze away from the Vavoom! and saw that Tyler had rocked back on his heels. He watched me closely. "Why? You think there was a reason to worry?"

I shook my head, ordering my thoughts. "I didn't have a reason. Not a real reason. I just thought it was unusual that he didn't show up when he said he would, that's all. I wasn't really as worried as I was just curious. I just thought that the whole thing about him not coming to Bellywasher's, I just thought it was—"

"Suspicious?"

Leave it to Tyler to think the worst of somebody. I dismissed the word with a wave of my hand. "I was going to say odd," I told him. "I thought it was odd. Monsieur is dependable. And he loves talking about this shop. He'd never miss an opportunity to do a little self-promotion. And that's what he was supposed to do at tonight's cooking class. He even said he'd bring giveaways, a Très Bonne Cuisine shopping bag for each student, with a kitchen gadget and a recipe inside."

The bell above the front door rang, announcing someone had walked into the shop. I saw Tyler's gaze dart that way.

"They're not going to let her in."

Since he pretended not to know what I was talking about, he gave me no choice but to go on.

"Eve," I said. "She's going to try to get in, but you know she'll never get past the cops at the door. She's too conspicuous. It's easier for me to get into places. No one notices me."

"What makes you think I was looking for Eve? Why would you assume I was even thinking about her?"

I could have pointed out that I saw the way he perked up when he heard that bell ring. Like one of Pavlov's dogs. But I knew that putting Tyler on the spot would get me nowhere.

"You're right, of course," I said, not bothering to mention what I thought he was right about since—truth be told—I found it hard to believe that Tyler was ever right about anything. "It was only natural for me to come down here to see what was going on. Then to find this." This time I couldn't help myself; I glanced over my shoulder. "Poor Greg."

"You knew the guy?"

"Not well." I wished now that I had. "He was quiet and considerate. I can tell you that. He loved to cook. Monsieur said that after Jim, Greg was the best employee he ever had. He was never late for work. He never closed up early, even when the shop wasn't busy. I remember Monsieur saying that if there was nothing else to do, Greg would refold all the linens or clean off shelves even when they didn't need to be cleaned. He was that kind of guy."

"And his boss, this Lavoie fellow, he kept a lot of cash around?"

"You think this was a robbery?" My blood ran cold and I hugged my arms around myself. "It's awful to think that some thug off the street wouldn't be satisfied with the money. That he thought he had to take Greg's life, too."

For all I knew, Tyler was about to agree with this. He never had the chance. One of the cops studying the crime scene called him over. He never told me to stay out of the way and mind my own business, so, naturally, I followed along.

"Looks like the cash register hasn't been touched," the man told Tyler. "And look here." He pointed toward Greg's feet. "What do you make of that?"

I looked at Greg's feet, too. I remembered now that he'd once mentioned that he was prone to gout, so I wasn't surprised to see that he was wearing brand-name sneakers with good arch supports and sturdy laces.

Or at least he was wearing what was left of them.

Greg's feet had been shot. Both of them.

As far as I could see, there wasn't another mark on his body.

"That's strange," I said.

Tyler didn't have to turn around to know I was right behind him. "What's strange is that you're poking your nose into this when it's none of your business." He turned my way just so I didn't miss his sneer of epic proportions. "On second thought, I guess that's not so strange after all."

"But there wasn't any money taken," I said, just to remind Tyler we were talking about the crime and not the way I had of getting myself embroiled in these kinds of things. "It wasn't a robbery. And if somebody shot Greg in the feet, it wasn't like they wanted to kill him."

"They wanted to hurt him." It was an understatement, but I didn't point this out to Tyler. "It's almost as if—"

"They wanted to make him talk."

My comment settled between us and we each in our own way thought it over. I didn't have to think for long to know what I'd said made perfect sense. Why shoot a man in the foot—and twice? I mean, if you weren't trying to get something out of him? Tyler, it seemed, was not so easily convinced.

He snorted. "You can't possibly know that."

"Of course I can't." There was no use arguing the point. "But it just doesn't make sense otherwise, does it? I mean, why just hurt a person like that? Unless you're trying to make him—"

"Talk." This time Tyler didn't sound so skeptical. He glanced my way. "You know anything about this Greg guy that would make it seem likely someone would want to make him talk?"

I wished I did. I shrugged. "If you mean did he owe somebody big bucks for gambling or something like that . . ." Another shrug. "I can't say."

"But we can say this is strange."

"I already did say that."

Tyler wasn't talking to me; he was talking to the crime-scene technician. He turned his back to me just so I didn't think he was. "It must have hurt plenty, sure, but two shots to the feet . . . that shouldn't have killed the guy."

"Unless he was taking some kind of medication that made him more likely to bleed."

My comment worked just as I'd intended it to. Though Tyler was trying his best to turn me off and tune me out, he had no choice but to face me.

"Greg had a heart problem," I explained. "I know this for a fact because we were discussing healthy cooking once and he talked about how he was cutting fat from his diet. You know, on account of his heart condition. And I was here just last week when he went out to lunch. I walked to the pharmacy on the corner with him. He went there to pick up a new prescription for Coumadin."

"The blood thinner." The crime-scene examiner was listening as intently as Tyler was, and he nodded. "That would explain why he bled out the way he did. Poor bastard. If it wasn't for him taking that medication, he might be here to tell us the story."

"And let us know who did this." Tyler looked my way. "Or do you have a theory about that, too?"

"Nope. No theories." Just to prove that I wasn't about to start a crime-scene investigation of my own, I clasped my hands together behind my back. "I can only assume that the person who shot Greg never meant to kill him. He couldn't have known Greg was on the medication. He must have been stunned when Greg collapsed. How did you know, anyway?"

"About the medication?" Tyler looked at me as if I'd suddenly started spouting Chinese. "I didn't. Not until you told me."

"Not about the medication. About the shooting." I glanced around. Except for the swarms of police officers in the place, there was no one else around. Nobody who looked like a customer, anyway. "If there was nobody here but Greg and the shooter, how did you know about the shooting? Theoretically . . ." This was a new thought, and it caused my stomach to swoop. "I should have been the one who walked in and found the body. But you were already here. Was there someone else in the shop when all this happened? Is that how you knew?"

"Does it matter?"

"It certainly must matter to you. If someone else was here, that means you've got a witness. It also explains how you knew about the shooting. I mean, if someone called you . . ."

I could tell when Tyler surrendered. That would be when he grabbed my arm again and tugged me back toward the Vavoom! display.

"I don't need your help solving this case," he said.

"I never said you did."

"Then why are you asking so many questions?"

"I care. Is that some kind of crime? I liked Greg. I'm sorry he's dead. And Monsieur is a friend of mine. If Greg is dead, maybe he's in some kind of trouble, too."

"He's the one who made the call."

I wasn't expecting this, and it brought me up short. But only for a moment. I heard the undertone in Tyler's voice and I didn't like it. Not one little bit.

"You're nuts," I told him, and believe me, I wasn't worried about being politically correct or about keeping my relationship with Tyler on an even keel. Thanks to what he did to Eve and how much he'd hurt her and how she was my best friend, Tyler and I didn't have a relationship, so I didn't have anything to worry about. "You can't possibly think that—"

"Why not? You said it yourself. You said that whoever shot Greg didn't mean to kill him. You said that he
must have been plenty surprised when he saw the way
Greg bled out. That would explain the panicked, muffled
call we got from your friend Lavoie. If he wanted Greg
to talk—"

"If Monsieur wanted Greg to talk, he would have baked
him a flourless chocolate cake. Or opened up a pricey bottle of wine and poured a couple glasses. He wouldn't have
shot Greg in the feet, that's for sure."

"Is it?"

"Damned straight." I didn't back down from my position, not even when Tyler turned the full force of his icy
glare my way. I raised my chin. "Besides," I said, "Monsieur knew that Greg was taking Coumadin. He's the
one who referred Greg to the doctor who prescribed it. I
heard them talking a couple times about the right way to
take the medication and how Greg had to be careful
about eating green, leafy vegetables while he was on it.
Monsieur Lavoie would know that an injury might kill
Greg."

"Maybe that was his intention the whole time."

I was so incensed by his stupid theory as well as his re-
fusal to listen to reason, I couldn't face Tyler. My anger
choking me, I whirled around, then spun back to him just
as fast. "In case you didn't hear me the first time, you're
nuts," I said, and I poked a finger at his expensive silk tie
just to emphasize my point. "Jacques Lavoie is a food
lover, not a killer. And I'm sure he has an ironclad alibi to
cover what happened here tonight. He's the one who
called you. That's what you said, right? Did he call and
say Greg needed help?"

"He called and said someone was in the store and he
thought Greg was in trouble."

"See." I was so pleased that Tyler had finally divulged

this important part of the story, I practically crowed. "Maybe Monsieur had just walked in. Or maybe he was in the storeroom or something. Maybe that's why he didn't know what was going on. As soon as he saw that Greg was in trouble, he called the cops. That just about proves he didn't have anything to do with what happened to Greg."

"Yeah, that's pretty much what I thought."

Tyler had been toying with me and when I realized it, my mouth dropped open. I propped my fists on my hips.

"Don't take it so hard." He boffed me on the arm. "I just wanted to see what kind of response I'd get from you. You know, see if my gut reaction and your gut reaction matched up. You'll be happy to know they do."

"And you should be happy I don't take a poke at that smug expression on your face." I glared at him, just for good measure.

But Tyler was already past that. He looked over to where a team of paramedics was putting Greg's body into a bag and hoisting it onto a stretcher. "We're right back where we started from," he said.

I thought about everything he'd said. "Maybe not. Why not just ask Monsieur Lavoie? If he knew Greg was in trouble, he must have seen what was happening. He'll tell you. Just ask him."

"I'd love to. If I could find him."

That jumpy feeling in my stomach solidified into a block of ice. I looked at Tyler hard. "You mean . . ."

"He's nowhere in the store, that's for sure. In fact, the back door was wide open. Like maybe he left that way and didn't bother to close it behind him. He called from his cell phone, but there's no answer on it now."

"Yeah." Thinking, I worked over my lower lip with my teeth. "That's what happened when I called him. You've tried—"

"His home? Right before you walked in, we heard from the team of officers we sent over there. There's no sign of Lavoie there, either."

"That means—"

"Yep." Tyler didn't look any happier saying it than I did hearing it. "Your friend Jacques Lavoie has disappeared."

Three

✖

HAVE I MENTIONED THAT JIM IS A CONSUMMATE professional?

I suppose I have. I mean, it's impossible for me to talk about Jim and not sing his praises to the high heavens. Yeah, he's that terrific. On the personal side, he's always been there for me. Professionally, I've seen him come through in a cooking pinch so many times, I'm pretty much convinced he's a bona fide kitchen superhero.

But if I needed more proof, it came the day after Greg's murder.

In spite of the fact that he'd soldiered through with the rest of the cooking class even after I called him to tell him what had happened at Très Bonne Cuisine and that we'd been up half the night in an effort to find Monsieur Lavoie, Jim was at Bellywasher's at his usual early hour. When lunchtime rolled around, he directed the kitchen staff like a conductor in front of his orchestra.

No missteps.

No miscues.

No sour notes.

Me? Well, after calling Monsieur's cell phone a couple of dozen times an hour the night before, going along with Jim when he visited every one of the haunts he knew Monsieur frequented, and just basically pacing my apartment as we wracked our brains to try to figure out what had happened to our friend, I was a little less perky.

The latest batch of supplier invoices was on my desk in front of me, but the numbers swam in front of my bleary eyes.

When my office door snapped open and Jim stuck his head in, I was grateful for the break. "Anything?" he asked.

I shook my head. "No answer," I said, with a look toward the phone on my desk. "I've been calling every half hour or so. But there's no answer at his house. No answer on his cell, either."

Jim's white apron was a stark contrast to the smudges of exhaustion under his eyes. He looked over his shoulder, quickly checking to be sure that for the moment, everything was under control out in the restaurant. Only when he was sure did he step into my office and close the door behind him.

"What are we going to do?" he asked.

In all the hours we'd worked on the problem, I'd never heard Jim sound this discouraged. Or this worried. I rose from my chair and crossed the room (it didn't take long; my office is lilliputian). I would have given Jim a hug if there wasn't a smear of marinara across the front of his apron and I wasn't wearing a white sweater.

I put a hand on Jim's arm and gave it a squeeze. "We're going to find him," I said, and honestly, I believed it. "Monsieur can't have just disappeared off the face of the earth. He has to be somewhere." I was grateful that Jim was listed as the emergency contact on the note that hung over the cash register at Très Bonne Cuisine. That meant the cops had contacted him directly the night before. He was in the loop, and he wasn't getting all his information about the murder and Monsieur's disappearance second-hand from me. "You heard what Tyler said when he called you last night," I reminded him.

"You mean about Jacques making that phone call. The one that alerted the police to the trouble." Jim nodded. A lock of hair fell onto his forehead, but he didn't move to brush it back. The curl of hair made him look younger. And more vulnerable.

I'd heard people talk about heartstrings, and at that moment, I knew for certain they were real because mine tugged in sympathy.

"Tyler said that phone call means Jacques is as right as rain," Jim said. He didn't have to; I remembered the call as well as he did. But I let him talk. He was bolstering his own spirits, and trying to buck up mine, too. "Jacques was able to make the phone call, so he must not have been hurt. Tyler said it means we shouldn't worry that he might be . . . you know."

I couldn't blame Jim. I didn't want to say it, either. I didn't even want to think about what he was thinking about, so I didn't. I concentrated on the facts instead.

"When I was at the shop, Tyler told me the back door of Très Bonne Cuisine was open when the police arrived. I think that means that when the killer came into the store, Monsieur must have been loading his car with the stuff he was supposed to bring over here for your class. Of course, I didn't get a chance to look around the store. If I could have gone back there, maybe I'd know for sure." A stab of embarrassment reminded me that after Tyler had given me more time than he probably should have at an active crime scene, he unceremoniously escorted me from the premises and told me to mind my own business.

Which was exactly what I was doing, I reminded myself.

Monsieur was our friend. This was our business.

With that in mind, I went right on. "He didn't come right out and say it—you know how Tyler can be—but I got the feeling he thinks that Monsieur walked back in and realized something was wrong. I'll bet Monsieur was all set to help. You know he wouldn't just turn tail and run. Not when a friend is in trouble. He's not that kind of person. But then he must have heard the shots, and that's when he called 911 and got himself out of there. It was the smart thing to do and it also means that he's safe. He's just—"

"Missing? Disappeared into thin air? Hiding? That makes the least sense of all. Why would he want to hide? Why would he need to?"

These were the same questions that we'd been over the night before—again and again, until our heads spun and our brains were as fried as the ravioli on the day's menu. Before I could try to drum up some answers that sounded new, different, and even vaguely plausible, there was a rap on my door.

Heidi, our waitress, opened it and came inside. In my office, three is the proverbial crowd and when Jim stepped closer, I stepped back to keep my sweater from getting ruined. Heidi, smart girl that she is, didn't waste any time.

"The party at table four is ready for their birthday cake," she told Jim, and he assured her he'd be right there. I knew the Tennessee whiskey cake Jim had made the day before was a special order for a group of regulars and that he was proud of his recipe. There was no way he wasn't going to serve it himself.

Before he stepped back into the restaurant, he looked toward my phone. "You'll try again?"

I didn't have to answer. He knew I would.

Before he closed my door, though, he turned to me one more time.

"He was the one who gave me my first real job when I came to this country, you know." Jim's smile was brief. "I was barbacking here for Uncle Angus, but there's only so much of that a young fellow can do, especially one who's itching to cook. Jacques' shop was brand new and when I stopped in to look around, he saw that I was interested, and knowledgeable. I'd taken a few cookery courses back in Scotland, but I'd never seen anything like that shop of his. I started out unpacking boxes, stocking shelves. I learned a lot there, and Jacques gave me a chance to cook, and to teach."

I knew the story, of course, but I didn't bother to point this out to Jim. As I'd seen in so many investigations, those left behind to deal with the aftermath of a tragedy needed space to explore their feelings and a chance to talk.

"But this isn't a tragedy," I told myself the instant Jim was out the door. And then I felt guilty. Because of course Greg's death was exactly that. Monsieur's disappearance, on the other hand?

Right now, that was a mystery.

As always, my mind and Eve's were apparently moving in the same direction. That would explain why the moment I was back at my desk and staring at those endless columns of blurred numbers again, she slipped into my office and plunked into the chair next to my desk.

"You're going to take the case, right?" Eve didn't wait for me to answer. She'd left her purse in my office that morning and she got it out of the bottom drawer of my desk, dug inside, and pulled out a tube of lipstick. "I mean, you pretty much have to, don't you? What with Monsieur being our friend and all."

"I dunno." I rolled my chair back. "It's not that I wouldn't like to know more—"

"Of course you would." Eve uncapped the lipstick, applied it, and smacked her lips together. "You're a smart woman with an inquisitive mind."

"But we don't have much to go on."

"You mean the cops don't." Eve pulled a mirror from her purse. She pouted into it, checking her lipstick. "You're oodles smarter than they are, Annie. You've proved that more than once."

"I have, but—"

"And you know you could do it again."

"I might be able to, but—"

"And you want to, don't you?" She looked directly at me when she said this and, face-to-face with the sheen of excitement in Eve's blue eyes, I found it impossible to speak anything but the whole truth and nothing but.

"It is interesting to investigate," I said, my words tentative. "I'll admit that. I like solving the puzzle of a case. I like knowing that a victim has found justice and the person responsible will be punished. But—"

"But? But what?" She shoved both lipstick and mirror back in her purse, tucked the purse in the bottom desk drawer, and sat up straight. "You are not telling me that you're going to give up on Monsieur Lavoie, are you, Annie? Because I just know that can't be true. He's our friend. And you're the best detective this side of the—"

"Oh, no. Don't try to pull that on me!" I was up and on my feet even before I realized it. "Being curious about what happened to Monsieur is one thing. Being thought of as some kind of Sherlock Holmes is—"

"The absolute truth. And you know it. You've got a gift."

"Maybe. Possibly. OK . . ." I indulged in a little vanity, not a weakness that usually plagued me. "OK, you're right. I'm pretty good at this detective thing. That doesn't mean—"

"Of course it does. You don't think the police are any-where near as concerned about Monsieur as we are, do you? I mean, truly, they might want to be, but they're just as busy as can be. And they don't know Monsieur like we do. They don't like him as much as we do. I mean, how can they, when they don't know him. Unless some of them do. I mean, if they're cooks. And they shop at his store. But I don't think they all could. I mean, every single cop on the Arlington force? That seems a bit unlikely. And it would mean Monsieur would be busy. All of the time." She must have seen my eyes go glassy. Eve twitched away the rest of her convoluted theory.

"Why, if we don't take charge and take on this investi-gation," Eve said, her voice as rock steady as her shoul-ders, "the mystery of what happened to Monsieur might never be solved."

I hadn't failed to notice how the *you* had somehow morphed into *we*. It didn't matter and, besides, like I've said before, there's no one I'd rather have with me on an investigation than Eve.

"We could go back to the places Jim and I stopped last night," I told her. "Those couple little bars in Clarendon, and that coffee place that Monsieur likes so much. Maybe there will be someone there today who wasn't there last night." It was an idea, sure, and it was better than sitting around doing nothing, but honestly, it felt useless. I twitched my shoulders, but that did nothing to get rid of the uneasiness that sat on them like a weight. "I don't know. It just doesn't seem like enough."

"It's a start, and it's better than doing nothing. The whole thing is just so odd, isn't it? I mean, Monsieur, he's anything but a shrinking violet. You'd think he'd want to come forward and tell the world what happened at the shop last night. He'd get interviewed on the news if he did. And there's nothing he likes better than pub-licity."

Leave it to Eve. The PR angle was one I hadn't thought of, but I knew she was absolutely right.

"He loves his friends, too," I said. "He must know we're worried about him. If nothing else, you'd think he'd give Jim a call just to let him know that everything's OK." My shoulders drooped. "Unless everything's not OK."

"Which we have no way at all of knowing until we get to the bottom of this crazy thing." Eve stood. It wasn't as if I hadn't seen her earlier in the day, but I guess I'd been preoccupied and hadn't noticed that she was dressed in a creamy skirt and pink blouse that made her look as fresh and bright as the flowers that grew in the boxes outside Bellywasher's front door. Eve always dresses to impress, but that Tuesday, she looked even more spectacular than usual.

It didn't take a detective to figure out what was going on.

"So . . ." In an attempt to look as casual as possible, I shuffled and reshuffled the papers on my desk. "When I walked out of Très Bonne Cuisine last night . . . when Tyler walked me out and walked me to the car . . . did he say anything to you? Anything about maybe stopping here today to talk to us all again?"

"Goodness no!" Eve's petulance was a little too . . . er . . . well, petulant to fool me. She folded her arms over her chest in a classic defensive posture if I ever saw one. "You were right there, Annie. You know what happened. Tyler said hello. Then he gave me that little arctic smile of his. But he never said . . . I mean, even if he had, you don't think I'd actually care, do you? He wasn't any happier to see me last night than I was to see him."

"Eve?" It was Heidi again. This time when she opened my office door, she left it open. "There's someone here to see you."

"Really?" As Eve had proven over the years, she

could be cool and calm up in front of dozens of beauty pageant judges, but even so, she wasn't much of an actress. Her faked surprise at hearing she had a visitor didn't fool me. When she threw back her shoulders, lifted her chin, and walked out into the restaurant, I didn't even need to confirm my suspicions. I did, anyway. I wasn't surprised to see a single customer sitting at the small table near the front window. He looked an awful lot like Tyler Cooper.

Maybe it was a good thing the lunch hour rush was in full swing. From the looks of the crowd waiting near the front door, I could tell Eve wouldn't have much time to chat with Tyler.

While I thought about all this and what it might mean, I tried Monsieur's phone again.

I didn't get any better results.

With no other options and no hope of making any sense of those invoices stacked on my desk, I sat back down and took out a legal pad.

What could have happened to Monsieur? I wrote at the top of the page.

Under that, I made a list of the spots Jim and I had stopped the night before and next to that, the names of the people we'd talked to at each one. A couple minutes' time on the computer and I had phone numbers for each of those places, too. I promised myself I'd call them to see if anyone was there I could talk to who hadn't been there the night before—*after* I finished half the invoices.

With that bit of incentive, I might actually have gotten back to the work that was from that day forward supposed to be my full-time job if Jim hadn't popped into my office again.

"Did they like their birthday cake?" I asked, and I swear, he was so distracted, he had to think about it for a couple seconds before he knew what I was talking about.

His quick smile told me the celebration had gone

well. "I've been on the phone," he said without preamble. He sat in the chair Eve had so recently vacated. "Arranging for a cleaning crew to get over to Très Bonne Cuisine once the police are done with the place."

I hadn't thought of this, but it made sense. I remembered once reading something about how the owner of a property is responsible for cleaning up after a crime. I didn't want to consider the task that waited for them. Just the memory of all that blood on the floor . . .

I wiped the image out of my mind and listened as Jim got down to business.

"Jacques and I . . . I don't think I've mentioned it . . . there was never any reason . . . but Jacques and I, we had an informal agreement of sorts. If anything ever happened to me, he was to see that things here ran smoothly. And if anything ever happened to him—"

"You're in charge of keeping the shop open for business."

"Aye."

I knew Jim was feeling sentimental, not to mention obligated. That's exactly why he wasn't thinking clearly. What kind of girlfriend would I have been if I didn't point this out?

I leaned forward. "I know you'd love to keep your word to Monsieur, but it's not going to work, Jim. You realize that, don't you? You're so busy here, there's no way you can run the shop."

"That's true." He took my hand. "I can't manage Très Bonne Cuisine, but you can."

While I was still at a loss for words and with my mouth wide open, Jim saw his chance and took the opportunity to explain.

"It's the perfect setup," he said. "You know Jacques will appreciate your help. When he gets back, I mean. You know he'll be thrilled to learn the shop's been in good hands."

"Sure, but . . ." I teetered on the edge between laughter and tears. Just to remind Jim of who—and what—I was, I looked him in the eye. "It's me, Annie Capshaw. I'm the world's worst cook. You remember that, don't you?"

"You won't have to cook."

"I'm the world's least likely person to know my way around a kitchen."

"Bah!" He dismissed this objection in an instant. "It's naught but cooking supplies, Annie. Pots and pans and the like. There's nothing to it. And who has a better head for business than you? That's all it is, you know. A business like any other business. A business just like this one. Only you're not dealing in food, you're dealing in—"

"Ice cream makers and roasting pans and pot holders I can't afford to buy."

His blank expression told me I wasn't getting through to him. I tried another tack. "The shop is a crime scene."

"Tyler's out front." He didn't know that I already knew this so he tipped his head in the direction of my closed door and the restaurant beyond. "He says they'll be done there by tomorrow. Which is why I felt free to schedule that cleaning crew. If you could be there to supervise . . ."

Supervising was something I knew how to do. I nodded. "Of course I'll do that if you can spare me here."

"And when it's all cleaned up and all ready to open again, then you'll work the shop."

"I never said that."

"But you will, won't you, Annie darling? We can't let the business go to pot just because Jacques isn't there. That's not how friends respond to their friends in trouble."

"It isn't. And I wouldn't want to leave him high and dry, but—"

"And it will give you the perfect chance to get a

closer look at the place. You know, for a little investigating. Detecting, Annie. Not cooking."

Call me cynical. I knew as sure as I was sitting there that Jim had planned out this speech to the very last word.

How?

Because he'd used the bait he knew would hook me.

Number one, there was that word, *cooking*. Oh, sure, coming from most of our mouths, there's nothing special about it. But coming from a Scotsman with a knee-melting accent . . .

Jim knew I was a sucker for those long *o*'s, that mellow tone when his voice wrapped around the vowels, and the way his lips puckered the slightest bit.

I could no more resist the temptation in his voice than I could the promise of a little detecting.

He knew that, too.

"But you hate it when I investigate," I said. Since it was true, I figured I had every right to call him on it. "You always worry when I'm looking into murders."

"But it's not the murder you'll be investigating. Not technically, anyway. The police will take care of that. You'll be looking into finding Jacques."

I had to admit the idea was tantalizing. But before I could say as much, Jim went on with the rest of his argument.

"You're good at this, Annie. You know you are. You have a way of getting to the heart of matters. And that's what we need, isn't it? Someone who cares enough to try and find out what happened to Jacques."

It was practically the same thing Eve had said. I'd been convinced then. Looking into Jim's eyes—more gray today than they were green—I was more convinced than ever.

"All right. I'll do it."

He patted my hand.

"But I'm going to need help," I told him, just so he

didn't think I was caving completely. "I don't know anything about kitchen shops, Jim. I can't answer customer questions." A new thought hit me and my blood turned to ice water. "Monsieur isn't still doing the cooking classes upstairs, is he?"

"Now, Annie . . ." He wound his fingers through mine. "There's nothing to worry about on that front. He's been talking about opening the cooking school again, but not until fall. By then—"

"Monsieur will be right back where he belongs."

I said this mostly to convince myself. I didn't need to throw the possibility of teaching a cooking class into the mix. Just the idea of spending time at a cookware store was enough to send chills up my spine. I shivered.

"You'll be fine." Laughing for the first time since the news of the murder at Très Bonne Cuisine broke, Jim rose and opened the door to go back out into the restaurant. "Think about it, Annie," he said to me over his shoulder. "It's a natural sort of job for someone with your organizational skills."

"And my cooking skills?"

My question stopped Jim in his tracks. He turned and grinned. "Cooking," he said, emphasizing those *o*'s like there was no tomorrow. "What can possibly go wrong with cooking?"

I'd heard that question before, and I didn't like to remind myself of the answers. Dead cooking students, suspicious cooking students, murderous cooking students.

Plenty could go wrong in cooking classes.

"Only there won't be any classes," I told myself in that lay-it-on-the-line voice I used to talk to myself and calm my nerves. "Only pots and pans. Heck, there's more cooking going on in this place, and lately, things here couldn't be going any better."

That cheered me right up, even if I was a little apprehensive, and I went into the restaurant to get an iced tea and to find out what time I needed to be at Très Bonne Cuisine the next day.

I guess my timing was good.

Or maybe it was very, very bad.

That would explain why when I stepped out of my office, I ran smack into a man standing just outside my door.

Did I say man?

This wasn't just any man and the second I realized it, my stomach hit the floor, then bounced up again to stick in my throat.

That's when I realized I was face-to-face with someone I hadn't seen since the day we faced off at the courthouse over a stack of divorce papers.

Four

✖

I LOOKED UP INTO THE CHOCOLATE EYES THAT USED to smile at me every morning from the pillow next to mine. I backed away from the body that was just as familiar and did my best (it wasn't good enough) to try not to remember that once upon what seemed like a lifetime ago, these were the arms that hugged me and that was the mouth that kissed me good-bye each day as we headed off to our jobs. His was the heartbeat I'd listened to, my head nuzzled against his chest as I fell asleep each night.

Now my own heart slammed against my ribs, counting out the seconds I was unable to find my voice: One, two, three, four . . .

I could barely keep up with the thoughts that sped through my head, and that was too bad. If ever there was a time I needed to be my usual rational and well-balanced self, this was it. But instead of being logical, I was dizzy. Instead of thinking, I was running on pure emotion and a shot of adrenaline so strong, it pumped through my veins, heightened my senses—and left my brain so far behind,

I was pretty sure it would never catch up. Pity, because without my reason to guide me, I didn't know how I felt. Heck, I wasn't even sure what I was supposed to feel.

Regret? Denial? Longing? Anger?

They were all possibilities, and I suppose each was legitimate in its own way. It wasn't until after the initial pikestaff of shock settled, after my heartbeat racheted back and my stomach stopped jumping around as if it was filled with grasshoppers, that I realized I felt one thing and one thing only—surprise.

"Peter!" I congratulated myself when I managed to say his name without the slightest trace of breathiness, and because I knew emotions were unreliable, I stuck with the only thing I could count on—my logic.

"What on earth are you doing here?"

"It's nice to see you, too, Annie." Like we were old friends, he leaned forward and gave me a peck on the cheek. A wave of familiar, peppery aftershave enveloped me and a stab of memory came right along with it. Old Spice was Peter's favorite. I'd always put a bottle of it in his Christmas stocking.

I also remembered that after he told me he'd never really known what love was until he met the girl who worked behind the counter at the dry cleaner's, he'd stopped wearing good ol' Old Spice and switched to a pricey, metrosexual scent she picked out for him at the mall.

I pretended not to notice he'd switched back. Just like I pretended not to make note of the fact that he was once again dressed in khakis and a tan polo shirt, and not the black and white, sort of noir, maybe goth look I'd seen him in the day our divorce was finalized.

"You're here for lunch," I said, because of course that was the only possible reason he could be at Bellywasher's. "You're not at school. You should be at school. It's the middle of the day."

"It sure is, and summer vacation has started." I should have remembered this and he was kind enough not to point it out. "I don't start teaching summer school for another two weeks."

"Summer school?" It was the one thing he'd been adamant about back when we were married. Summer, Peter always said, was his hard-earned vacation time, and he didn't want to spend it teaching remedial chemistry to kids who didn't want to be there and weren't going to learn anyway. "You always hated summer school."

He shrugged. "The mortgage has to get paid," he said, and yeah, he was so casual about it, I couldn't help but bristle.

The mortgage, you see, had always been a bone of contention between Peter and me.

I wanted one. In the worst way. Because in the worst way, I wanted to own a home of my own.

Peter was a little more blasé about the idea of home ownership. He finally gave in to my years of poring over the home section of the newspaper and sighing, and right before we separated, we started looking at (inexpensive) homes.

When our assets were divided, he took half of the down payment with him, and pulled my dream of home ownership out from under me.

Was I bitter? Absolutely! But this wasn't the time or the place.

I pasted on a smile. "Table for two?" Automatically, I checked behind him to see if Mindy—or was it Mandy?—was with him. "Or one?"

"One." As if to prove he was alone, he spread out his hands and looked around. "I hear the food's good here."

"It isn't good, it's fabulous." We were on firmer footing now, and I was in my element. I never get tired of talking about how wonderful Bellywasher's is. "The lunch crowd has thinned so you've got your choice of tables. You can sit over there if you want." I grabbed a menu from the bar and waved it toward the small table near the sandalwood screen that separated our entryway from the tables beyond. As I did, I caught Eve's eye. She was in the middle of saying something to Tyler, but when she saw who I was talking to, her mouth dropped open.

I could just about see the wheels turning in her head, and when she made a move to get up, I stopped her with a look. I had not one shred of doubt that she was about to come over and tell Peter to take his lunch business somewhere else. Call me shallow: I wasn't about to turn down a paying customer.

Call me curious: I was dying to know what he was doing here.

Because I didn't want Eve to get involved and say all the things I would have said to her ex-husband (if she had one) if he appeared out of the blue, I showed Peter to his table myself.

"How did you know about this place?" I asked him. "I can't believe it's just—"

"Coincidence? You know me better than that." When he sat down and looked up at me, his eyes gleamed. "I'm a science teacher, Annie. I don't believe in coincidence. I stopped at Pioneer this morning."

"The bank? My bank?"

"Apparently, it isn't your bank anymore. They told me you quit."

"You went to my bank? To see me?"

Back when we met, Peter's laugh was one of the first things I'd noticed about him. It was deep and rich, and it always had a way of warming through and through.

That was then, and this was now. I told myself not to forget it and stared down at him, so anxious for answers, I was able to ignore his deep-throated chuckle and the way it tickled its way up my spine.

Peter opened his menu, but he didn't glance at it. He was looking at me as carefully as I was watching him. "I never thought you'd do something that foolish."

"You mean show you to a table and hand you a menu? Or are we talking about something else? Like the bank. Was that foolish?" I'd thought the same thing myself not twenty-four hours earlier, but somehow, hearing the sentiment coming out of Peter's mouth brought everything into perspective. "You can't possibly know what's foolish for me to do and what isn't. You don't know me anymore, Peter. You gave up the privilege of commenting about my decisions the day you cheated on me. Which also means that what I do and where I work . . . well, it's really none of your business."

"Sorry!" When I stepped away from the table, Peter grabbed my hand. "I didn't mean to ruffle your feathers. Knowing you, I was surprised, that's all. All those years of seniority . . . all those contributions to your 401(k) plan. You never would have done anything so out of character back when we were married. You must like this place a whole lot."

"I do." I cringed at the phrase and its connection to the past—and to Peter—and, anxious to fill the silence, I'd already opened my mouth to tell him about the daily specials when I realized Jim was standing just a couple feet away. He wasn't watching us. Not exactly. I mean he wasn't looking at our faces. He was staring at the place where Peter's hand and mine were linked.

I had nothing at all to feel ashamed of, but that didn't stop the guilt from seeping into every pore. I yanked my hand out of Peter's and backed up a step, distancing myself from him at the same time I gestured to call Jim closer. "There's someone I want you to meet," I told him. "This is Peter. Peter Capshaw."

It took him a moment to put the pieces together, but I knew exactly when they clunked into place. Jim can be cool, calm, and collected in the face of the worst kitchen calamities. This didn't exactly qualify, but his reaction was no different. His eyebrows rose just a smidgen and he stuck out his hand in a friendly enough greeting. Still, I couldn't help but notice that his shoulders were rigid.

"Good to meet you," he told Peter. Like I said, Jim is a born pub keeper. Throwing a line of bull when necessary is part of the job description. "You've heard about us, eh? Stopped in to see what all the fuss is about?"

Peter scraped back his chair so that he could get a better look at Jim. "Actually," he said, "I stopped in to see Annie. I was surprised to hear she'd left the bank, but I'm starting to get the picture." He slid his gaze from Jim to me, and I was tempted to tell him that whatever picture he was getting, it was one he should erase from his mind. Like where I chose to work, who I chose to work with was none of Peter's business.

"Well, I hope you don't mind if I borrow Annie for a second." Since Jim already had a hand on my arm and was piloting me toward the bar, this seemed an unnecessary statement. "We have business to discuss."

"Do we?" I asked, as soon as we were out of Peter's earshot. "Or was that a little caveman grandstanding?"

"Is that what you think?" There was a rag on the counter next to the sink where the glasses were washed, and Jim grabbed it and wiped off the bar. Even though it didn't need it. "Actually, I do have something to talk to you about." I could tell he was trying not to, but he couldn't help himself; he looked over to where Peter sat with his back to us. "What's he doing here?"

"That's what I'd like to know."

Yes, it would have been perfectly legitimate if I had said that, but it wasn't me talking, it was Eve. She scampered over to join us, her voice a harsh whisper. "Annie, that's Peter. What is Peter doing here?"

I closed my eyes and gritted my teeth, gathering my patience. "I know it's Peter. And I don't know what he's doing here," I said, and when I opened my eyes again, I gave both Eve and Jim a laser look. "The two of you didn't leave me alone with him long enough to find out."

"It's not that I'm jealous or anything. You should know that," Jim said.

"But, Annie, honey . . ." This from Eve, who shot a look over her shoulder to where Heidi was taking Peter's order. "This is peculiar."

"As peculiar as Tyler showing up here to talk to you?"

Tyler had left the moment Eve came to stand behind the bar with us, and in Eve's slightly warped way of looking at things, I guess that meant his visit didn't count. That would explain why she clicked her tongue. "We have had dealings with Tyler in the recent past," she reminded me. "We have not"—she repeated this with emphasis—"we have not had dealings with Peter. Not since the day we saw that weasel at the courthouse and you signed your final divorce papers."

I didn't need the reminder. I steered the conversation back to where it started. Or at least to where I wanted it to start. "Which doesn't explain what Tyler was doing here."

Eve could roll her eyes with the best of them. "Annie, are you forgetting? We keep tripping over him when we're investigating our cases."

"But he wasn't here to talk about Greg's murder. If he was, he would have asked to see Jim because Jim is the emergency contact for Très Bonne Cuisine. Or he would have talked to me if he wanted to know what I may have noticed at the shop last night. Or because he wanted to gloat about something he'd noticed that I hadn't. Or just to tell me to keep my nose out of places where it doesn't belong. He didn't do any of that. He didn't even order lunch, or a Pepsi from the bar. All he did was talk to you."

"Why, yes, I suppose you're right." Eve tried her best,

but it wasn't good enough. A smile broke across her expression. "Tyler and Kaitlin have postponed their wedding," she said.

This was a surprise, and while I processed it, I thought about everything it might mean. The implication hit like a Metro train. "Oh, no!" I backed away, both my hands out to keep the idea at bay. "You and Tyler . . . that doesn't mean that the two of you . . . you can't be serious."

"You are such a worrywart!" Even though it didn't need it, Eve smoothed a hand over the pink blouse that matched the stilettos that added three inches to her already towering height. "Tyler stopped in. Just as a courtesy. He said he didn't want me to hear the news through the grapevine. He said he thought he owed me that. You know, as a friend."

"Uh-huh." I crossed my arms over my chest and stepped back, my weight against one sensible, flat-soled shoe. "You and Tyler were never friends."

Eve's lips thinned. "Which doesn't mean he can't stop by for a chat now and then," she said before she gave me that look only a best friend can get away with—the one that pinned me to the floor, demanded the truth, and pretty much screamed *You ain't getting away with nothing, girlfriend.* "Is that why Peter is here to see you?"

"Now, now, ladies." He really didn't have to step between us, but Jim did anyway and I was grateful. This wasn't a discussion I wanted to have with Eve in Bellywasher's, not with Jim standing by and Peter in the wings. "We'll talk about all this later, why don't we. When there aren't any customers about. For now . . ." He looked around, scrambling to find something for Eve to do. "If you could check with Damien and see if the crab cakes are ready for table five, that would be a godsend."

Of course she agreed. But not before she raised her

perfectly arched eyebrows in a look that promised we had a lot to talk about.

We did.

As soon as I could sort through what the hell was going on.

"I didn't know he was coming," I told Jim the moment Eve was gone. It wasn't as if I felt obliged to provide some sort of excuse, I just wanted to be up front with him. "I'm not especially happy to see him."

"Of course I know that, Annie." His smile came and went. "And I'm sorry if I came across like some antediluvian throwback. You have every right to talk to anyone you like. More right to talk to him than others, I suppose." Again, he looked Peter's way. "He's not what I expected."

"Really?" I looked that way, too, and while I was at it, I elbowed Jim in the ribs. "You thought he would have cloven hooves, horns, and a tail, right?"

Jim grinned. "I didn't think he'd be that nice looking. I mean—" Like most guys, he was embarrassed to admit he even noticed what other guys looked like. But then, Peter's hard to ignore. Not that he's drop-dead gorgeous or anything. He's not. He's not as tall as Jim. He's not as broad in the shoulders. I suppose he's technically not more than average looking, but somehow, for Peter, that's more than enough.

He's got dark hair and a great smile. He's got a rugged, square chin that I used to think indicated strength of character, and a kind of swagger that has less to do with his opinion of himself than it does with self-preservation. When you teach chemistry to hormone-driven teenagers, you'd better be all about attitude. Or they'll eat you alive.

"He's a fine-looking bloke," Jim finally said, because really, there was no way out of it. "You must have made a handsome couple."

"Handsome is as handsome does." Just so he didn't

forget it, I stood on tiptoe and planted a kiss on Jim's cheek. "What Peter did to me . . . no way does that qualify as handsome."

"Neither would me marching over there and dragging you away from him. Not if I wasn't telling the truth. I really do have business to discuss with you."

Jim pulled a key chain out of his pocket and handed it to me. It held three keys and had a little corkscrew on the end of it. I recognized it as the extra set of keys Monsieur Lavoie kept at Bellywasher's as a backup. "I need you to go over to Monsieur's."

I thought about the shop and the blood on the floor and how it wasn't supposed to be cleaned up until the next day, and my stomach flipped like it hadn't flipped in a long time. Well, at least not since a couple minutes before when I ran into Peter. "Of course, if there's something you need . . . ," I said, and I didn't sound convincing, even to me. "But I doubt the cops will let me in. They're probably still processing the crime scene."

"Oh, no, not to the shop." Jim gave me a quick, apologetic smile. "It's his home where I'd like you to go. I think we should pick up the mail, maybe turn on a light or two. You know, make the place looked lived in so that no one notices he's gone and gets it into their heads that this might be a good time for a burglary."

"Of course. I should have thought of that myself."

"I'd go on my own, but there's a bride coming in just a bit for a consultation on a wedding luncheon next month." He glanced up at the clock that hung above the bar. "The lunch hour is just about over. Take Eve with you, why don't you. That's better than you going off alone."

Grateful for the distraction and glad to have a legitimate excuse to tell Peter we'd have to catch up another time, I went into the kitchen to find her.

"This is perfect, Annie." She practically purred when I told her we were going out. "A chance to dish the dirt on Tyler and Peter and investigate, all at the same time."

It was exactly what I had been thinking.

Except for the Peter part, of course.

The Peter part I still wasn't ready to talk about. At least until I could think it over and figure out what the heck had just happened.

Of course, that didn't prevent Eve from trying to get every little morsel of info out of me. She talked all the way to Cherrydale, a stone's throw from the Clarendon neighborhood where Très Bonne Cuisine is located. She was still talking when we maneuvered our way around a dark sedan just pulling away from the curb. We parked in Monsieur's driveway.

I'd been to the house a couple of times before, and this time, just like then, I was impressed by the charming 1920s bungalow. Monsieur had owned it for little more than a year, and he'd renovated it from top to bottom. I knew that though it was small, it was packed with every modern convenience, from a media room to the kind of sleek and well-stocked kitchen most food lovers only dream of.

I also knew that if I was going to find out where Monsieur was and why we hadn't been able to find him, this was the perfect place to start.

"Wait." I put a hand on Eve's arm and stopped her when she was about to pop out of the car. "Let's take a couple minutes and just look at the place. Anything seem weird to you?"

She stared at the house. "Not a thing. You?"

"No." I hated to admit it, but facts were facts. My hopes dashed, I pushed open the car door. "I was hoping we'd see something glaring. You know—"

"Like a written note from Monsieur, telling us exactly where he is and why?" I didn't have to look Eve's way to know she was smiling.

"That would be nice, but I'd settle for the next best thing."

"Which is . . . ?"

We stepped into the house and I picked up the mail that was lying on the floor near the chute. "Nothing interesting here, that's for sure," I said, thumbing through Monsieur's mail. That day, he'd gotten a cell phone bill, a cable bill, three catalogs from cookware suppliers, and an invitation to join a cookbook-of-the-month club. All of the mail was ordinary. "Maybe there's something here in the house that will give us a clue."

There wasn't. Not in the sleek, modern kitchen or the media room or the living room with its stylish furniture and walls faux painted to look like seude.

By the time I worked my way upstairs to Monsieur's bedroom, I'd pretty much given up hope of finding anything at all.

Of course, that was before I was brazen enough to look through Monsieur's dresser drawers. And what I found there . . .

"Eve!" She was checking out the bathroom and I guess she heard the hum of excitement in my voice, because she showed up lickety-split. "Take a look at these."

I held out a handful of driver's licenses for her to look at.

"They're from different states," she said, shuffling through them. "This one's from Nevada and this one's from Maryland and this one's from West Virginia. And they all belong to different people. Why would Monsieur have all these folks' driver's licenses?"

I couldn't blame her for missing the point. Even though it was practically screaming at us. I mean, after all, who would have imagined . . .

My hands trembling and my mouth suddenly dry, I took the licenses from her and fanned them out. "Sure,

the states are all different," I said. "So are the names.
But look at the pictures, Eve. The pictures are all—"

"Oh, my goodness!" Eve's mouth dropped open. Now
that I was holding the licenses, she was free to point one
perfectly manicured finger at them. "Annie, do you see
what I see? All those pictures on all those licenses . . .
they're all Monsieur Lavoie!"

Five

✖

I DON'T KNOW WHAT THE CLEANING CREW USED TO get the bloodstain off the floor at Très Bonne Cuisine, I only know that whatever it was, it worked like a charm. By the time they were there for a couple hours, there was little sign left of the horror that had happened in the shop only two nights before.

I watched as they finished the floor and started in on the counters, the front display window, and the area around the cash register. There wasn't any blood in any of those places—not that I could see, anyway—but Jim had put me in charge, and as the person in charge, I decided that I wasn't taking any chances; a thorough cleaning was definitely in order.

Besides, if I worried about the work crew and (since we were paying by the hour) how much the whole thing was going to cost, I wouldn't have to think about those—

"The drivers' licenses, Annie. We really need to concentrate on those licenses."

Eve was right, but even as she zipped past, refilling

the stock of the store's trademark mint green shopping bags that were kept behind the front counter, I kept my sights—and my mind—on the cleaning crew.

It beat going over what I'd already gone over so many times in my head.

What were all those licenses doing in Monsieur's house? Why was his picture on them? What was Monsieur up to, exactly?

And could it have had anything to do with Greg's death and Monsieur's disappearance?

"I dunno." So much for my resolve. Sure, I'd sworn I wasn't going to talk about it, or even think about it, for that matter. But as Eve worked on stowing the bags within easy reach of the cash register, I just couldn't help but tell her what I was thinking. The whole thing was eating at me, and as always, it was easier to talk out the problem than it was to let it bounce around inside my head until my brain hurt. "It just doesn't make sense, Eve. Those drivers' licenses, they can't have anything to do with Monsieur's disappearance."

She paused in the middle of what she was doing, wrinkled her nose, and tipped her head. "No. They can't. But we should look into them anyway. What if Monsieur is a Russian spy? Or an undercover agent for some rogue dictator state? What if he's an alien and their technology is better than ours, of course, so they've learned how to make their people . . . or beings . . . or critters . . . or whatever they are, look just like us, and they're living among us and we don't know it?"

I could tell that after work the night before, Eve had gone home and watched the Sci Fi Channel. Or truTV. Or a little of both.

"I don't think so," I told her, and left it at that. What was the point of debating her theories, anyway? "But it sure is strange. And I sure would like to find out what's going on. But where would we even begin? Even murder is more straight-up than identity theft. If that's what it is. Fake driver's licenses . . . I'm out of my league." Just thinking about the possibilities—all of them terrible—made my heart pound. I told myself to get a grip. "There's got to be some logical explanation for Monsieur having those licenses. I mean other than the spy/covert agent/alien angle. All we have to do is figure it out."

This did not cheer me in the least. We had a murder on our hands already, and I had enough on my plate. Like a store to run. And all the paperwork piling up at Bellywasher's. Not to mention the not-so-insignificant fact of Peter walking back into my life.

It was overwhelming, and because it was, I stuck with the tried and true.

"Monsieur's not a crook," I said, trying to convince Eve at the same time I tried not to think about the neatly stacked display of Vavoom! jars nearby. Seasoned salt that passed for some magical seasoning was one thing, sure, but it was a far cry from identity theft.

I went on putting words to my thoughts. "So if Monsieur isn't a criminal, the licenses can't mean anything. They sure can't have anything to do with what happened here at the shop. Monsieur's not even a suspect. At least I don't think he is. Tyler didn't make it sound that way."

"No, he's not a suspect." For the second time in as many minutes, Eve was deep in thought. It was probably a record. "Monsieur's a . . . a material . . . a material something."

"Material witness?"

"That's right." Eve said this with so much conviction, I couldn't help but look at her carefully, surprised. As soon as I saw a flush race up her neck and darken her cheeks, I knew what was coming.

"Tyler called last night," she said, and if the confession wasn't enough to confirm my worst suspicions, the fact that she wouldn't look at me was. "He mentioned it, that's all."

"He stopped at Bellywasher's to see you yesterday. He called you last night. Eve, I'm not liking the sound of this. Are you and Tyler—"

"You watch your mouth, Annie!" As if she'd touched her finger to a live wire, Eve backed up until she was standing against the lighted cubbyholes that lined the wall behind the cash register. Each one featured a Très Bonne Cuisine product, artfully displayed. The light glanced against a copper saucepan and made Eve look as if she was surrounded by a metallic halo. "Don't you even suggest anything like . . . like what you're suggesting. It's bad luck to talk about things like that. Or bad karma. Or something. Tyler and I . . ." She swallowed her words along with a breath of horror. "The man is despicable."

"So you've been telling me for a whole year." I leaned against the counter, the better to catch her eye. "But when I saw the two of you at Bellywasher's yesterday, you didn't look like you thought he was despicable."

"Annie, you know me better than that."

I did. Which was why when Eve went back to straightening the shopping bags without giving me details, I knew something was up. Eve is all about details.

"I was just being polite," she said, her voice tight and her shoulders rigid. "You know, the way I would be to any customer. I wasn't about to turn Tyler away. Not when he was going to buy lunch."

It was the same thing I'd told myself about Peter.

The trick was, I knew how I felt about Peter and I had the sneaky feeling it wasn't anything like what Eve was feeling for Tyler. Was I worried? Absolutely!

Which was why I had to probe—at least a little more.

"Only Tyler didn't," I reminded her. "Buy lunch, that is."

I knew the moment she gave in because her shoulders heaved. She stood, her voice as pleading as her look. "It's just that, with the wedding being postponed and all, . . . well, you understand, Annie. Tyler just needs someone to talk to."

"The way I remember it, you and Tyler never talked."

"And the way I remember it, you and Peter always did."

She had me there.

Before I could admit it, though, Eve went right on. "But I didn't see much talking going on between you and Peter yesterday. You made sure you hightailed it away from him before the boy could even begin talking."

"Not true," I pointed out. "Jim needed us to go to Monsieur's. And we did. And then we found the IDs and . . ." We were back to where we started, and I was no happier now than I was then.

"Maybe we're looking at this all wrong," I said, far more comfortable with the puzzle of Monsieur's vanishing act and Greg's death than I was speculating about what Peter had up the sleeve of his suddenly-not-so-trendy polo shirt. "Monsieur's disappearance is somehow connected to Greg's death. That's pretty obvious. So maybe we shouldn't be looking at it from the perspective of him disappearing. Maybe we should be looking at this like a murder investigation."

I think Eve was just as grateful to change the subject as I was. She grinned. "Now you're talking, girlfriend! Where do we start?"

"At the scene of the crime." I made a wide gesture to include the entire shop. "When I walked in, Greg was lying right . . ." I went to the spot. The floor was still damp and I didn't want to take the chance of marking it with my shoe prints so I skirted the edges of the wet spot and pointed into the center of it. "Right there. And Tyler said that Monsieur's phone call was muffled." I looked around.

From where I stood, I couldn't see much. Rents in Arlington are at an all-time high and shop space is at a premium. Like most retailers in the area, Monsieur had learned to maximize his square footage.

Directly in front of me was the counter and the cash register, but as I mentioned, even the space behind it wasn't wasted. Cubby after cubby featured some speciality cooking item. To my left was the big front window where, once the cleaners were done, I'd have to set up some sort of display. Behind me was a wall of shelves made from glowing oak where gadgets were displayed alongside most of the other, smaller items the store sold: knives and corkscrews and ready-to-cook mixes for everything from southern food specialties like corn bread to soups the likes of which never came in the cans I bought at the grocery store.

To my right were the aisles that led to the back of the store. There were four altogether, and they were packed with merchandise. From where I stood—from where Greg must have been standing when he was killed— there was only one aisle with anything like a clear line of vision to the back of the store. It was the aisle that led straight to the room that doubled as Monsieur's office and stockroom.

I stabbed a finger in that direction. "That's the only place he could have been and seen anything," I told Eve, and I didn't have to explain. She started down the aisle and toward the back of the store even before I did, and waited for me to catch up outside the office door.

"We're not going to find anything," I said, just so I didn't get any crazy notions about clues that had been overlooked or mysterious messages only we could understand. "The cops have been all over this place. If there was any evidence in there, they already found it. Of course"—I grinned—"that's not going to keep us from looking." I stepped into the office.

Like the rest of Très Bonne Cuisine, the room was
well planned and tastefully decorated. It was a nice size,
maybe fifteen feet long and half as wide, with two doors
leading into it, the one we'd entered directly from the
store and another on the wall to our left that led to a
small entryway and the back door. A counter ran along
the far wall. There were shelves above it and plenty of el-
bow room. I wasn't sure exactly how Monsieur used the
space, but as long as I was working there, I knew it would
be perfect for checking in and pricing merchandise. On
the wall just to the right of the door was a copier and next
to that, a coffeemaker, one of those dorm-sized refriger-
ators, and a small microwave. On the other side of the
doorway was a desk that contained a laminator, a computer, and a phone. It was all pretty standard.

Until I turned and looked back into the shop.

Thanks to a display of poolside acrylic glasses, the
view of the front of the store wasn't perfect, but it was
plenty good.

"This has got to be the place where Monsieur was
when he made that call," I told Eve, and since she
was standing closer to the back door, I grabbed her and
marched her over so she could see what I saw. "Look. He
could have come in here." I raced over to the other door,
opened it, and stepped into the entryway where Monsieur
hung his coat and kept the trash containers. Just as
quickly, I walked back in, certain I was retracing Monsieur's steps.

"He could have come in here from the back parking
lot. I'll bet he was loading up the stuff to bring to Bellywasher's, just like I told Jim. And then when he looked
into the store . . ." I did just that, imagining the terrifying scene that unfolded in front of Monsieur's eyes. "He
probably couldn't see everything . . ." I moved to my
left, then my right, peering into the store as I did. From

one angle, all I could see were stainless steel roasting pans, heavy-duty mixers, a display of flatware that would have put my plain-Jane silverware at home to shame—and a sliver of the front of the store. The other angle provided a view of the glassware, a line of Tuscan pottery, small kitchen appliances—and a similar peek at the front of the store.

"I'll bet he saw enough," I mumbled to myself, then raised my voice so Eve could hear me clearly. "Maybe he heard something, too. Go ahead," I instructed Eve. "Go up front and say something. I'll see if I can hear you."

This sort of reenactment is right up Eve's alley. Her face shining with anticipation, she scurried to the front of the shop, and a moment later I heard her growl, "Stick 'em up," in a deep voice that I guess was supposed to pass for the killer's.

"Yes. I can hear you perfectly," I called. I raced to the front of the shop. She came toward the back. We met in the middle of an aisle that featured dish soap, hand cleaners, and lotions made from all-natural, earth-friendly ingredients. I couldn't even begin to imagine how anyone could pay thirty-seven dollars for a soap dispenser refill, and, rather than think about it, I stuck to my case.

"He heard something," I told Eve. "He must have. That's how he knew Greg was in trouble. Monsieur's taller than me and shorter than you . . ." I craned my neck, checking my theory against the evidence one more time. "He probably saw something, too. He might have seen the killer. He might have recognized him." I looked to the back of the store and the back door that led into the tiny lot where Monsieur parked his silver Jaguar. "And then he took off."

"I can't blame him." Eve shivered. "It must have been terrible."

"But why won't he come forward and tell the police about it?" Frustration bubbled in my voice, and I struggled for answers. Before I had a chance to find any, someone tapped on our front door. Through the glass panel on the door, I could see that it was a man, and I stepped around the cleaning crew just finishing (I made a mental note of the time so we weren't overcharged), unlocked the door, and opened it just enough to deliver my message.

"We're reopening tomorrow. Right now—"

"I'm sorry to bother you." The man touched a hand to the bill of his baseball cap. "My name is Len, Len Dean."

Surprised, I opened the door a bit wider. "Len Dean the English teacher who teaches with Peter Capshaw at Wakefield?"

A smile twitched across Len's expression. "Don't tell me you were one of my students. I hate it when I realize the years have passed and you kids are all grown up." He peered into my face. "Maybe you were a student of mine. You look awfully familiar."

"That's because I'm Annie. Annie Capshaw. Peter's wife." Heat raced into my cheeks. "Peter's ex-wife," I added as quickly as I could. "I remember chatting with you and your wife at a couple of faculty Christmas parties. And I think we chaperoned the prom together three or four years ago."

"That's right." Len's smile was genuine. "I should have recognized you; I just didn't expect to see you here. I just wondered . . ." He glanced into the shop and the smile fled his face. "I just came around to see if it was really true."

"You mean about Greg? Yes, I'm sorry. It is. You knew him?"

"Greg and I . . ." Len swallowed hard. "Sorry," he said. "You know how English teachers can be. Big softies.

That's what my wife always says. She says it comes from reading all that poetry, says the humanities teachers aren't as tough as math and science teachers. Greg was a math teacher, you know. Over at Jefferson. We never worked together, but we knew each other. You know how it is in the education community. As a matter of fact, we played cards together every Wednesday night." Once again, Len's gaze strayed into the store. He didn't know exactly where the murder had happened, of course, and his gaze wandered from the front counter and down the nearest aisle. I could only imagine what he was imagining—what had happened; where; if Greg had suffered—and since I'd always liked Len and his wife, Marissa, I took pity on him and opened the door so he could step into the shop.

"It's going to seem weird tonight," he said, settling himself near the display of cookbooks. "We're playing over at Guy Paloma's place. You remember him."

I did. I had always liked Guy and his wife. In fact, when news of Peter and my separation ran rampant through Wakefield High, Gina Paloma was one of the few faculty spouses who called me to express her concern even though I didn't know her well.

"We talked about canceling," Len said, pulling me away from my thoughts. "But heck, Greg loved our Wednesday night games and we figured it wouldn't hurt for us to get together and talk. You know, sort of like a wake. Or therapy."

I did know, and I told Len I thought it was a good idea. Right before I realized that a perfect investigating opportunity had landed on my doorstep. Literally.

"I met Greg a few times when I stopped here at the shop," I told Len. "He seemed like a nice guy."

"He was great." Len wiped a hand over his eyes. "Always real positive. Always upbeat. Even when he was diagnosed with that heart problem of his. He wasn't going to let that stop him, he said. Now that he was retired, he had too much life to live."

"Which is why this is so horrible." I didn't need to point this out to Len; he already knew it. I did it anyway, as a way of easing into some serious questioning. "Do you suppose there's anything about Greg's life that would have . . . I don't know . . . I mean, do you think he—"

"Had any enemies? Ones that wanted to see him dead?" Len pulled off his baseball cap and ran a hand through hair that was thinner than last time I saw him. "If you knew him at all, you knew Greg wasn't the kind of guy who made enemies. Except in school, maybe." He chuckled. "I imagine a math teacher makes plenty of enemies. Especially in those middle school grades. But that's just kids being kids. You know the way they are. You remember from when you and Peter were—"

"I do." There was that phrase again, and, rather than think about all the promise it held and all the misery it ended up causing, I thought about the students in Peter's classes who were special cases. Some were just plain hard to teach. Others had chips on their shoulders the size of the Washington Monument, and they weren't about to let anybody—especially a chemistry teacher—knock them off. All of them were challenging. None of them were seriously dangerous.

"This doesn't feel like it has anything to do with school," I said, and Len nodded in agreement. "If Greg was a card player, was he involved in any other gambling?"

"I don't think so. Not that I know of, anyway. And our card games, they were always friendly."

"And Greg always won?"

Len smiled. "Greg? Greg was the biggest loser to ever sit around our card table." The smile faded, and his eyes narrowed. "Until last week, that is. Last week, Greg was the big winner. I wouldn't even remember except that it was so unusual."

"Did anybody take it too hard?"

His eyes snapped to mine. "You don't think . . . ?" Len clamped his ballcap back on his head. "You've been reading too many books. It's a friendly card game. Just a friendly game, that's all. Yeah, there was a little grouching last week. Somebody accused Greg of cheating and, being a math teacher, well, I guess he might have been doing something like counting cards. But really, Annie, I don't think anybody took it too bad. Not bad enough to . . ." Again, his gaze roved the store.

I knew I had to keep him on track. "You don't seem too upset about Greg winning last week."

Len shrugged. "I'm not the guy who lost big," he said, and he stepped back to the door. "I'll bet Marissa would love to see you. We're playing at our house next week. Stop by, why don't you."

I told him I'd think about it, and I would. I did. Because even as I watched the cleaning crew pack up . . .

Even as I said good-bye to Eve as she headed to Bellywasher's for the dinner hour, and locked up and checked to make sure the door that led upstairs to where Monsieur used to conduct cooking classes was locked . . .

Even as I went into the back office to look over the lay of the land and try to figure out what, exactly, was involved in running a high-end kitchenware shop . . .

Even as I did all that, I thought about that Wednesday night card game.

And about how even the mildest-mannered player might make an enemy or two if his fellow gamblers thought he was cheating.

I was still thinking about all that later that evening when I parked my car in front of Guy and Gina Paloma's house.

All right, yeah, I hadn't been invited to stop in until the next week, but that was just a technicality. On my way up the front walk, I reminded myself what I was going to say to explain my presence before I started asking questions about that big win of Greg's:

I just saw Len.

I just learned he was a friend of Greg's.

I just wanted to say hello and express my condolences to the card players.

I would have done all that, too, if when the front door snapped open, I wasn't too surprised to speak.

But then, I hadn't expected to see Peter.

Six

❖

NOT BEING PREPARED FOR THE SURPRISES THAT WERE suddenly popping up in my life—surprises like running into Peter twice in close succession—was turning into something of a theme. Which would explain why I wasn't ready—again—the next morning when I opened Très Bonne Cuisine and was inundated with people.

Notice I said *people*, not *customers*.

I quickly picked up on the fact that the flood of folks who packed the store were mostly gawkers.

"This is where it happened, right? Did you see the body? Was there a whole lot of blood?"

I'd heard the same sort of questions so many times that morning from the morbid thrill seekers waiting out on the sidewalk when I opened the shop, that when I heard them again—this time from a kid in droopy shorts and a T-shirt emblazoned with the name of a heavy metal band—I snapped.

"Greg Teagarten was a nice, kind, gentle man," I told the kid, and since he wasn't expecting either the response or the vehemence in my voice, he jumped back and eyed me carefully. "How can you come in here like some kind of vampire, just looking for thrills and maybe the sight of a little blood? How dare you! How dare any of you!" OK, it might have been bad for business, but speaking my mind made me feel better. Since I was planning on speaking it some more, I raised my voice.

"If any of you are here to shop, I'll be more than happy to help you," I said to everyone and to no one in particular. "If you're here because you want to see where the murder happened, or if you're from the press and you're expecting a story . . . well, then, you're not welcome, so just get the hell out."

Did I think this would work? Not really. So I was plenty surprised (see, it was a theme!) when a dozen or so people, including the kid in the droopy shorts, shuffled out and refused to meet my eyes.

There were three shoppers left and while I still had their attention (OK, they were staring at me like I was some kind of nutcase), I took the opportunity for a little PR.

"Sorry," I said, and really, I meant it. "I didn't mean to be rude, but—"

"Hey, no apologies necessary." A bald man, a little older than middle-aged and wearing jeans and a black-and-white-patterned golf shirt, stepped toward the front counter where I was standing. When I realized my fists were on my hips and that probably wasn't the way to greet a customer, I pressed my arms to my sides and smiled.

He smiled back. "Not to worry," he said. He adjusted his thick glasses on the bridge of his nose, the better to see the other customers, who had gone back to browsing the aisles. "Everyone left is a regular. But you're not." He was a tall man, and he stepped back and looked me over. "I've never seen you in here before. Where's Jacques?"

I had expected that, sooner or later, someone would ask the question and I had a story of sorts all prepared. "He needed a couple days off. You understand. I mean, after all that happened here the other night . . ."

"Of course." The man was carrying a couple of pale green linen dish towels and a set of pot holders in shades of cantaloupe and watermelon. He set them on the counter. "I hope that means we'll see you here more," he said. "It's nice to have a woman around. Adds a little class to the place."

I knew he was kidding, so when he laughed, I did, too.

"Jacques should have hired you sooner," he said. "Sure, the guy's a cooking legend, and so many of the great chefs are men, but I'll tell you what, for my money, nobody can cook like a woman. Maybe I'm just old-fashioned, I don't know, but I'll bet you're a dandy cook."

"Cook? Oh, you know . . ." I didn't think this was the time or the place to admit that cooking and I really didn't get along, but the last thing I needed this early in my gourmet-shop career was for someone to get the wrong idea. "I'm just a friend of Monsieur's. I'm just helping out. As soon as he's feeling up to it, Monsieur will be back. He'll be in charge. And I'll go back to my real life over at Bellywasher's."

"Well, I'm glad he's taking some time." The man reached for the display of Vavoom! I'd moved to the front counter. I'd gotten there extra early that morning and before the store opened for business, I'd repriced all the Vavoom! at two dollars and ninety-five cents. It didn't exactly make up for the exorbitant price of twelve ninety-five that Monsieur had been charging, but it made me feel less guilty about taking so much of his customers' hard-earned money for the seasoned salt inside the jars. My display wasn't nearly as artistic as the one Monsieur had designed. What it was, though, was very, very neat.

The man plucked a jar from the even, careful Vavoom! pyramid I'd built and added it to his pile of purchases. "Jacques is a sensitive kind of guy. I can only imagine how much this whole thing has upset him. So tell me, where's he hiding out? The Ritz? Or is it the Willard? Knowing him, I'll bet he went for upscale. One look at this place and even somebody who doesn't know him would figure out that he loves his creature comforts."

"Oh, I don't think he's staying at either of those places," I said, and since I'm not really much of a liar, I left it at that. "I only hope that I can handle things for him while he's gone."

"You're off to a good start. Only, when you talk to him, tell him his regular customers are worried about him and anxious to have him back. Not that I don't trust you!" His smile was genuine. "But I always appreciate Jacques' recommendations and his advice." Before I could wonder who in their right mind would spend twenty-two dollars for two dish towels and ten bucks apiece for pot holders, the man pulled out his wallet, paid for his purchases in cash, and left.

He was barely out the door when Eve walked in.

"Lunch can't be over at Bellywasher's!" I said, but when I glanced at the clock, I realized it was. That's how fast the morning and the early afternoon had sped by.

"Thought you might need some moral support of the good old chocolate kind." Eve handed me a small white bag and I didn't have to peek inside to know what it was. I could smell the heavenly aroma of Jim's flourless chocolate cake. There were dishes and silverware in

Monsieur's office, and while she stayed up front to help the customers who'd just finished picking out their purchases, I went back and got them. The cake was supposed to be a single-sized serving, but I sliced it in half and put a hunk on each of our plates. Even at a half portion, we were flirting with caloric overload. I, for one, was willing to chance it.

When I got back up front, I saw that the customers were taking full advantage of the sale on Vavoom! One lady bought three jars. The man in back of her in line was thrilled by this first-time-ever sale on the product he claimed he couldn't live without; he promptly asked Eve to put four in his bag. As soon as she was finished with them and the customers were out the door, Eve got down to business.

"Here's what I don't get." She made herself at home behind the front counter. I stayed on the other side of it. "I mean, when you called last night and told me you'd run into Peter at that card game . . ." She took a bite of cake and rolled her eyes in a *Man, this is the best thing since sliced bread* sort of way. "It's no wonder you're crazy about the boy."

I knew she was talking about Jim, not Peter. "He was just as surprised to see me as I was to see him." I was talking about Peter, not Jim. I took a bite of cake and grinned, both at the taste and at the memory of the look of shock on Peter's face when he opened the door of Guy Paloma's house and found me on the front porch. "Imagine, he'd just gotten there for the card game and he was closest to the door. So when I rang the bell, he just naturally answered it."

Eve made a face. "I can't picture Peter playing poker. He's not that—"

"Daring?" With a nod, I agreed. "He sure never was back when I was married to him. He said he started playing after our divorce. I guess it was all part of the

new, cooler, expensive-aftershave-wearing Peter he became to satisfy Mindy. Or is it Mandy? Anyway, as it
turned out, it was perfect that he was there. I was able to
talk to him and find out about that card game last week.
You remember, the one Greg won. The one I tried to
tell you all about yesterday, only you didn't give me a
chance."

I looked at Eve hard when I said this. Too bad she was
busy looking at her chocolate cake. She didn't see that I
was leaning forward just a bit, my eyebrows raised, waiting for her to explain herself.

When she didn't, I had no choice but to call her on the
carpet. "You remember, Eve. We were on the phone together. We were talking. The way best friends—and fellow investigators—do. But then your phone beeped
because you had another call coming in. And even though
you told me to hold, you never came back on the line."

"Technical difficulties." Eve finished the last of her
cake and licked her fork clean. "It happens."

"So I hear." I wasn't buying it, but, hey, who was I to
criticize? If Eve dropped my call because she was talking to Tyler (and I'd bet a lifetime supply of Vavoom!
that she was), I'd spent part of the evening with my ex. I
guess that made us even.

"Peter was at last week's game, too," I said. "When I
asked about what Len Dean had said . . . you know,
about how Greg was the big winner and someone was
the big loser and I wondered if the big loser was also a
sore loser . . . well, Peter just laughed."

"It wasn't him, was it? Oh, my gosh!" Beneath their
dusting of Precious Posy blush, Eve's cheeks paled.
"Oh, Annie, I always knew he was a first-class weasel.
Greg won all Peter's money and then Peter . . ." She
swallowed hard. "He had no choice. I mean, he had his
honor to think about. And what was he going to tell
Mindy/Mandy when he came home with no money?

You said he was teaching summer school this year. He must be desperate. I mean, who wouldn't be with huge gambling debts? He needed vengeance. That's why Peter came in here and—"

"Peter did not kill Greg."

"Oh." Eve frowned. "I was sort of hoping he did. Wouldn't it be fun to see him behind bars?"

Maybe.

"That's beside the point," I said because the thought of Peter in an orange jumpsuit was far more appealing than it should have been. "I asked, you know, in a round-about kind of way. I asked Peter what he'd been doing Monday evening when the murder went down. He told me he was at a faculty meeting. You know, about summer classes."

"But he could have lied about it."

"He could have. He didn't. Peter was never much of a liar. Even after he met what's-her-name. He never lied about cheating, just came right out and told me about it. Besides, I called the school and checked. There really was a meeting that night. Peter really was there." We were getting so far off track, I wasn't even sure where we were headed anymore. I finished my cake, cleaned up the plates, and took them to the back room. When I'd put on a pot of coffee that morning, I'd realized there were perks (pun intended) to my job at Très Bonne Cuisine. Monsieur kept a personal supply of expensive Jamaican coffee on hand. It was leagues better than the off-brand stuff I bought at the grocery store, and I didn't feel the least bit guilty about using it. After all, I was minding the shop.

I made a fresh pot and, while it was brewing, I found a big earthenware mug for myself and I got out a matching one for Eve. I filled hers, then mine, and since there wasn't anyone in the shop at the moment, I sat down at Monsieur's desk.

"Peter told me that another one of the players was the big loser last week. A football coach named Bill DiSantis."

Eve nodded. "And Bill is the killer."

"Bill lost twelve dollars and fifty cents."

"Huh?" She set down her mug, the better to prop her fists on her hips so she could quiz me. "What on earth are you saying, Annie? Are you serious? This Bill character killed Greg over twelve dollars and fifty cents? That's sick. It's twisted. It's—"

"Bill didn't kill Greg, Eve. Don't you get it? When Len told me that Bill was the big loser, he didn't bother to mention that in their game, twelve dollars and fifty cents is high stakes. It's penny-ante poker. That's one of the biggest pots they ever had. That's why Bill made a big deal about Greg cheating. Peter introduced me to Bill. He's a regular kind of guy, and I don't think he'd hold a grudge, not over twelve dollars. Heck, that's what a jar of Vavoom! used to cost."

"So Bill didn't kill Greg?"

"You got that right."

"Then who did?"

The bell on the front door sounded. "I wish I knew," I said, hurrying to the front of the shop. "Really, Eve, I wish I knew."

ON THURSDAYS, TRÈS BONNE CUISINE IS OPEN UNTIL nine, and by eight thirty, I was beat. I was tired of fielding questions about Greg's untimely end, sick of reminding people that murder is not a spectator sport, and so truly weary of selling Vavoom! that I thought I'd drop where I stood. Yeah, word had gone out that for the first time since Monsieur had introduced it to the culinary community, the seasoning was on sale. I can only describe the result as an epicurean stampede.

When the crowds finally dispersed, I took the opportunity and headed into the back room. I grabbed a ladder and dug around in the boxes stored on the shelves above the work counter until I found what I was looking for—dozens of empty jars bearing the distinctive Vavoom! label, a five-pound box of bulk seasoned salt, and a note written by Monsieur that was, apparently, all there was of a proprietary Vavoom! recipe.

To five pounds of seasoned salt, it said in Monsieur's twig-thin, soldier-straight handwriting, *add one cup garlic powder, one-half cup dill, three tablespoons lemon pepper.*

Knowing that he actually altered the original product made me feel better about selling it. And still glad I'd put it on sale.

A little more digging, and I found all the ingredients I needed to concoct my own batch of Vavoom!, as well as a little scoop and funnel. At just a minute before nine when I was all set to lock up and begin filling jars, the bell over the front door rang.

"I'll be right with you," I called out. I hoped my exhaustion didn't register in my voice. As I had learned in the restaurant business, customers were customers. Even late customers. I wiped my hands against my white apron and started out of the office.

"No need!" came the reply.

I'd recognize that voice—and that sexy accent—anywhere. In spite of my fatigue, I found myself smiling. There's nothing like a visit from a honey of a hunk to brighten a girl's evening.

I greeted Jim with a kiss. Right before my throat tightened and panic closed in. "You're here. You're not busy at the restaurant tonight. What's wrong? We didn't get a bad review somewhere, did we? We couldn't have. But it's Thursday night. You should be slammed."

"And you shouldn't be so worried about business all

the time." Jim was clutching a small bouquet of flowers in shades of pale mauve, purple, and cream. "The bride," he said. "The one I quoted the wedding luncheon for. She had flowers shipped in, to see how the colors would look with our decor, and said I could use them on the tables. I thought you might appreciate them."

"They're beautiful." They were, and when I stuck my nose into the middle of the bouquet, I found that they smelled good, too. One of the cubbyholes behind the front counter featured a ten-inch crystal vase and I appropriated it and stuck the flowers in. I'd fill the vase with water when I went to the back room to get to work on the Vavoom!

"So what's up?" I asked Jim. "Why are you here?"

"To see you, of course." His smile was a little too bright.

"You mean to make sure I'm OK."

I knew that sometimes he hated having a detective for a girlfriend. He was nice enough not to point this out.

"Is there anything wrong with being concerned about you?" He glanced around the store and, satisfied that all customers were gone for the night, he went over to the front door and locked it. "There's been a murder here recently. I don't need to remind you of that. It's only natural that I worry."

"And I appreciate it. I really do. Truth be told . . ." I came back around to the front of the counter and looped my arm through Jim's. "This is the first time all day that I've been alone. I've been so busy, I haven't had a chance to sit down for more than a minute at a time."

"I'm glad to hear it. But I can't have you working yourself to a frazzle. That's why I've hired you some help."

I wasn't expecting this, and I stepped back, surprised. "You think I can't run the shop on my own?"

"I think you could rule the world if you were so inclined. But I don't like the idea of you working such long hours."

"And if I have help, I won't be alone."

"Aye." He gave in with a smile. "Raymond starts on Monday."

"And Raymond is . . . ?"

"A customer. Has been for years. Used to come around back when I worked here. He's devoted to the place. He's one of those brainy types, runs a computer company or a Web site or something. But he fancies himself a cook. I offered him a chance at some hours here at the shop, and he jumped at it. Don't look at me that way," Jim added, though what way I was looking at him, exactly, I wasn't sure. "Is that such an awful thing, to be worried about you?"

"Actually, it's sweet." It was, and something a lot of guys wouldn't have thought about. Peter never would have.

I caught myself as soon as the thought formed and ordered it out of my head. I'd spent the better part of the last couple years banishing all thoughts of Peter. I didn't need to get into any new bad habits.

"It will be nice to have some help," I told Jim. It was the truth, and better than what I'd been thinking about. "Truly, I never imagined I'd be this busy."

"And no wonder." What was left of my display of Vavoom! caught Jim's eye and he untangled my arm from his so he could step closer to the front counter and read the computer-generated sign I'd taped there. "Sale?" He considered the concept. "That's one product Jacques has never put on sale. Said he never had to. That it practically sold itself, no matter what price he put on it."

"Well . . . yes . . ." I had never told Jim the truth about Vavoom! Partly because I didn't think there was much point. Mostly because I didn't want him to think less of Monsieur. I edged into the subject now with something less than enthusiasm.

"Vavoom! is pretty good stuff, and I used to use it all the time myself, but you know . . ." Like a diver going off the high board, I pulled in a breath and took a leap. "It's seasoned salt," I said. "Vavoom! It's seasoned salt with a bit of lemon pepper and dill and garlic thrown in for good measure. I should have told you sooner, but . . . well, want to see? Come on."

I grabbed Jim's arm and tugged him down the aisle, and once we were in Monsieur's office, I showed him the empty jars and the bulk seasonings and the handwritten recipe.

"That's why I put it on sale, Jim," I confessed. "It just didn't seem right charging that much for the stuff. I've seen the invoice for the bulk salt. Monsieur hardly pays more than ten dollars for five pounds of it, then turns around and—"

"The cheat." Jim shook his head. He didn't look angry, exactly. He looked exasperated. And more than a little disappointed. "I never suspected."

"I knew." At this point, I had no choice but to explain how I'd discovered Monsieur's scheme back when I was a cooking student at Très Bonne Cuisine. "I never wanted to tell you. I didn't want you to think less of him."

Jim glanced at the recipe. "Well, he is changing it somewhat. I suppose that excuses Jacques to some extent. But honestly, I never thought . . ." He blew out a breath of annoyance. "It's quite a scam, isn't it? And he's got everyone believing it's a gourmet treat."

I moved over to the counter and measured the additional ingredients. I added them to the salt, stirred, and started filling jars. Without me asking, Jim stepped up beside me to help.

I'd barely finished one when what he'd said struck a chord.

"It's a scam!" I repeated Jim's words. They didn't provide all the answers, of course, but suddenly those IDs we'd found at Monsieur's . . . suddenly, they made a lot more sense.

Seven

✖

I QUIT MY JOB AT PIONEER SAVINGS AND LOAN BE-
cause running back and forth between the bank
and Bellywasher's was too much to handle.

Great plan, yes?

It had worked for exactly . . . er . . . let me do a little
math here.

It looked like my plan had worked for less than
twenty-four hours.

Now, nearly a week after I walked into Très Bonne
Cuisine and saw Greg's body lying on the floor, my life
was more hectic than ever. The shop was open six days a
week and yeah, once in a while Eve came in to help or
Jim stopped by to lend a little moral support. But by and
large—at least until that happy day when the help Jim
hired actually started—I was pretty much a one-man . . .
uh . . . one-woman show.

And there were still invoices to pay and file at Bellywasher's.

And invoices to pay and file at Très Bonne Cuisine.

And shipments to check, and bank deposits to take

care of, and tax papers to prepare, and cash registers to balance and stock with proper change.

At both places.

Not to mention the whole taking-care-of-the-customers part, which I didn't have to deal with at Bellywasher's, thank goodness, but did have to handle at the shop. The problem with customers, see, is that they ask questions. About cooking. And cookware. The problem with me is that I don't know any of the answers.

To say that my stress levels were to the moon would be completely understating the problem.

It should come as no surprise, then, to learn that as much as I was itching to look into Monsieur's disappearance and that tantalizing stack of licenses and how they might (or might not) be related to his Vavoom! scam, I never had much of a chance until Sunday. That was the one day of the week that Très Bonne Cuisine was closed, and after the brunch crowd at Bellywasher's had finally cleared out and before the dinner crowd could arrive, Eve and I took some time and convened in my apartment.

I was sitting at my computer. She was on a chair next to mine. I gave her a sidelong look and made sure not to sound too critical when I said, "You know, there are no dogs allowed in this apartment complex."

"Doc isn't a dog." Eve had the critter in her lap, and she lifted him so they could rub noses. He looked an awful lot like a dog to me. Even if he was wearing a red cotton sweater that matched Eve's tank top. "Doc is my itty-bitty friend. And besides . . ." She scrubbed a finger behind one of the dark, V-shaped ears of the tiny Japanese terrier. "It's not like he lives here or anything. He's just visiting. With me. Nobody could complain about that. Nobody would even know he was here. He's so well behaved and so quiet. Like a little angel in a dog suit!"

"Uh-huh." Pardon me for not sounding nearly as enthusiastic. I clearly remembered the night she snuck Doc into the back room of Bellywasher's and he escaped, walked out into the restaurant, and barfed all over the place. "My neighbors will not be happy if he starts carrying on."

"He's not going to carry on. He's too good to carry on." Eve planted a kiss on top of the dog's head before she lowered him into an oversized white leather tote bag studded with rhinestones that matched the ones on Doc's collar. At least I hoped he was wearing his rhinestone collar. During one of our investigations, we'd discovered that the sparkly collar Doc was wearing when Eve got him (the one we'd always assumed was just a showy fake) was the real deal. The thought of that many genuine diamonds in my plain ol' middle-class apartment was enough to make my blood pressure soar.

Ever practical, I decided it was best not to think about it.

"Here's what we're going to do," I told Eve, partly because it took my mind off the diamonds, and mostly because time was a-wastin'. "We're going to do a little research. About Monsieur. I figure if we find out all we can about him, then we'll be able to figure out what he's up to with the IDs. And where he might be."

Eve had recently seen her aesthetician, so when she shook her head, her blonde hair gleamed in the glow of my desk lamp. "I don't know. Think about it, Annie. We know all there is to know about Monsieur. He's our friend."

"Do our friends tell us everything?"

I paused here. A long time. Which gave Eve the perfect opening to bring up Tyler. She hadn't said one word about him in days. Naturally that made me suspicious. I was dying to know what was up with him. And her. And them.

When she said not a thing, I waited even longer.

That didn't work, either, so I puffed out a breath of

exasperation and went right on. "I've asked Jim," I told her. "We sat down together last night and talked for a long time. I told him to tell me everything he knew about Monsieur." There was a yellow legal pad on my desk and I picked it up and handed it to Eve. "That's all he knows."

She read over my neatly written notes. "French. Owner of Très Bonne Cuisine. Lives in Cherrydale." Eve wrinkled her nose. "See? I told you so. We know all that."

"Except there's more." I pointed to the next lines.

"Loves to cook. Good businessman. Reasonable boss, though not especially generous when it comes to salary and raises. Cares about his customers. Except for the Vavoom! thing."

Eve wasn't around the night Jim found me filling the Vavoom! jars so I filled her in about that part of the story. "Jim was disappointed," I said. "He didn't think his friend could ever be that—"

"Dishonest?" Eve flipped the page on the legal pad, but since there was nothing written past the first page, she flipped it right back. "It doesn't say here that he thinks Monsieur is dishonest."

"No." The thought sat uneasily with me, and I twitched my shoulders. "Jim didn't want to come right out and say it, so I didn't add it. But that's not the point." I reached for the pad and tapped a finger against the list. "The point is that it's a pretty short list. And pretty basic, too. Even though Jim has known Monsieur for years, he really doesn't know that much about him."

"Monsieur is a private person."

"But he's not." I thought about all those smiling faces on all those jars of Vavoom! "Monsieur is a showman. He loves publicity. He adores the spotlight. He's got a following in the area and he loves that, too. You've seen the way he perks right up when somebody walks into the shop and says they saw his picture in the paper or in some culinary magazine or another. The same thing happens at Bellywasher's when he's there and someone walks in and recognizes him. He's as happy as a kid on Christmas morning when that happens, and he's not shy about talking to anybody or about posing for pictures. So why is it that a man who loves to be the center of attention—a man we think of as our friend—why is it that we really don't know that much about him?"

Eve tipped her head. "I never really thought about it before," she admitted.

"Why would you? Why would any of us? We all meet people and we take those people at face value. They tell us they're cooks, and we believe them. Why shouldn't we? They tell us they're rocket scientists or horse trainers or that they work behind the counter at the local Starbuck's, and there isn't one reason in the world for us to stop and consider if they're telling us the truth or not."

Eve still wasn't sure where I was headed. At the risk of ruining her perfectly put together look, she worked her lower lip with her teeth. "Are you saying that Monsieur might not be who he says he is?"

"I'm saying we don't know. Maybe one of those licenses we found . . ." I looked toward the drawer of my computer desk because that's where I'd stashed the IDs. "I'm saying that maybe one of those people is the real Monsieur."

"No way." Honestly, I couldn't blame Eve for sounding so dead set against my idea. I didn't like the sound of it, either. I didn't like the way it made my insides uneasy, or the way just thinking that our friend may have deceived us made my skin crawl. "You can't fake being French, Annie. Everybody knows that. French people are . . . well . . . they're French."

"I'm not saying he's not French."

"Then what are you saying?"

I wasn't sure, and I didn't like admitting it. I sighed. "I'm saying we should check. That's all. How could it hurt? And how much can we possibly know about a person who wasn't born in this country, anyway?"

"You know a lot about Jim."

"That's different." It was, and Eve knew it. Which was exactly why she brought it up. That would explain why her eyes sparkled, too.

And why she smiled when she said, "You and Jim are falling in love, aren't you?"

The question wasn't out of line. I mean, Eve is my best friend.

"Jim is terrific." It was the truth, and I wasn't shy about admitting it.

"And?"

I didn't even try to hide my smile. "And we're falling in love."

"I knew it!" Eve was so happy for me, she shrieked. "I can't wait, Annie! I can't wait until he asks you to marry him."

When I think about Jim, I get all warm and fuzzy.

When I think about matrimony, my insides freeze up.

I guess that explains why I was suddenly feeling like a Slurpee.

I hugged my arms around myself. "There's been no talk of marriage," I said.

"But if there is—?"

"There isn't. There hasn't been. Marriage is a big step. Bigger than quitting my job at Pioneer. I wouldn't even think about it. I mean, after—"

"Peter?"

As a best friend, Eve should have known better.

She didn't. She gave me that look of hers, the one that's innocent and probing—all at the same time.

"Peter is a nuisance," I said. "I don't feel a thing for Peter. Not anymore."

"Then why has he been hanging around?"

"He hasn't been hanging around." I hadn't even thought about it, but now that I realized it, I was relieved. "I haven't seen Peter since the night of the poker game. He's ancient history. Like Tyler used to be to you."

Remember what I said about Eve being my best friend? Well, I was her best friend, too, so she shouldn't have sloughed off my comment like it was nothing at all.

"Are we going to tell Tyler?" she asked. "I mean, about Monsieur's IDs? I wonder if it's something the police should know about."

I was nobody's fool. I knew a change of subject when I saw it. Or heard it.

Like I was going to let that stop me?

Remember, we were talking best friends here, and best friends have a dispensation of sorts; they don't have to back off. Not when the subject is l-o-v-e.

"I think it's too soon to involve . . ." I made sure I put so much emphasis on this word that anybody could have seen—or heard—where I was headed. "I don't know if we should get Tyler involved." I said it again, just the same way. "Unless he is already. Involved, that is."

"Well, aren't you about as subtle as a presidential motorcade?" Eve tried to look put out, but a smile played around the corners of her mouth. "Truth be told, Tyler is not involved. Not currently, anyway. I mean, not in the immediate future."

It took a moment for this momentous news to sink in. Even after it had, I wasn't sure I'd heard her correctly. "Are you saying . . . ?"

"The wedding has been postponed again. They set a new date. They pushed it back again." Eve looked much too pleased by this announcement, but before I even had a chance to feel

A) appalled
B) frightened
C) worried
D) all of the above

she breezed right on, "Tyler says it was by mutual agreement. That's how he put it. Mutual agreement. He said
that over the last months, he and Kaitlin have grown
apart. You know, the way some couples do. They thought
if they postponed the wedding, they might be able to
work things out." She shrugged. Not like she'd been
thinking about it and couldn't make sense of the situation. More like *Oh, well, what the heck, Kaitlin's loss is
my gain*.

Which I'm pretty sure is why my stomach did a flip-
flop.

"You know how it is sometimes, Annie," Eve said,
ever the bearer of wisdom when it came to any relation-
ships but her own. "You and Peter, you could never work
things out, either."

"I tried. Peter wasn't interested." I would have
thought she'd remember. "But that's beside the point,
which is—"

"That we're supposed to be talking about Monsieur.
Research, isn't that what you said?" In a message as un-
subtle as that presidential motorcade, Eve reached over
and flicked on my computer screen. "It's nearly three,
Annie, and I have to be back at Bellywasher's in a little
bit. We'd better get down to business."

There was no use arguing and, hey, since I'd probably
spend the rest of the years I knew Eve worrying about her
romantic entanglements—and since I planned to know
her for the rest of my long, long life—I figured there
would be time enough later to quiz her about Tyler. For
now, we had Monsieur to think about.

With that in mind, I Googled his name.

"Eight pages of citations!" I bent closer to the screen for a better look. "Here's the Très Bonne Cuisine home page," I said, pointing to each line as I went. "Here's an article about the appearance he's scheduled to make at the big D.C. food show in a couple weeks. He's one of the main presenters. That's what Jim says, anyway. Monsieur is supposed to be doing a demonstration of French cooking."

"I wonder what they'll do if we don't—"

This was something else I didn't want to think about. Two weeks was a long time. Too long to go without word of our friend. Rather than consider it, and the emptiness that assailed me when I thought about the way I'd feel if we hadn't made some positive progress by then, I kept on reading.

"Here's a page that talks about Vavoom! and how popular it is." I shook my head and clicked to the next page.

"Look! Here's one that says something about Monsieur's early life in France. That's exactly the kind of information we're looking for." I clicked on the article and when it popped up, Eve and I both bent forward, eager to read more.

The article was a profile piece that appeared in *D.C. Nights*, the local (and locally influential) culinary magazine, seven years earlier, long before I'd known Monsieur, or Jim, or that a place as terrifying to a kitchenphobe as Très Bonne Cuisine even existed. The headline declared Monsieur the "King of D.C. Cuisine." It appeared right above a full-color photograph that showed a beaming Monsieur in a blinding white chef's jacket. He was smiling in that devil-may-care way of his while he motioned in a very Gallic, *voila!* sort of way to the sign over the front door of Très Bonne Cuisine.

"Gosh, I hope he's all right." Eve's sentiments pretty

much echoed my own thoughts. I glanced over to see that, as she looked at the photo, her eyes filled with tears. "What if he's—?"

"Not going to talk about that," I said, and because the photo of Monsieur made the same impression on me, I scrolled down to the body of the article as fast as I could. "Not even going to think about it. All we're allowed to think about is what we can do to find Monsieur. For now, this is what we can do."

Eve agreed, and reached into her purse for a tissue.

At the same time that I instructed my computer to print the article, I started skimming.

"He's been in this country for seventeen years now," I told Eve, and without me even asking her to do this, she grabbed the legal pad and added the information to my list. "His mother was named Marie. She was a pastry chef back in France and he credits her for giving him a lifelong interest in food and a desire to prepare it correctly and serve it with flair. His father was Pierre Lavoie, a sommelier. That's a wine expert," I added, because I knew even without her asking that Eve didn't have a clue.

"Monsieur was born in a little town in France called Sceau-Saint-Angel. The family bloodlines go back there for hundreds of years. Wow. Imagine having that kind of wonderful, rich heritage. I'm surprised he didn't talk about it more. I've never heard him even mention Sceau-Saint-Angel, have you?"

"No." Eve squinted at the screen so she could copy down the proper spelling of Monsieur's hometown. "Maybe he had an unhappy childhood."

I read some more. "Maybe not. He talks about accompanying his parents on trips to wineries and orchards and to the markets where they purchased the freshest ingredients for their cooking. Look, here he says something about the first time he went to Paris and ate at Lapérouse."

I added another aside for Eve's benefit. "It's an old, old restaurant. Very famous. Supposed to be romantic, and with fabulous food."

"So we know Monsieur had a happy home life." Eve rapped the pen against the pad. "Maybe something terrible happened to him after he came to this country. You know, unrequited love. Or a love triangle with another chef and a gorgeous food critic. Or—"

When Eve got this way, it was best to stop her before things got out of control. That's why I asked her to get the article out of my printer and put it in the file folder I'd left on my desk, the one where I'd written *Monsieur* on the tab.

I printed out some of the other information we found out about him, too, but honestly, by the time we were finished, we still didn't have much to go on.

Except for that information about Sceau-Saint-Angel, of course.

I checked the clock, did some quick mental calculations, and Googled the name of the town.

A couple minutes later, I had the phone in my hand.

"How's your high school French?" I asked Eve.

 AS IT TURNED OUT, EVE'S HIGH SCHOOL FRENCH WAS nonexistent.

I should have remembered that.

Eve took four years of Spanish. It wasn't that she was some kind of fortune-teller who anticipated our current global economy. Or that she had an inkling of how valuable it would become to be truly bilingual.

The way I remembered it, there was a cute football player who Eve had her eye on back in our high school days, and since he was Puerto Rican by birth, he was taking Spanish for an easy A. While I muscled my way through French I, II, and III under the eagle eye of Sister

Mary Nunzio, Eve struggled just enough in Spanish class to make sure she needed extra tutoring from you-know-who. She went steady with that cute linebacker for the better part of our junior year.

Funny, isn't it, how even incidents like that from years ago have repercussions in the present.

That's why I found myself with the phone in my hand, listening closely as the person on the other end spoke slowly in the hopes of getting through to me.

"Cent dix-sept?" Just to be sure I got it right, I repeated what the kind gentleman from Sceau-Saint-Angel had told me. *"Êtes-vous certain?"*

I nodded in response to his answer. *"Je comprends,"* I told him, then thanked him and hung up.

"You don't look happy." Eve's comment was an understatement.

"Monsieur Brun . . . he's the owner of the one and only local bed and breakfast in Sceau-Saint-Angel . . . Monsieur Brun has lived there all his life." I thought back to our conversation. "I'm not exactly sure, but either he said he's two hundred and eleven or he said he's seventy-one. I'm guessing the seventy-one is right. Either way, he's been there a long time and he knows every single person in town. Everybody knows everybody else in town. They know everybody's families. And their families' families."

"And?" Eve leaned forward, anxious to hear more.

"And there are only one hundred and seventeen people in Sceau-Saint-Angel," I told her. "So it isn't hard to know what's going on there. Monsieur Brun . . . he says he's never even heard of a family named Lavoie."

Eight

✖

MAYBE COOKAHOLICS GET ANTSY WHEN THEIR FA-
vorite shop is closed. Maybe they spend their
Sundays pacing their kitchens, or poring over cookbooks
and planning the meals they'll prepare in the coming
week. I didn't have to try hard to imagine legions of
them taking the seasonally color-coordinated notepads
we sold in aisle one (shades of sherbet this time of year)
out of the modular drawer organizers they'd bought from
aisle two and scratching their lists of ingredients and the
details of the pricey cookware they'd need to make their
culinary dreams come true.

Maybe that's why Monday at Très Bonne Cuisine
was so incredibly busy. I couldn't see straight much less
take the time to consider what we'd learned the previous
afternoon from Monsieur Brun in Sceau-Saint-Angel.

Why had Jacques Lavoie lied to us, his friends?

Why had he concocted a history for himself that
didn't jibe with the facts?

If his background was phony, what did that have to
do with the IDs?

And with his disappearance?

Too bad I didn't have a second to spend on the problem. I was so busy during the day that when five o'clock rolled around and I finally remembered it was class night at Bellywasher's and I was supposed to supply the gadgets Jim would demonstrate that evening, I panicked.

I raced to the back of the shop and printed out the e-mail Jim had sent earlier in the day. Then, like a deer in the headlights of a fast-moving catering truck, I stood in the middle of the shop and stared at it.

"Rasp?" My voice was a little edgy (OK, it was whiny, I'll admit it), but it didn't matter. For the first time since I'd opened the front door that morning, I was alone. My desperation echoed back at me from the hardwood floors and the granite countertops. It was not a pretty sound. "What in the world is a rasp?"

"I might be able to help." The answer came just after the refined ring of the bell over the front door and I turned just in time to see a man close the door behind him.

I did say *man*, right?

I think I might have been more accurate describing him as a mountain.

The guy was well over six feet tall and his shoulders were so wide that when he stood in the doorway, he blocked the outside light completely. He wore crisp khaki pants and a pressed-to-within-an-inch-of-its-life white cotton shirt with short sleeves that showed off biceps where muscle bulged on top of muscle. His neck was as thick as the ham Jim prepared for the last week's class at Bellywasher's, and his chest looked to be chipped from granite.

"I'm Raymond," he said, moving forward to shake my hand. "You look a little surprised to see me. You knew I was coming tonight, right?"

Somewhere in the back of a brain crammed with information I'd never known existed, been concerned about, or wanted to know about cooking and cookware, a memory floated to the surface, and I recalled that my new assistant was set to arrive that evening. In fact, a long time ago in a galaxy far, far away (actually it was right there at Très Bonne Cuisine the week before when Jim brought up the subject), I'd heartily approved of the plan. With someone else working the shop, I might be able to get over to Bellywasher's in something close to reasonable time on nights like this, and, once I was there, I could try to clear my desk of the papers that were piling up on it like sand dunes on a windy beach.

I had not, though, expected Raymond.

At least I hadn't expected the Raymond that Raymond turned out to be.

Jim had told me the man he hired to help out was a Très Bonne Cuisine regular. I knew he was in his forties and that he was some kind of IT genius who ran his own incredibly successful business but longed to leave the corporate world behind and become a chef.

Go figure.

Raymond was gay, Jim had also told me. He was also helpful and friendly and when it came to food and cooking, he had encyclopedic knowledge. He lived in one of the million-dollar town houses that had just been built nearby.

All that was well and good. But whatever picture had formed in my mind, it was not a buttoned-down African American version of the Incredible Hulk.

Sometimes I catch on slow. But eventually I do catch on. At the same time I gave Raymond a welcoming smile, I realized that in the last week, Jim had come into the shop to help a couple of times, and always in the evening. Not coincidentally, evening was when Greg had been killed. Sure, Jim had hired Raymond to provide the culinary expertise the shop was sorely lacking now that I was in charge. But he was also looking out for me. He was worried about me. Jim had not just hired an assistant, he'd hired some muscle. Some incredibly amazing muscle.

"Raymond! I can't tell you how glad I am to see you!" True on both counts, the culinary count and the muscle one. "It's going to be so nice to have help here. We've been slammed."

"And from what I hear, when it comes to cooking, you're not exactly Martha Stewart."

Raymond said this with so much good humor, I couldn't help but laugh along with him. "You got that right," I admitted.

"Then I'm going to assume Jim was right about everything else he said about you, too."

I should have accepted the compliment at face value, but who could blame me for being a little curious?

"Oh?" I had to crane my neck to look up at Raymond. "What, exactly, did Jim say?"

Looking me over, Raymond ran a hand through his close-cropped hair. "Pretty, Jim said. He got that part right. He said you were smart, too, and I'm betting that's also correct since you single-handedly took over this place and it's looking as good as ever. He did not, however . . ." He plucked the list from my hands. "He did not tell me that you didn't know what a rasp was. Do you even know what it's used for?"

"Rasping?"

Raymond was kind enough not to point out that my guess was lame.

Instead, he strode down the nearest aisle (he practically filled it) to where the gadgets were displayed. He pulled what appeared to be a giant (and dangerous-looking) file from the shelf and held it out to me, its bright yellow plastic handle pointed my way.

"Rasp," Raymond said. "Sometimes called a rasp grater or a zester. What's Jim making?"

I stood on tiptoe to point to the printed e-mail message

in Raymond's hand. "Broiled lamb chops with lemon caper sauce. See. It calls for lemon zest."

"And it sounds divine!" He smacked his lips. "What he's going to do . . ." Raymond grabbed another rasper and demonstrated. "The rasp is run across the skin of the lemon. Like this." He pretended to hold a lemon in one hand, then glided the rasp over it. "That will shave off the zest, and it will gather here." He pointed to the underside of the grater blades, which, the way he was holding the rasp, were facing up. "Then Jim can measure the zest and put it in his recipe. See, it's really pretty easy when you just know what to look for. What else do you need, babycakes?"

I doubt I've ever been called babycakes by anyone, much less six feet four inches of muscular man. Had I been thinking clearly in an I-am-woman-how-dare-you-minimize-me sort of way, I actually might have been offended.

If I didn't like it—and Raymond—so much.

I motioned for the e-mail and read over Jim's message. "Grapefruit citrus sectioning tool," I said. "That's for the spinach, chicory, and grapefruit salad he's making." Raymond handed me something that looked like it belonged in the garden. "These aren't pruning shears?" I asked him.

He smiled like I was kidding.

I wasn't, and since I didn't want to break his heart, I kept reading. "Baked bananas and blueberries. Which means we need—"

"A banana slicer." Like a magician pulling a rabbit out of a hat, Raymond whisked a weird, banana-shaped item off the nearest shelf and held it up for me to see. "Clever little object. You put your banana here and just slice along the lines. Every home should have one."

Mine didn't. Rather than get into it, I went right on, reading from the list again. "He's also going to make glazed apple slices. Don't tell me, let me guess. That means we need an apple peeler."

"One that can also core and slice would be perfect." He marched down the aisle, reached to a top shelf, and produced the gizmo. "I bought one of these from Jacques right before Christmas last year so I could make my chicken breasts with slivered apples when one of my clients and his wife came to dinner. It works like a dream."

"And . . ." I checked Jim's list one last time. "A pineapple slicer. That's for the Jamaican punch the drink folks will be making."

"Done." Raymond added one last device to the pile. It reminded me of a small cordless vacuum, only more compact and skinnier. He must have been reading my mind. "Easy to clean up. Very simple to use. Perfect pineapple rings every time," he said.

And I knew that when it came to hiring help, Jim had found us a gem.

I was past the point of proud and, as the day had proved all too clearly, I was heading straight to desperation, so I wasn't even embarrassed when I blurted out, "How often can you work?"

Raymond's grin was infectious. "You're open late Mondays and Thursdays. I'll be here for sure those two nights. Need me on Saturdays?"

"I need someone who knows what a pineapple slicer looks like every day of the week."

"I'm going to take that as a yes."

"Yes!"

"I've got water aerobics on Wednesdays, and Fridays are always my night out so I'd rather not work that day. I have to get my beauty nap, you know! But except for the pesky meetings that keep getting in the way of my social life, I make my own schedule. If you need me during the day, I can probably make it. And don't you dare thank me," he added quickly, probably because he saw that my mouth was open and he knew I was going to thank him.

"This is the opportunity of a lifetime for me. It's a dream come true. As a matter of fact, I checked my schedule before I came over here and I'm free and clear tomorrow. If you need some help during the day cleaning up or stocking shelves—"

"Would you? Really?" I could feel the tears welling in my eyes, and rather than have Raymond think I was some kind of weirdo, I balanced my armful of gadgets and took them to the front counter. "I can't tell you what a wonderful help that would be."

"Hey, I love this place. And I miss Jacques. Any idea when he'll be coming back?"

"Soon. I hope." The reminder put a damper on the excitement I felt at having a new helper, and a new friend. "Not that I don't like working here or anything, but—"

"Jim told me." Raymond patted my shoulder in a friendly sort of way. His hands were as big as frying pans and I had to brace myself against the counter or risk falling over on contact. "He says you're not-so-good at cooking and great at everything else."

Yeah, that sounded like Jim. He was a gem, too.

I was thinking exactly that as I loaded my cargo of gadgets into a shopping bag and gave Raymond some last-minute instructions about the cash register and locking up. While I was at it, I'd noticed earlier that our supply of soup mixes was dwindling. I didn't remember selling any, but, hey, I was willing to chalk that up to a case of trying to do too many things at the same time. I told Raymond where the extras were kept and asked him to please restock the shelves, and I'd already hoisted my shopping bag into one hand when the front bell rang again.

I wasn't worried. Très Bonne Cuisine was in good hands.

Of course, that didn't stop me from freezing in my tracks when I saw who stepped into the shop.

"Hello, Annie."

Tonight, Peter was dressed casually in jeans and a T-shirt the color of the paprika in little containers on our herb and seasoning shelf. He glanced at the bag I was carrying. "You're leaving."

"I've got to get to Bellywasher's for a cooking class. Raymond will take care of you." I motioned toward Raymond, who was just coming up the aisle from the back office where he'd gotten one of our white aprons and was tying it around his back. On him, the apron looked as if it came straight from the store's Kids Cook section.

"Oh, that's OK." Peter barely looked at Raymond before he turned his attention back to me. He stepped toward the front counter. Since I was standing directly between it and him and the displays all around us made it impossible to get by without getting too close, I had no choice but to step back. "I just need a couple of things," he said. "I won't keep you long."

I wanted to say, *You won't keep me at all since I'm leaving*, but I remembered what Eve had said last time Tyler came to Bellywasher's. Paying customers were paying customers and as caretaker of his establishment, I had an obligation to Monsieur Lavoie to treat everyone who walked through the door with respect. Even a weasel like Peter.

I motioned to Raymond that I'd take care of things and watched as his eyebrows rose in an expression that clearly said he realized I knew Peter—and that he couldn't wait until we were alone so we could dish the dirt.

I ducked back behind the counter and from there, I saw that Raymond was straightening the shelves of stainless-clad cookware that was not so far away that he couldn't hear exactly what was going on.

"I didn't realize you were into cooking," I said,

watching as Peter took a quick look around. "Is it like poker, another new hobby?"

"Oh, you know how it is." Peter stepped closer. "Everybody cooks." His eyes lit. "Everybody but you. What are you doing here, Annie? The most cooking you ever did was grabbing a box of Hamburger Helper and—"

"Ancient history." It wasn't that I was ashamed of my cooking skills, or my lack of them. It was just that I didn't need to be reminded. Not by Peter, anyway. And not in front of Raymond. I sloughed off his comments with a laugh and a lift of my shoulders. "You learned to play poker. I learned to cook."

"Amazing." He said it in a way that made me feel a little queasy. Like he really meant it. Like he was impressed.

I pretended to fiddle with the cash register.

"But what happened to the restaurant?"

Peter's question snapped me back. "Bellywasher's?" He looked at me with those melting brown eyes of his. "You told me you were the business manager there."

"I am the business manager there. And I'm the business manager here. It's a long story."

"And again, I say, amazing. You're . . ." Peter took a step closer to the counter. Call it instinct. Even though there was a slab of polished granite between us, I took a step back. "You're like a different person," he said. "You're so accomplished. So professional."

"Which means I wasn't accomplished and professional before."

"Not what I meant."

"What you said." There was a time this would have cut me to the quick. Now, I simply cocked my head and stared at him, expecting him to back down not because he had to, but because it was my due.

It was.

He did.

And somewhere deep down inside, I actually felt a little sorry for him. "I've got to get going," I said, stepping to my right so that I could move around to the front of the counter. "We've got a cooking class at Belly-washer's tonight, and—"

"I won't be another minute." Peter grabbed a pig-shaped wooden cutting board from a nearby shelf and plunked it on the counter. From another display near the front window, this one intended to attract mothers and grandmothers for those last-minute impulse buys, he reached for a tube of pink cake icing. As if that wasn't enough, he added two boxes of the red, white, and blue citronella candles I'd put out in honor of the upcoming Fourth of July holiday.

"That ought to do it," he said.

I look at the disparate assortment. "You're sure?"

"Sure."

"You don't need anything else?"

He reached for his wallet. "Nope."

"Then how about if you tell me what you're really doing here."

Just as my professionalism and business acumen apparently had done, my question caught Peter off guard. I would have known that even if we hadn't been married for eight years. It was the uneasy, embarrassed way he smiled, I guess. Or maybe it was the uncomfortable way he shifted from foot to foot.

"I was just passing by," he said, and I actually might have believed it if he didn't push a hand through his dark hair when he said it. I remembered that gesture. I'd seen it a thousand times. Always when Peter was feeling guilty about something.

Oh, how well I remembered that he'd never once resorted to that gesture when he fessed up about Mindy/Mandy!

Keeping the thought firmly in mind, I wrapped the

pig cutting board in tissue and tucked it into a shopping bag along with the candles and the icing. "You were just passing by and you decided you couldn't live without a wooden pig cutting board? Or maybe it's Mindy/Mandy who needs the cutting board. What, is it some kind of romantic anniversary for you two? Maybe you're commemorating the first time you cheated on me with her? There are some who would see the pig as wonderfully symbolic."

In my peripheral vision, I saw Raymond give me the thumbs-up.

That was far more encouraging than the pained look on Peter's face. "That's not fair, Annie," he said. Leave it to Peter to try to defend the indefensible. "I didn't come here to argue with you. I just wanted to . . ." He was never the hemming and hawing type. He hemmed and hawed. "Actually, I just wanted to see you."

I was about to ring up his purchases, and my hands stilled over the keys of the cash register. "That's not a good idea," I told him.

Peter shrugged. "You can't blame a guy for trying."

"I can blame a guy for not trying back when we were married and you didn't give a damn."

At this, Raymond's eyebrows rose even more, and his eyes went wide. He had given up all pretense of not eavesdropping, and he stood with his colossal arms folded over his enormous chest, just listening.

I don't think Peter noticed. He wasn't looking at anyone or anything but me. "That was a long time ago, Annie. You haven't forgiven me?"

I'd like to say I took Peter's cash from him gracefully. It was more like I yanked the money from his hands. I punched the keys on the cash register, fished out the proper change, and shoved it in Peter's direction. "If you're looking for forgiveness, you've come to the wrong place. That's not my job."

"But—"

"Thank you for shopping at Très Bonne Cuisine." I gave Peter the smile I offered every customer as they left.

Right before I stepped around the counter, grabbed my shopping bag, and called a good night to Raymond.

"You're making a mistake, Annie." Peter's words followed me to the door. "You're forgetting that not everyone is what they seem."

Yeah, I already knew that. Peter had taught me that lesson.

But as I got to my car and headed over to Bellywasher's, the truth of what he said hit like a ton of bricks.

"Not everyone is what they seem," I mumbled to myself, and I knew exactly why it bothered me in the context of Monsieur's disappearance.

It was exactly the reason I hadn't done more to pursue that stack of suspicious IDs. Or the telltale information I'd received from Monsieur Brun, the innkeeper, the day before.

Not everyone was what they appeared to be, and if I dug a little deeper into Monsieur Lavoie's background, I was afraid I wasn't going to like what I found.

Did it matter?

Personally, yes, it mattered a whole bunch. To me, to Jim, to all Monsieur's other friends.

Professionally . . .

I knew exactly when I made up my mind, because my hands tightened on the steering wheel and my spine stiffened with resolve.

Professionally, I had to find out what was going on.

No matter what the consequences.

Nine

 THE BAD NEWS WAS THAT ON MONDAY, HER DAY off, Eve twisted her ankle.

No, it didn't happen at the gym. Eve and sweat are not on a first-name basis.

She told everybody that the accident happened as she was chasing after Doc, racing to save him from meeting a tragic and horrible end under the wheels of an oncoming bus.

I knew better.

Number one, because Doc is too lazy and far too spoiled to ever think about running away from Eve. I mean, why should he? The dog lives better than a lot of people. He certainly has a bigger wardrobe than mine.

Number two, I knew that just like Eve and sweat, Eve racing anywhere is a statistical improbability.

Unless she's racing to a sale at Nordstrom.

She finally fessed up with the truth—I knew she would—and the truth was that my instincts were right on. It was her own fault, Eve admitted. She had tried to outpace a woman who had her eye on the same pair of alligator slingbacks Eve saw from the other side of the shoe department. Eve darted. The other woman rushed forward. Eve sidestepped, pivoted, slipped.

The good news?

Well, according to Eve, the good news was that she got to the shoes first. Even though by that time, she was limping.

As far as I was concerned, the good news was that the injury wasn't serious. However, Eve had been ordered by her doctor to stay off her feet for a couple days. And that was the second piece of good news. Because she is the hostess at Bellywasher's and because a restaurant hostess is always on her feet, Eve was forced to take a couple days off. That meant she was free to investigate with me.

After all, Eve riding in the passenger seat while I drove qualified as staying off her feet, right?

Eve pulled down the visor on her side of the Saturn and peered at herself in the little mirror, checking to make sure her makeup was just right. Of course it was. "So, you think Raymond will work out well?" she asked me.

The way I grinned at the very mention of his name should have been a clue, but since Eve was so busy looking at herself, she didn't notice. "He practically begged me to let him work today," I said. "This is my first real day off in as long as I can remember. Raymond is my hero! He's going to be perfect. I talked to him before I left home, and he's in his glory. He actually thinks working at Très Bonne Cuisine is the best job in the whole, wide world."

"You don't." Eve snapped the visor back into place. "I don't know how you're doing it, Annie. I mean, with the way you feel about cooking and all. And I miss you at Bellywasher's."

"I miss being there." Who ever would have thought I'd say that about working at a restaurant! My grin stayed

firmly in place. "I just don't fit in at Très Bonne Cuisine.
Sure, the shop is gorgeous, and most of the customers
are nice. Except for the ones who come in just to see the
place where Greg died."

After a week, I should have been used to the scenario, but it still gave me the creeps. We were headed
south and the early morning sun was blazing through
my window. My air-conditioning was on the fritz so it
wasn't nearly as cool in the car as I would have liked.
Still, I shivered.

"We need to get to the bottom of this," I told Eve. As
if she didn't know. "The whole thing is weird, and it's
driving me crazy. Has Tyler said anything . . ."

OK, so subtle, I'm not. Since Eve was being less than
forthcoming about her contact (or lack of it) with Tyler,
it was only fair for me, as her best friend, to force the
subject.

"You mean about Greg? About Greg's murder?"
Even though she'd just checked her makeup, she
checked it again. "The only thing he's said—"

"Aha! You have talked to him again!" I was so proud
of my detective skills and so jazzed about catching Eve
in my little trap, I didn't realize how hard I was pressing
on the accelerator. It wasn't until I saw my speedometer
inch up to seventy-five that I caught myself, and slowed
right down. Sure, everybody on I-95 exceeds the speed
limit. All the time. But I am not everybody. Especially
when it comes to driving.

Careful to keep my speed exactly where it belonged,
I moved over to the far right lane to stay out of the way
of the speed demons on the road with me. The driver of
the dark sedan behind me must have been gauging his
own speed against mine. He slipped right behind me
into the lane.

I gave Eve a sidelong glance. "You've been seeing
Tyler."

"That's exactly why I haven't told you. I knew this was how you'd take it."

"Take it? Take what?" My heart thumped like the bass line in the music of the overloud stereo of the Hummer that whizzed by us as if we were standing still. "Eve, you and Tyler . . . you're not . . ." I swallowed hard. No easy thing, seeing as my mouth was suddenly so parched I could barely get the words out. "You're not engaged again, are you?"

Eve's only reply was a squeal of laughter.

It wasn't much, but it did make me feel better, and my heart rate ratcheted back. If Eve was laughing at the very idea of marrying Tyler, then it couldn't really happen.

Right?

I never trust cars that actually drive slower than me. Or maybe I should say more accurately, I never trust the drivers of those cars.

As I was thinking all this, I checked my mirrors—twice—before I passed the red Camry crawling along in the right lane. The car behind me did the same. It wasn't until I settled back in the lane and well in front of both the red Toyota and the dark sedan that I felt safe giving Eve another probing look.

"You didn't answer me."

"About being engaged? To Tyler?" Eve picked at her white linen pants. Not that there was any lint on them or anything. "Don't be silly, Annie. Tyler is still engaged to Kaitlin. Technically. And even if he wasn't . . . my goodness, Annie! Even if he wasn't, a man who's been engaged, then gets unengaged, he wouldn't be ready to get engaged again."

"Would you?"

"To Tyler? My goodness, you don't have any faith in me at all, do you?" Eve sniffed in the way she always does when she's put out.

I guess I couldn't blame her.

Tyler had sliced and diced her heart. He had pureed her self-esteem, stir-fried her self-confidence, and served it all up on the platter of his own huge ego.

Maybe I was starting to think like I worked in a gourmet shop after all.

"So let's go over our plan." I figured I owed Eve for questioning her judgment, and I engineered the change of subject without any fanfare. "I'm glad you're investigating with me, Eve. Want to grab that file folder I gave you when you got in the car?"

She did, flipped it open, and squinted at the copy I'd made of one of the licenses we'd found at Monsieur's. "The name on the driver's license is Bill Boxley." Thinking, Eve cocked her head. "Do you think Monsieur's real name is Bill Boxley? If it is, I can't say I blame him for changing it."

"I think it's a distinct possibility that Bill Boxley and Jacques Lavoie are one and the same person. That would explain why he has the license, right?"

"Yeah, but . . ." Eve hesitated.

I was negotiating my way past a van driving too slowly in the left lane and an eighteen-wheeler in the right that didn't seem to recognize that such things as speed limits exist. Only when we were safely by the van and watching the truck disappear into the distance in front of us, did I feel safe getting back to the conversation.

So safe, in fact, that I barely noticed that when I maneuvered my way between the van and the truck, the dark car behind me did, too.

I'd heard the uncertainty in Eve's voice, I knew where she was headed. "Yeah, but . . . ," I echoed her comment. "You don't think Monsieur might really be Bill Boxley? Or Bill might really be Monsieur?"

"I don't know what to think. And I'm not sure I

understand what you're thinking. What are we trying to prove with a trip to Fredericksburg?"

The answer was simple enough. "Fredericksburg . . ." Without taking my eyes off the road, I pointed to the photocopy of the driver's license. I'd meant to point out the address, but instead, I poked Bill Boxley in the nose. "Fredericksburg is the home of Bill Boxley. Of all those driver's licenses we found at Monsieur's, Bill Boxley's is the most recent. Check it out. It expired just a couple years ago. All those other licenses are older."

Eve squinted at the picture of Monsieur that graced the license. In it, his hair wasn't quite as silvery, and he was a little thinner than the man we knew. "And . . . ?"

"And I chose the newest license because it seems to make more sense starting there than it does starting with the older ones. My guess . . ." I paused here because, after all, it was something of a ta-da moment. "My guess is that we're going to go to the address on that license, and we're going to find Monsieur Lavoie there."

"You mean Bill is Monsieur? Or Monsieur is Bill? But why?"

I knew Eve's question had nothing to do with my logic, and everything to do with why people thought the way they did and did the things they did. That's why I shrugged. "Who knows. I mean, maybe Monsieur has a wife and seven kids living out here in Fredericksburg. Though why he wouldn't want anyone to know it, I can't imagine. Maybe he's gay. Or maybe—"

"Maybe he's a spy or an agent for a rogue government."

Just like the first time Eve had raised these possibilities, I was not about to let them distract me. "It's the whole Vavoom! scam thing that got me thinking in this direction, Eve. I'll bet Monsieur is up to something. Maybe not something as illegal as being a spy or the agent of a rogue government, but something he shouldn't be up to. I'll bet that's why he's got a couple of different identities. Theoretically, I suppose it's none of our business. Unless Monsieur's involved in something that's going to get him into a whole bunch of trouble. Considering what happened to Greg, I think that's a very real possibility. And even if it isn't . . ." I chose to think of the problem from this angle because thinking about the myriad illegalities I didn't even understand scared me so. "We can at least talk to him. We need to let him know we're worried about him. And if there's anything we can do to help him get out of whatever trouble he's in, we need to do that, too."

"We should also tell him the police still want to talk to him."

I bit my tongue. It was better than bringing up Tyler's name again and, besides, our exit was fast approaching. I had Eve consult the MapQuest directions I'd printed out before I left the house and we found Bill Boxley's address with no problem. It wasn't until I pulled my car into the driveway that I realized the dark car that had been behind us on the freeway was still on our tail.

Suddenly uneasy, I craned my neck, hoping for a look at the driver, but when he passed the house and continued down the street and around a corner, I reminded myself we were not the only ones allowed to drive the freeway between Arlington and Fredericksburg. My nerves calmed by a dose of common sense, I told Eve to stay put so as not to irritate her swollen ankle and walked to the front door, wondering as I did exactly what I'd say when Monsieur answered it.

I guess I shouldn't have worried.

Because Monsieur Lavoie didn't answer the door.

A Confederate Civil War soldier did.

*   *   *

"YOU'RE BILL BOXLEY?" NOT THE BEST WAY TO START a conversation. I shook away my surprise and tried again. "Hi! I'm looking for Bill Boxley."

"You found him." The man who answered the door was as round as he was tall. He had a shock of salt-and-pepper hair and a beard to match. It hung down to his chest, brushing his gray wool coat with its crimson cuffs and gold curlicue embellishment.

"My goodness, aren't you hot in that thing?" Leave it to Eve not to miss a trick. Especially when it comes to overlooking the big picture so she can glom on to the fashion consequences. She rolled down her window and called out, "It's the middle of the summer, sugar, you must be roasting in that big ol' coat!"

Bill Boxley laughed. I guess there's nothing like the thick accent of a true Southern belle to warm the cockles of a Confederate officer's heart. "Now that you mention it, young lady, I am a tad uncomfortable out here in the heat," he called back to her at the same time he opened the front door wider so that I could step inside. "Come on. Come on in," he said. "Your friend is welcome, too. The AC makes it much easier to tolerate this scratchy wool. On my way to get some regimental photographs taken," he explained, glancing down at his uniform. "You know, reenactors."

I was glad he told me. Then the house wasn't as much of a surprise. It was a medium-size Greek Revival, complete with white columns and a covered front porch. Inside, it was furnished with antiques. The walls were dotted with tintypes of men in uniform and women holding umbrellas and wearing bustles. From where we stood in a foyer papered with cabbage roses and violets, I could see into the living room. A musket hung over the fireplace.

"So . . ." Bill looked at me closely. "You with the Prize Patrol?"

I guessed he was going for funny so I laughed. "That's not it at all," I told him. "We just . . ."

Just what?

I'd been so certain the door would be opened by our friend Jacques Lavoie, I hadn't even planned for this contingency.

Like I was going to let that stop me?

I was on the trail, and, like any good detective, I wasn't going to lose the scent this early. "My friend Eve and I . . . she waited in the car because she hurt her ankle . . . we're just doing a little research," I said, trying to look and sound more professional than any gourmet-shop/restaurant business manager had the right to. "Has your driver's license ever been stolen?"

Bill had eyes the same nondescript color as the mousy brown in his hair. They opened wide. "It has. It has, indeed. But my goodness, that was years ago. You're with the police, right? I can't believe you'd care about a crime so old."

"Oh, you know how it is." I smiled widely at the same time I was careful about not answering Bill's question. "No one ever found the license?"

"Well, no." Leaning against a nearby wall was a sword hanging from a belt, and Bill reached for it and strapped it on. "Why does it matter after all these years? I got a new license. And that one's not expired or anything. If you'd like to see it . . ." He made a move, but I stopped him, one hand briefly brushing the elegant gold cord trim on his jacket.

"That won't be necessary," I told him. "We're just confirming the information. Tell me . . ." Considering that Bill wasn't Monsieur, Monsieur wasn't Bill, and Bill's license had been stolen, a whole new world of possibilities presented themselves—all of them with *fraud, felony*, and *identity theft* written on them in letters three miles high.

Almost afraid to ask, I eased into a new avenue of questioning. "Your license, was it taken from your wallet? Or did the whole wallet go missing?"

"The whole wallet. You can read that part in the police report if you look it up. If they even keep reports as old as that."

"And were there . . ." I told myself not to lose heart. Whatever Bill had to tell me, it might be important to the investigation. Even if I didn't want to hear it. "Were there credit cards in your wallet? Were those missing, too?"

"Well, that's the strange part, isn't it? All the credit cards and the wallet itself . . . they were all returned to me. Sent right here to me at home in a big manila envelope. I called the police and told them. They came and took the envelope away. Never heard another word about what they did with it, or what they found out. But I guess you know that, too, right? The only thing I never found again was the driver's license."

I breathed a little easier. "And your credit card accounts . . . were there ever any charges associated with them from the dates they were missing? You know, purchases you hadn't authorized and couldn't explain?"

"Nah, nothing like that! I told the cops I'd call if there were. Believe me, I went over my credit card statements with a fine-tooth comb. Still do." Bill took out a pocket watch and checked the time. "You will have to excuse me," he said. "I've got to get over to Marye's Heights before the photographer decides he can't wait around any longer." He checked his reflection in a nearby mirror and fluffed a hand through his beard. "You've got all the information you need?"

I did.

But notice I said that what I'd gotten from Bill Boxley was *information*.

I was still no closer to finding any answers.

* * *

THOUGH I WOULD HAVE BEEN HARD-PRESSED TO make a list of them, I guess there are some distinct advantages to working in a gourmet shop. I was able to prove it the next day when I used a pricey paring knife to slice apart the Bill Boxley license we'd found at Monsieur's. My knives at home would have chewed through the plastic and left behind a mess. This one, with its handle of crafted African blackwood, full-tang blade, and double bolsters (I have no idea what any of that means, but I heard Raymond describe the knives that way to a customer), slipped through the license like magic, right under the lamination, and after that, right under the photo of Monsieur that had been carefully pasted over the one of Bill Boxley.

I'd recognize that beard anywhere.

Truth be told, I sat there for a while, staring at my handiwork, completely stumped.

Monsieur took Bill's license and altered it to make it his own. But he didn't touch Bill's credit cards.

That was a good thing, right?

But it didn't explain why Monsieur wanted to be Bill Boxley.

Because Raymond couldn't help me out at the shop on Wednesday, I was working at Très Bonne Cuisine alone. I stewed over the problem (there I go, using cooking analogies again) all that day. But Raymond being Raymond, he felt awful about leaving me in the lurch. Me being me . . . well, I'm not usually one to take advantage of other people, but this situation seemed to call for serious measures. So I took advantage of Raymond's good nature and his guilt and asked him to work on Thursday. He agreed—I knew he would—and, armed with the next most recent license in Monsieur's stash, I got up bright and early that morning and headed north to Allentown, Pennsylvania.

Too bad Eve was feeling better (I don't mean that to sound as callous as it does), because she was back at work at Bellywasher's. That meant I had to make the three-and-a-half-hour drive by myself.

While I drove, I thought over what I was going to say when the man who owned this driver's license, Fred Gardner by name, answered his front door. Would I ask all the same questions?

Have you ever lost your wallet?

Was the license taken?

How about your credit cards?

And whatever Fred Gardner told me, where would it get me?

And what would I do next?

I guess the entire experience should have been a lesson in not worrying until it was time to worry. Because when I went to the address listed on the license, I didn't find Fred Gardner. Or a house, for that matter. All I found on the corner of two busy cross streets was an empty lot.

Curious, yes?

And while I thought it over, I stopped at a nearby mom-and-pop diner for lunch.

I already had my burger and fries in front of me when I realized I was wasting a perfect opportunity. My waitress was named MaryAnn. She was a thin woman with strikingly red hair and even more startling gray roots and since everyone who walked in seemed to know all about her and her family, I guessed she'd been around for a while.

"Excuse me." She was walking away when I said this, and she held up one finger to tell me she'd be with me in a jiffy and fetched the coffeepot. It wasn't what I wanted, but I didn't object when she refilled my cup. "I wonder if you can tell me about someone who used to live around here. His name is Fred Gardner."

"Fred Gardner, the music teacher? You bet I knew Fred. Everyone in town knew Fred. I played in the high school marching band back when he was the director. Clarinet. If it wasn't for Mr. Gardner . . ." MaryAnn wore a red-and-white-striped apron. It was decorated with the kinds of pins school booster clubs sell, the ones with kids' pictures on them. She touched a hand to a picture of a prepubescent young man with short, sandy hair and big ears. He was holding a tuba that was practically as big as he was.

"Learned to love music from that man," she said. "And I passed that on to my kids and my grandkids. This is Jacob, my grandson. He can't wait until he's old enough to play in the same marching band as his granny did." She smiled down at the button. "He's a fine young man."

"I'm sure." I was. MaryAnn was just that kind of person. "Does Mr. Gardner still teach music at the high school?"

"Fred?" MaryAnn shook her head. "He's been dead for twenty years at least. They knocked down his house just a couple months ago. His kids sold the property. You know how it is. They live out of town somewhere and they don't give a damn. I hear they're gonna be building a car wash over there where Fred's house used to stand. Too bad. Used to be kids and music there all the time. Now, a car wash." She shrugged, surrendering to the inevitability of progress.

"Then maybe you can tell me . . ." I'd made a copy of the picture of Monsieur—younger and thinner even than he had been on Bill Boxley's license—from Fred Gardner's license. I pulled it out of the file folder next to the plate where my burger and fries were getting cold and held it up for MaryAnn to see. "Is this Fred Gardner?"

She took the picture out of my hands and looked at it closely. "No way!" She'd already made a move to hand the picture back to me when she took another look. "But you know, it looks like . . ." She turned the picture this way and that, her eyes narrowed.

"I've lived around here for a long, long time," she finally said. "That picture there . . . that looks like an older version of one of the boys I went to school with. He sat next to me in Mr. Gardner's music class one year . . ." A lightbulb went on inside her head. I could see the glow of it in her eyes.

"Norman Applebaum," she said, handing the picture back to me. "Can't say for sure, but it looks a whole bunch like him. We graduated together from William Allen High. Class of '67. My goodness, I haven't seen Norman in years. But I do recall hearing something about him." Again, she stopped to think. "That's it!"

Someone called to her and MaryAnn turned away. As she headed back into the kitchen to pick up an order, she delivered her final piece of information over her shoulder.

"He went out to Las Vegas. Yeah, that's what I heard. He went out to Las Vegas years and years ago. Last I heard, he came to a bad end out there."

Ten

✠

I HAD STARTED OUT ON THE SLIPPERY SLOPE TO A LIFE of crime. I knew it, and I wasn't at all comfortable with it.

I guess that's why, that night as I slid a copy of the William Allen High School class of '67 yearbook across the bar at Bellywasher's, my hands shook just like they had back at the Allentown Public Library when I swiped the book.

Yes, I said swiped. As in filched, purloined, lifted, (gulp) stole.

"I'm going to send it right back," I said, even though Eve and Jim hadn't asked where the book came from or what I was planning on doing with it. "The folks at the library wouldn't let me check it out. I don't have a library card for their system, plus, they said yearbooks can only be used for reference in the library. And I could have just photocopied Norman Applebaum's senior picture, but there are other pictures of him in there. He was in the drama club. And on the newspaper staff. And I thought we could take our time and really look at the pictures and we could make our own copies, and I wanted your opinions, and I promise, I really will send it back. I'll even send a note of apology." I swallowed hard. "I don't think I'll sign it."

Jim kissed me on the cheek. "You'd make a terrible criminal. It's one of the things I love about you. That, and the fact that I never have to worry about the bev naps going missing." He held up one of the little square napkins that were stacked on our bar and every other bar in America. "You'd take one to wipe up a spill and buy me a case to replace it."

I wasn't just reinforcing my position when I answered him. I wanted to make sure Jim wouldn't think less of me now that he knew I had felonious tendencies. "But I really am going to send the book back."

"As well you should." Jim skimmed a hand over the cover of the book. It had been a busy night at Bellywasher's and he'd taken a break from helping Marc and Damien clean up after the pub closed. There was a smudge of something chocolate across the front of Jim's white apron. "This yearbook is more than forty years old." He said *book* the way he said *cook* and it speaks to how upset I was that I hardly even noticed (hardly) the little thrill that raced along my skin at the sound of those delicious, long *o*'s. "There probably aren't many yearbooks left from back in '67. No doubt this book is valuable to the people in that town. Even more valuable to all the alumni."

"It's a one-of-a-kind treasure." Eve joined in, as serious as I'd ever seen her. "In fact, I just heard something on the radio. There's been an all points bulletin issued. They said something about being on the lookout for a gourmet-shop worker with curly hair. They said she's shifty."

That's when I realized they were teasing. It helped. A little. So did the vision in my head, the one of me taking the yearbook to the post office first thing the next morning, putting it in an overnight envelope, and sending it right back to Allentown where it belonged.

Before I could do that, though, we needed to get down to business.

I told my conscience to shut up and flipped open the yearbook to the section where the seniors' graduation pictures were prominently displayed. The photos were arranged alphabetically. It didn't take long to find Norman.

I didn't need to ask Jim and Eve to take a gander. Even before I poked my finger at the black-and-white photo, they bent closer for a better look.

While they did, I bit my tongue, the better to keep my opinions to myself. After all, I'd had three and a half hours in the car with the William Allen High School yearbook, and in those three and a half hours—the yearbook open on the front seat beside me—I'd had plenty of opportunities to glance over at the picture of the young man with shaggy hair and wearing a Nehru jacket.

"So?" I'd waited long enough. I wanted to hear what they thought. After all, that was why I'd pilfered the yearbook in the first place.

My impatience didn't stop Eve from peering at the picture a while longer. Jim did her one better. He took the book over to where an overhead light shone directly above the bar cash register. He stared at the photograph of Norman for a long time before he shook his head.

"That's the hell of it, isn't it?" he said. "A person changes a great deal in forty years. I've seen pictures of my own mum from way back then. Wouldn't even know it was her if she didn't tell me."

I was hoping for something more conclusive, and I guess my expression gave me away, because Jim handed the book back to me. "There's a resemblance, sure enough. If you add more than forty years, and more than forty pounds, and a whole lot of gray to his hair . . . yeah, this Norman fellow might look like Jacques. But if it's really him . . ."

"Let me see it again." Eve reached over and grabbed the book out of my hands. She wrinkled her nose. "Yeah," she said. "It's him. For sure. Maybe. Or maybe not."

My spirits sank. I'd already been over the *definitelys* and the *maybes* and the *maybe nots* inside my head. All the way back from Allentown. I was hoping Eve and Jim would be more help.

I squinted at the picture, trying to imagine the fresh-faced boy in it wearing a crisp, white Très Bonne Cuisine apron and smiling back at me from a jar of Vavoom!

"Let's say it is him." I threw out the suggestion because standing there wondering was getting us nowhere. "That leaves us with even more questions. If Monsieur started life as Norman Applebaum and then he was all those other people . . ." I thought about the stack of phony IDs and my spirits slumped even lower. "It's overwhelming. I mean, where do we even begin?"

Pub keeper that he is, Jim knew exactly where. He poured a glass of white wine for me, a glass of red for Eve (her current favorite was Shiraz), and a bitter, dark beer for himself. He put the glasses on the tray, carried the tray to a nearby table, and pulled out chairs for Eve and me.

"We're getting ahead of ourselves," he said. "And that's going to accomplish nothing at all."

"But—"

He stopped me with a look. "It isn't like you to get so discouraged," he said. "You've never lost faith in yourself and your detective abilities before. Not with any of your other cases. You're feeling down because you're worried about Jacques."

"Sure. Of course." I dropped into the chair and when

Jim put the glass of wine in front of me, I took a sip. "He's our friend. And so far, nothing we've done has brought us any closer to finding out what happened to him. What if . . ." I took another sip of wine. When it slid past the lump of emotion in my throat, it hurt. "What if he's dead?"

"If he's dead, the police would have found his body by now." This comment came from Eve, and I turned her way. It wasn't the time to bring up Tyler so I kept my mouth shut on that subject and simply listened. "They've looked in all the logical places," she said. "I mean, they checked the parks and the Potomac. They even took a close look at all the johns in the morgue."

"That's John Does," I told her, but I don't think she saw the difference.

"So all that's good." Jim licked a bit of beer foam from his lips. "Until we hear differently, we're not going to panic. We're going to assume Jacques is alive and well."

"And all we have to do is find him." I plunked my elbows on the table and cradled my head in my hands. "We could always look into what the waitress in Allentown told me," I said, thinking out loud. "She said Norman Applebaum came to a bad end in Las Vegas. What do you suppose that means? Does it mean Norman died there? If he did, and if we could get some kind of confirmation about that, then we'd know for sure that Norman's not Jacques and Jacques isn't Norman."

"That's a good start." Jim had an order pad in his shirt pocket and he pulled it out and scribbled a note.

Back when we met at that cooking class at Très Bonne Cuisine and I got involved with my first case, Jim had opposed the very idea of me sticking my nose into a murder investigation. Don't get the wrong idea; he's not the Me-Tarzan-You-Jane type. Even back then, he tells me, he knew I was smart and capable (I love it when he says things like that). But like most regular people—me included before that fateful cooking class—Jim had never been so close to a murder. He knew nothing about investigating. And he was worried about my safety.

Recently, he'd learned to be more tolerant. Oh, I suspected that he still worried, but I knew that if I kept him in the loop and bounced my ideas and theories off him, it made him more comfortable. It was also a no-brainer from my point of view: If Jim knew where I was going and who I was going to see, it provided me with a safety net. I liked that, too, especially since Jim had already proved himself something of a superhero when it came to saving me.

There was the time he raced into a dark alley to whisk me away from danger and keep me from getting arrested. And the time he dove into the path of a giant vase that was headed right at me. And . . . well, I could go on and on. The point being that when it comes to my well-being, Jim is fearless.

It seemed even the perfect boyfriend could get better and better. Jim had never done anything as tangible in regard to one of my investigations as keeping a list for me, and watching him scribble on the order pad, my heart warmed.

"So you'll do the computer work, right?" He pointed my way with the pen he was holding. "What do you want me and Eve to do?"

"Well, while we're at it, we should all take a look at these other pictures. We might as well start there." I'd flagged the pages with sticky notes, and I flipped to the one that showed the drama club arranged on the gym bleachers. "There." I poked a finger at Norman, standing in the back row. "What do you think?"

"It looks more like Jacques there, for sure," Jim said, and I wondered if he really meant it, or if he was just trying to boost my spirits. I appreciated it, but really, I was searching for the truth.

He glanced at the photos on the opposite page. They showed scenes from a school production of *Our Town*, and according to the caption on the photo of the curtain call, Norman Applebaum had played the Stage Manager. Norman stood in the center of the line of teenage actors to take his bows.

"There's no denying that looks like Jacques," Jim said. "I've seen him smile that way dozens of times, usually when he's being interviewed by the press or when he's onstage at a food show. He loves being the center of attention."

"And Norman loved writing, too." I turned to the page that showed the school newspaper staff. In that particular picture, Norman was wearing a cardigan sweater. He was seated at a desk in the newspaper office.

"On this picture . . ." Jim examined it closely. His expression fell. "Not so much," he said.

He was right.

I sank back in my chair. "Well, I'll make copies of the pictures, just in case we want to refer to them. For now, I guess it's all we can do. I'll work the Las Vegas angle, too. If MaryAnn's right about Norman going out there and we can find out what really happened to him, we can take it from there. Only . . ." I glanced at the clock above the bar. "I can't do it tonight. I'm whooped, and I have to stop at Très Bonne Cuisine on my way home. I know there isn't much change in the cash register and I'll need to get some for the morning, but I need to get some tens and twenties out of the drawer and I'll pick up the day's deposit while I'm at it. That way I can stop at the bank on my way in tomorrow."

"I'd come with you, but—"

The same apology came from both Eve and Jim at the same time.

I looked from one of them to the other.

"I've got to meet someone," Eve said.

I didn't ask who. I didn't want to know. Besides, I already did.

That left Jim. He grimaced. "We've got a hell of a mess in the kitchen that needs to be cleaned up before anyone can go home," he said. "I can't leave Marc and Damien high and dry."

"Of course you can't." I popped out of my chair. "And you don't need to. I can certainly go over to Très Bonne Cuisine on my own." I reached over to grab the yearbook. It was still open to the picture of Norman in the newspaper office.

Maybe it was the way he was sitting, facing the desk and looking over his shoulder toward the camera. Maybe it was the light. Or the fact that his hair was cut shorter than it was in his graduation photo.

Whatever the reason, something struck me as different, and I took another, closer look at the kid.

When I did, I fell right back into my chair.

"What?" Eve wasn't one to pick up on nuances so I guess that shows how obvious my surprise must have been. She leaned forward and grabbed my arm. "What is it, Annie? You're looking at the picture of Norman as if you've seen—"

"A ghost? Maybe I have." I flipped the book around so that Jim could see Norman better. "Take a look," I said. I turned the book again, this time so that it was facing Eve. "I can't believe I've been staring at this kid all day and I never noticed it before." Let that be a lesson to me. I was so busy looking for any resemblance between Monsieur and Norman, I was blind to looking at anything else. It wasn't until I'd given up on the problem that this new possibility presented itself.

With one finger, I pointed at Norman. "OK, don't try to add on forty years when you picture him; try thirty. And don't imagine that he's gained much weight. Think of him as thin. Who do you see?"

Eve squinted.

Jim cocked his head.

I gave Norman's nose another tap. "I think there's a re-semblance to Monsieur, all right," I finally admitted. "But there's a resemblance to someone else, too. In this pic-ture, Norman looks a little like Greg Teagarten."

Jim nodded.

Eve's eyes flew open.

"Then you think that Norman isn't Monsieur, he's re-ally Greg?" When Eve is thinking really hard, she wrin-kles her nose. I wondered if she knew it wasn't an especially attractive expression and knew in an instant that of course she did. That's why she made it a rule never to think very hard.

"I don't think Norman is Greg," I said. "Because Greg isn't the one with all the phony IDs. But maybe . . ." I was about to propose a theory so preposterous, I won-dered if even my friends would believe it. "I think there's a good chance that the resemblance between Greg and Norman is the reason Monsieur hasn't been heard from since the night of the murder."

They waited for me to say more, but I needed a mo-ment to organize my thoughts. It wasn't until I was sure I could explain at least semiclearly that I gave it a try.

"Monsieur made that call to the police from the back room at Très Bonne Cuisine, right? That means he wasn't out in the store, but he did see enough of what was going on to know that Greg was in trouble. And the killer didn't mean to kill Greg. We know that because he only shot Greg in the foot, like he was trying to make him talk. So maybe the killer—"

"Thought Greg was Norman, but he wasn't really Norman because Norman is Jacques and that's why he's hiding." Jim finished my thought for me, and I was grate-ful. It was a slippery theory and I was beginning to lose my hold.

I nodded. "It's possible. And it explains a lot. Not about the licenses, but about why Monsieur hasn't been seen or heard from since. If the killer was really after Monsieur—"

"Then Greg was killed by mistake." Jim's voice was as hollow as the feeling inside me.

"It also explains why Monsieur is hiding." This came from Eve, who was so proud of herself, she sat up and threw back her shoulders. "Annie, you're brilliant!"

"If I was, I'd know where Monsieur was. And who's after him. And why."

"Aye." Jim got up and collected our glasses. "But we have faith in you. You'll figure that part out soon enough."

I hoped so. Because I'd already figured something else out that, so far, had eluded both Jim and Eve. I would have mentioned it, but it was late, and there was no use in the two of them going to bed as worried as I was.

Why?

The answer was simple enough: If the killer was really after Monsieur and killed Greg by mistake, that meant Monsieur was still in a whole bunch of danger.

I ARRIVED AT TRÈS BONNE CUISINE A LITTLE WHILE later, and because it was late and most of the nearby storefronts were retail space, the block was pretty quiet. Some of the bars and restaurants in the area were still hopping, but they were farther up the street, and thanks to the distance and the fact that a steady, misty rain had started to fall, local partyers had opted for closer parking spaces. Rather than having to go around back to the lot, I had the luxury of pulling my car up to a rare open parking place right outside the front door of the shop.

In fact, the only other car around was a dark sedan parked three spaces farther up the street.

For the record, I do not have the gourmet-shop worker's equivalent of spider-sense. But I'm no dummy, either. When Eve and I drove to Fredericksburg, I'd noticed a dark sedan mirroring our moves. A car that got off at the same exit we did and followed us to Bill Boxley's house.

Was it the same car?

I squinted for a closer look and cursed my lack of sense (spider or otherwise) for not noting the sedan's license plates back in Fredericksburg. It might be the same car, I decided.

Or it might not.

Just to be safe, I kept my eye on it as I unlocked the front door of the shop. I didn't see a driver and there was no one else out on the sidewalk. No one I could see, anyway.

Not one to take chances, I locked the door behind me, disarmed the security system, and flicked the switch that turned on the light above the front counter cash register area.

Had I been thinking less about everything we'd discussed back at Bellywasher's and what it could mean in regard to Monsieur's disappearance and Greg's murder, I might have noticed that something wasn't right. As it was, it was late, I was in a hurry, and my brain was so busy spinning through the Norman Applebaum is-he-or-isn't-he scenario that it wasn't until I unlocked the cash register and took out the two twenties I would exchange for singles at the bank the next morning that I saw that our display of gourmet dried soup mixes was in disarray.

Yes, I am organized. Some say a little too much so.

Yes, I am a stickler for order.

No, I'm not obsessive. At least I don't think I am.

That's not why I noticed the mess.

This wasn't just a soup mix out of place here and there. The dried mixes had been completely removed from the shelf and dropped on the floor.

I was one hundred percent certain Raymond wouldn't leave such a mess. He simply wasn't the type.

Was I worried? Not really. After all, the front door was locked when I arrived. And our security company hadn't called to say there'd been an alarm. Maybe that's why I approached the problem—and the shelf where the soup mixes had been last time I saw them—logically.

When I did, I saw that there were a couple of wild rice and veggie mixes on the floor along with one chicken cheese tortilla and three white cheddar broccoli. There were also four packages of potato leek soup, and at the same time I remembered that the soup was Monsieur's favorite (he always added a healthy glug of sherry), I noticed that they were set to one side.

"Weird," I mumbled to myself, and it was a good thing I whispered the word.

Otherwise I wouldn't have heard a noise from the cookware aisle. It sounded a whole lot like footsteps.

At the same time I backed away from the soup mixes and toward the door, I realized I'd left my keys on the front counter. I couldn't get to them without wasting precious time and I couldn't get out of the shop without them.

With few options, I did the only thing I could think to do. I turned on every light in the shop and raised my voice.

"I know you're here," I said. At the same time I raced to the counter and grabbed for the keys. "I've already called the police so you might as well just stay put." I darted for the door and I would have made it, too, if not for those soup mixes on the floor.

I stepped on the chicken and cheese tortilla mix. My ankle turned and my foot went out from under me. I shot out a hand to grab the rack where the soup mixes were displayed, but I hung on too tight.

The rack tipped and the gadgets displayed over the shelves of soup mixes rained down on me. I covered my head with both hands, remembering too late that the only thing keeping me upright was that rack. My feet slid and I went down in a heap.

Even before I plucked a dozen garlic presses away from me and brushed away the barbecue brushes, the wooden kebab skewers, and the corn-on-the-cob holders that covered me, I knew I was in trouble.

Because even before I looked up, I sensed someone was standing over me.

Eleven

✛

"MONSIEUR!"
Even before Jacques Lavoie offered me a hand, I sat up like a shot. Kebab skewers rained down from my shoulders and peppered the floor.

"What in the world are you doing here?"

He made that very Gallic gesture of his. The one where he shrugs and turns over his hands. It said, *Why shouldn't I be here, it is my shop, yes?* even before he said, "Why shouldn't I be here, *chérie*? It is my shop, yes?"

"Of course . . . it's your . . . shop." I was so surprised, so relieved, and so completely bowled over, I could barely put together a coherent sentence. Maybe that's why I stayed put right where I was, right there on the floor amid a slew of kitchen gadgets and soup mixes. "But where have you been? Why didn't you come forward to tell the cops what happened to Greg? What on earth is going on?"

There was that gesture again. This time, it conveyed a message that was all about how it would take a while to explain. Before he could even begin, though, Monsieur looked toward the front door.

"I have been a little nervous," he explained, watching me watch him. "You understand this, yes? After everything that has happened . . . If we could turn out the lights, perhaps?"

"Of course." Before he could make a move toward the switch, I got to my feet and flicked off the lights, checking the sidewalk out in front of the store as I did. It was empty. Except for my car and that dark sedan still where I'd last seen it, so was the street. Even so, Monsieur's gaze darted to the front windows again and again, and I couldn't stand to see him look so uneasy. I took his arm. "We'll talk in the office."

"Oh, no, *chérie*. I have an idea even better than that." He bent to retrieve two packages of potato-soup mix. "The water is already boiling and the wine, it is open. If you hadn't interrupted me while I was searching for the soup mix, I would have put everything back where it belongs and be eating my dinner right now. You'll join me, yes? We'll go upstairs. To the cooking school."

I had already started down the aisle toward the back of the store, but when I heard this, I put on the brakes and fought to catch my breath. "That's where you've been all this time? Upstairs?" I was torn between giving Monsieur a hug and punching him in the nose, and he wasn't the only one I was mad at. After all, I was supposed to be the detective, and I hadn't even known the person I'd been looking for was living right over my head.

Good thing the lights were off. Monsieur didn't see when my cheeks flamed.

Or maybe he did. "I am sorry to cause so much trouble," he said. "*C'est vrai!* It is only just that . . ." Again, he glanced at the windows and, even in the dark, I could see that his eyes were round and his forehead was creased with worry. He ran his tongue over his lips.

And I decided right then and there that whatever he had to tell me, it could wait until we were upstairs and had the door closed and locked behind us.

We went to the back of the store and he punched in the security code to open the door at the bottom of the steps that led up to the cooking school. Even once we were upstairs, though, he didn't turn on any of the lights, and I knew why. The school has a gigantic window that looks over the street. It lets in an incredible amount of light. The design is pure genius. The natural light adds to the elegant ambience established by the stainless-steel appliances and the individual work stations with their sleek granite countertops.

But a window that lets in light lets it out, too.

I didn't need Monsieur to say a word. In complete darkness, I followed him to the back room where there was storage space, sinks for cleaning up—and no windows. Once we had the door to that room closed, he dared to turn on a light.

I saw that he had a nearby table set with a linen cloth, china, and a set of sterling flatware. There was a loaf of bread on the table, too, and an open bottle of wine. He got another glass, poured, and handed it to me.

"That is better, yes?"

"Yes. But . . ." I sucked in a long breath and forced myself to let it out slowly. "I'm confused. What have you been doing up here?"

Monsieur didn't look any happier saying it than I was hearing it. "Panicking mostly," he admitted.

"Then why not talk to the cops!" It seemed the simplest solution to me, and I cupped my wineglass in both hands and paced back and forth, waiting for some sort of explanation that would put the last week into perspective.

It was a long time coming. Monsieur drank some wine, poured the soup mix into the water he had boiling on the stove, got a bottle of sherry from a cupboard. He waved toward the table and I took a seat. He set a place for me, cut into the loaf of bread, and handed me a piece.

"It is difficult to explain," he said.

"As difficult as it's been for your friends to wonder if you're dead or alive?"

I hadn't meant to sound so furious. Or maybe I had. Now that my shock had settled into mere surprise, I felt bitter frustration nip at the edges of my composure. Like anyone could blame me? I scraped unsalted butter over my bread and chomped, chewing it over along with the thought that relief and anger can apparently go hand in hand.

"We've been worried sick," I said without apology. After all, I wasn't the one who needed to apologize. "And all this time—"

"I have been right here. Yes." At least he had the decency to hang his head. When the timer rang, Monsieur filled two soup bowls, added sherry to each, and served. While I waited for my soup to cool, I stared across the table at him.

"It is hard for you to understand, I know," he said. "Things are . . . how do you say this? These thing are confusing."

"That's putting it mildly." Now that I'd had a few minutes to think, my brain had finally started to work and my thoughts were lining up. Systematically, I went over everything I'd learned and seen since the day Monsieur went missing, including those driver's licenses.

My hands trembling with the effort to control my temper, I reached for another slice of bread and buttered it. "So tell me, what's really going on? And who are you, Monsieur? Who are you, really?"

He had been in the middle of ladling a spoonful of soup to his mouth and he stopped, the spoon raised and the soup on it sending a small cloud of steam in front of his face. It struck me as appropriate, seeing as how Jacques Lavoie's life was all about smoke and mirrors.

He put his spoon back into his soup bowl. "I am not surprised that you have discovered this about me," he said. "You are a very smart woman. This, I have always known."

"Not so smart that I can't be fooled."

"Oh, no. No, *chérie!*" Monsieur's laugh was deep and throaty. It always reminded me of Pepé Le Pew. "You are very bright. You have found out—"

"That there is not now and never has been a family named Lavoie in Sceau-Saint-Angel, France. That you own a truckload of false IDs. That you are not and never have been Bill Boxley, and that when you stole his wallet, you took his driver's license but not his credit cards." I took a deep breath before I added, "Oh, and I also know that Fred Gardner must have been one hell of a good teacher because folks in Allentown still remember him fondly even though he's been dead for twenty years."

As I spoke, Monsieur's face grew paler and paler. By the time I punctuated my last words by slapping my hand against the table, he was the color of the white apron he wore over a blue oxford shirt that looked as if it had been slept in.

"See?" He blinked rapidly and tried for a smile that never quite peaked. "It is just like I said. As a detective, you are brilliant. You must be, *chérie*, to know all this. You are as smart as you are beautiful. It is no wonder that my dear friend Jim thinks so highly of you. You are—"

In any other circumstances, I might have been all for basking in his praise. Right then and there, I was so not in the mood. I leaned over the table and cut him off with a look. "You can cut the crap and the phony accent—Norman."

If ever I hoped to find proof, there it was. Monsieur's mouth fell open and he collapsed back into his chair.

In spite of the fact that I was fighting mad, I was not heartless. Rather than continuing my attack, I backed away and gave him a moment to collect himself. He did, and right before my eyes, I saw a transformation. The swagger went out of his shoulders. The cocky Gallic smile fled his face. When he finally spoke, I wasn't the least bit surprised that there wasn't a trace of an accent anywhere in his voice. It was flat and nasal and East Coast sounding. Norman may have grown up in Allentown, and maybe he did come to a bad end in Las Vegas, but if I was a betting person (and it goes without saying that I'm not), I would have bet he'd spent time in New Jersey, too.

"It's a scam. All of it's a scam. Like all the other scams. You understand, don't you, kid?"

I wasn't about to let him off the hook so easily. I kept my eyes on him. "You mean like Vavoom!?"

With his spoon, he made figure eights in his soup. "Kind of." He shrugged. "I mean, the whole thing about being French . . . you can see how it helps with the business, right? Who's going to take cooking lessons from a guy named Norman from Allentown? Who's going to buy expensive cookware from him? Norman Applebaum . . ." He sighed. "Doesn't exactly have the ambience I was looking for when I bought this place."

"And Bill Boxley?"

He thought about it for a moment. "Boxley was the guy from Fredericksburg, right? That's where I was running a sweet little scam with this cleaning fluid." His shoulders shot back, his eyes lit, and I didn't have any trouble at all picturing him as Bill Boxley, hawking his product in front of an enthralled crowd. "Cleans. Shines. Polishes. Just a little dab on a rag takes care of all your cleaning needs. Tarnished silver? Just wipe it away! Dirty floors? Add a quarter cup to a bucket of warm water and they're hospital clean! Greasy dishes?"

He chanced a glance my way. When he saw I wasn't buying (his cleaning product or his attempt at winning me over), he went back to being regular ol' Norman. His shoulders slumped. His cheery, confident personality disappeared, and he made a face. "I made a bundle. Until folks found out my magic cleaning fluid wasn't so magical."

I'm not usually cynical. Which is why he was surprised when I sneered, "What, it ate through cloth?"

"It was fine on cloth. It was fine on everything. It should have been, it was dishwashing detergent."

"Which you repackaged and sold as something wonderful. Like the seasoned salt you sell as Vavoom!"

"And you put it on sale!" He tried to look outraged by the audacity of my management decision, but actually, Norman looked a little impressed. "You got guts, kid," he said. "You're good at setting things right."

If it was true, why didn't I feel better? I spooned up a mouthful of soup. "I'm getting nowhere on Greg's murder," I said. "But that's because I haven't been able to get all my questions answered. Because the person who has the answers . . ." I paused here so my words had a chance to sink in. "The person who has the answers was nowhere to be found." A thought struck and I set down my spoon and looked across the table at Norman.

"You said Monsieur was a scam. *Like all the other scams*. That's what you said. Do you think it's possible that any of those other scams has anything to do with Greg's death?"

He scratched a hand through his hair. "I don't see how."

"But you knew the killer was looking for you, and not Greg." I didn't say this like it was a question, but I was hoping for confirmation nonetheless.

Norman gave it to me with a brief nod. "That's why I've been hiding out," he said. "He wanted to talk to me. And I saw what happened to Greg. I'm not a brave person, Annie. If that guy gets ahold of me . . . well, I can't even think about it without having a panic attack. That's why I ran out of here the night Greg was killed. I was so upset, I didn't know what to do. By the time I calmed down and decided to go home, there were cops at my place. I wasn't sure why. I didn't know if they thought I shot Greg. I was so scared, I couldn't think straight. I spent that night just driving around and the next day after the cops were gone, that's when I came back here. I figured it was the last place anybody would look for me, the cops or"—he gulped—"the guy who killed Greg." Embarrassed, he looked away. "I thought I'd get up the nerve to go to the cops, but I haven't. I don't know if I ever will. I thought—"

"What? That you could hide up here forever?"

He answered with a shrug.

"Like it or not, you're going to have to talk to the police eventually. They'll protect you. You're a witness." When Norman didn't reply, I looked at him closely. "You are a witness, aren't you?"

He gave me another shrug.

"This is getting us nowhere!" Frustrated, I pushed back from the table and looked around the room. There was a stack of paper on a nearby countertop and I went over and grabbed it along with a pen. I plunked both pen and paper on the table next to Norman.

"We need to work our way through this thing, and as far as I'm concerned, there's only one place to start. Let's go out on a limb here and say I'm right. That guy was after you, Norman, and I'm thinking that if we try hard enough, we just might be able to figure out why. Go ahead." When he didn't make a move to pick up the pen, I handed it to him. "Write down the ones you can think of."

"The scams?" It was hard to look at the man seated in front of me and not think of him as the jolly Frenchman who had influenced so many people—including Jim— with his flair for food. When he looked up at me, he no longer looked larger than life. He was an ordinary guy. An ordinary guy named Norman. A little befuddled, he asked, "All of them?"

There was more frustration than resignation in my sigh. "We're not going to figure out what's going on otherwise."

Norman agreed, and while he worked on the list, I sat back down to finish my soup and another piece of bread.

Just for the record, he might really be Norman from Allentown, but the owner of Très Bonne Cuisine knew a thing or two about food, all right. Sherry in potato soup is a very good thing.

I FINISHED THAT BOWL OF SOUP AND A SECOND ONE. Norman had rummaged through the supplies upstairs and come up with what he needed to make chocolate mousse for dessert. Let's face it, nothing is going to keep me away from chocolate. Not even my shock, my surprise, and the fact that I was just plain annoyed at Norman and all he'd put us through. I dished up the mousse and, in a rare moment of culinary inspiration, added a few raspberries. Apparently, Norman had been sneaking out to the open-all-night grocery store. The fridge in the cooking school cleanup room was far better stocked than mine at home.

Good thing my mood was mellowed by the endorphins the chocolate had triggered in my brain. Otherwise I would have lost it as I read through the list of Norman's scams.

"You're kidding me, right?" I asked him, glancing up as I finished page three and flipped to page four. "You sold fake doctor's excuses to people so they could get out of work? A fake doctor selling fake excuses? People really fell for that? There's no way."

He slipped into the Jacques Lavoie personality and accent effortlessly and tossed out the Gallic hand gesture with a casual, "I am a genius, yes?"

I slapped the pages on the table. "You're a crook."

"Come on, Annie." Norman tasted his mousse and nodded, satisfied. "I didn't really hurt anybody with any of my scams. Yeah, I sold people a bill of goods. But hey, I didn't cheat anybody who didn't want to be cheated. Would you believe there's a magic cleaning fluid that can change your life?"

"Of course not, but—"

"Would you pay somebody to write you a doctor's excuse, just so you could get out of work?"

"Never, but—"

"Would you buy a college paper? I mean, if you were a student, would you pay money for a paper and turn it in as your own work? In any class? Would you pay somebody to write your paper on eighteenth-century English poetry? Or geology? Or—"

"You know enough about eighteenth-century English poetry to write papers about it?"

Norman grinned. "That's *paper*, singular. I only ever wrote one and I'll bet it's been turned in at least once on every college campus in America. The Internet is a wonderful thing. And college students are young and stupid and more concerned with partying than studying."

"And they have their parents' money to spend."

He winked. "You bet!"

I tapped the papers into a neat pile and set it down on the table. "Well, I don't think Greg was killed because of some eighteenth-century English poet, do you? It doesn't make any sense." My mellow chocolate mood was fading and I was getting crabby fast. Then again, by that time it was three o'clock in the morning, and I am not a night person. "There's got to be something you can think of, something that would explain—"

"Shh!" Norman put a finger to his lips and, just like he did, I bent my head and listened.

I heard exactly what he heard—the sounds of someone moving around downstairs in the shop.

For the second time that night, my breath caught and my pulse pounded triple time in my ears. In spite of the fact that I told myself there was nothing to worry about—that there was no way anyone knew we were up there and that even if they did, there was no way they could get to us—I thought of the nervous way Norman had looked at the front window while we talked downstairs. And the sight of Greg's body lying in a pool of blood.

"There's someone downstairs." Norman mouthed the words and pointed. "Don't move. We can't let them know we're up here."

It was the perfect plan and it actually might have made me feel secure if the next sound we heard wasn't the door at the bottom of the cooking-school steps creaking open.

"We've got to hide." That was me, mouthing the words and gesturing wildly, like we were playing some kind of weird version of charades. I looked around the cleanup room, but except for a big walk-in cooler that took up most of one wall, there really was no other place to hide.

And there was no way on earth I was going to hide in a walk-in cooler.

With no other options, I did the only thing I could think to do. I motioned Norman to one side of the door that led into the room and I took up position on the other side—but not before I armed myself with the copper pot Norman had used for the soup.

When the door snapped open, I was ready.

I raised my arm, swung, and—

"Annie!"

"Don't do that to me!" Since Jim was the one who'd nearly gotten beaned by the soup pot, I probably wasn't completely justified screaming at him. I clutched my chest to keep my heart from beating its way through my ribs and fell back against the wall. "What on earth are you doing here? Why didn't you let me know it was you? Why didn't you call?"

"I did call. A dozen times at least," he said. It was the first time I remembered my purse—and the phone in it—was still down on the front counter of Très Bonne Cuisine. "I thought something was wrong. I thought something had happened, and I looked all around the shop. And then I found your purse, but not you. Annie, you gave me quite a fright."

There was no easy way to tell him the surprises weren't over.

Rather than try, I turned Jim around. For the first time since he'd walked in the room, he saw Norman.

Jim's mouth opened and closed. He smiled. He looked to me for confirmation that he wasn't seeing things, and when I nodded, he raced forward and pulled his old friend into an enormous bear hug.

"It's you. It really is. You're not dead. You're alive. You're well. Annie found you."

"Not exactly." I didn't like to take credit where none was due. I stepped into the touching reunion scene. "This is Norman Applebaum," I told Jim, and it was a good thing he was in on my yearbook thievery; at least I didn't have to explain this part of the story. "Norman's been hiding out up here in the cooking school since soon after Greg's murder."

"Here? In the school?" I could tell exactly when Jim's relief turned to anger, just as mine had done. That would have been right about when his accent got so thick I could barely understand him. "And ye're tellin' me that all this while, we were a-frettin' and a-worryin' and thinkin' you'd been killed like poor Greg was, and Annie's been chasin' here and there and all this time . . ." His outrage choked him, and all Jim could do was stare at Norman in wonder.

"There's a lot I need to explain," Norman said. As understatements went, that one was a doozy.

BY THE TIME THE SUN PEEKED OVER THE HORIZON, I think we'd heard it all. Norman told us how, growing up, he'd always been antsy, eager to see the world. He explained that soon after he graduated from William Allen High, he went out to Vegas.

And did he come to a bad end out there?

When I asked, at least Norman had the decency to look embarrassed.

He told us that he worked in a tiny bar far from the neon lights of the Strip, and as a way to make a little extra cash on the side, he rigged a couple of the countertop slot machines.

MaryAnn the waitress was right. Norman's story did not have a happy ending. He was caught and did jail time for his crime, eighteen months to be exact.

When he got out . . .

Well, Norman didn't make any apologies, and though I may have expected a few, I guess I could understand. It was hard for a guy with a record to find a decent job, so Norman did the only thing that was logical. At least in his mind.

He became Bill Boxley. And Fred Gardner. And all the other people I'd found IDs for. And he'd run a series of scams along the east coast and the west, until that fateful day when the cooking skill he'd learned at the

Nevada State Prison led him to the opportunity to own his own gourmet shop.

"The rest . . ." Norman filled our wineglasses—again. "Like they say, the rest is history. I always liked cooking, and when the idea hit that I could own my own shop, well, I decided that would be like heaven on earth. I've established a great business, and I love doing what I'm doing. Très Bonne Cuisine is my life. This is where I belong. I've given up the scams . . . well, except for the Vavoom! I started an honest business and I want nothing more than to keep it going. I even thought about turning over a whole new leaf and letting the world know who I really am." He shook his head, dismissing the thought just the way he must have when it first occurred to him. "How can I? Would you shop here if you knew I was a con? Would anybody pay the least attention to a guy who learned to cook in prison?"

We'd been seated around the table for hours, and Norman got up and stretched. "I've never been happier," he said. "Until—"

"Until somebody walked in here and blew Greg away." Even the taste of the expensive wine Norman poured couldn't sweeten my words.

Norman shivered. "Just thinking about it makes me sick," he said. "I swear, I don't know what the guy wanted. He just walked in—"

"You saw him come into the shop?" Wine or no wine, late hour or not, I'd waited a long time to ask him these questions, and I wasn't about to let the opportunity pass. "Did you recognize the man?"

"I never got a good look at his face." The gesture Norman made reminded me of the old Monsieur Lavoie nonchalance. Except that now, Norman didn't look nearly as debonair as he did confused. "Tall. Dark jacket. Jeans. That's pretty much all I could see from the back office." This time his shrug was all about despair. "I can't really describe him. I wouldn't recognize him again if he walked in here right now and asked to sit down."

"Then how did you know he was looking for you?"

While I asked the questions, Jim pulled out the same notepad that had been in his pocket earlier that evening (I guess technically it was the evening before now that it was Friday morning). Norman talked, and Jim took notes.

"I was loading the car. You know, I was supposed to take stuff over to Bellywasher's. The steel-clad roaster and the ice cream maker and . . ." As much as he loved food and the expensive cookware he sold to prepare it, Norman shrugged it all off as inconsequential in the face of what had happened. "I was going in and out and I heard Greg talking to someone, but hey, that's not unusual, is it? The shop was open late that night and whatever the guy wanted, I knew Greg would take care of everything. He always did. He was—" Norman's voice got thick and he coughed away his emotion. "Greg was a nice guy. I hate that this happened to him. If I would have been braver. Or smarter. If I realized sooner that something was wrong—"

"When did you realize something was wrong?"

I could tell Norman had been avoiding thinking about the whole thing, that's how pale and shaken he was. I couldn't blame him. All the more reason we had to talk about it.

"What did he say?" I asked. "The guy Greg was waiting on, how did you know he was really looking for you?"

"I heard him . . ." Norman swallowed hard. "I heard the man raise his voice. He said, 'It's payback time, Norman.'"

Twelve

✖

"IT'S PAYBACK TIME, NORMAN."

Ignoring the confused looks on Jim's and Norman's faces, I drummed my fingers against the table and mumbled the words. "Don't you get it?" I said, looking from one of them to the other. "It's a clue."

"Well, it's how I knew the guy was looking for me, that's for sure." Now that it was morning and we didn't need the lights, we'd opened the door that led into the main room of the cooking school. A stream of mellow sunshine poked into the room where we'd spent the night. Norman stepped through the sunlight to retrieve the waffles he'd just made. He put them down in front of us, and added a scoop of fresh strawberries and a dollop of whipped cream.

Something told me they didn't eat like this back at the Nevada State Prison.

Norman sat down and cut into his own stack of waffles. "As soon as I heard him say that, I knew the guy was mixed up, that he thought Greg was me. I was in the back office and I was just about to step out front and tell him he had the wrong guy, but . . ." In spite of the sweetened whipped cream, Norman's expression soured. "That's when I heard the first gunshot. After that, I didn't know what to do. I guess I panicked. Instead of going out front, I called the cops."

"That's exactly what you should have done." I gave him a sympathetic smile because I could tell the memory was painful for Norman. Rather than risk losing him to it, I made sure to keep our discussion on track.

"The killer did think Greg was you," I said. "But not the you you are. The you you were." That didn't make any sense. Not even to me. I licked whipped cream from my lips and tried again. "You and Greg didn't look anything at all alike now. But we noticed the resemblance between the young you and Greg in the pictures we found of you in the William Allen High yearbook."

The look on Norman's face told me he was anxious to hear more of an explanation, but rather than get sidetracked, I put a hand on his arm to stop him.

"You see what this means, right?" I asked. "The killer is probably someone who knew you years ago. Or at least someone who's seen pictures of you from back then. He did what we did when we looked at your graduation picture. We tried to imagine what the kid in the photograph would look like with a few years and a few added pounds. So when he walked into the shop and saw Greg—"

"He thought it was me." Norman interrupted me. Which was just fine by me. It gave me a chance to take another bite of waffle. His expression fell and he set down his fork. "What a lousy way to die. Poor Greg. He didn't even know what the guy was talking about. He didn't know I was Norman. Nobody did. So why kill him? Why kill me? I mean, that's what the guy thought he was doing, right? He thought he was killing me." His pleading look pivoted between Jim and me. Which would have been just fine—if we had any answers.

The way it was, we sat in silence for a long while, eating our waffles and sipping the coffee Norman had brewed with just a touch of chicory. After a while, his shoulders rose and fell.

"I know I haven't given you guys much reason to trust me," Norman said. "I'm sorry for that. When I started this whole crazy Jacques Lavoie thing, I never thought I'd have friends who were so wonderful that I'd feel guilty for lying to them. But I do. I have you two, and Eve, and everyone over at Bellywasher's. Believe me when I say I thought of telling you all the truth a thousand times. I just never got up the nerve. And I loved the whole eccentric French chef thing." He gave us that Pepé Le Pew laugh, only this time it didn't sound as jolly as it did downright phony. I wondered how I'd never noticed before. "I loved being in the limelight, having all the D.C. foodies beating a path to my door. Now . . ." He sat back and raised his chin.

"I want you to know that I'm sorry you had to learn the truth this way, and from now on, I'm going to be one hundred percent aboveboard with you. All of you. Always. I swear . . ." He raised his right hand like he would have done if he were in court. "I swear I never did anything to anyone that would make them want to kill me. I'm not a violent man. Never have been. The only thing I ever did was take some people's money. And never a whole lot of it, either. Why would somebody want to kill me for that?"

I interrupted him because I didn't know if Norman knew this part of the story. "But he didn't want to kill you. The murderer just wanted to make you talk. That's why he shot Greg in the foot. He thought Greg was you, and he thought if he hurt him badly enough, Greg would tell him whatever it was he wanted to know. Only Greg didn't know, of course, because Greg didn't have any idea what the killer was talking about. And after he shot Greg—"

"He saw me." Norman's complexion was ashen. "I heard the shots and I was so startled, I knocked against something back in the office. That was the first the guy knew there was somebody else in the store. That's when I really got scared. I took off for the back door. But not before the guy got a look at me. I saw his face. Just for a moment. And I've got to tell you, there was such a funny expression on it, I couldn't make heads or tails of what the guy was thinking. But now I get it. That was the first he realized he'd shot the wrong man."

"And that's when you knew your life was still in danger." It was the first thing Jim had said in a while and I looked his way to find him deep in thought, his brows low over his eyes and his jaw firm. "It's no wonder you've been keeping yourself out of sight. He's still out there. And if he finds you—"

"That's not going to happen." I thought it important to point this out, mostly because I could see that the very idea was making Norman green around the gills. "We're getting ahead of ourselves," I said, not because we were, but because if I kept the conversation on our investigation, Norman wouldn't have to think about the vicious killer who was still out there somewhere looking for him. "What we really need to concentrate on is who the guy is, and what he wants."

Norman didn't look sure. "I keep wondering how he knew. I mean, about Très Bonne Cuisine. If the killer wasn't even sure who Greg was or what I look like, how did he know to come to Très Bonne Cuisine?"

I didn't have the answer and I didn't pretend I did. "What's even more important," I said, "was what he was trying to find out. He said, 'It's payback time, Norman.' That means he thought you owed him something. Even more important—"

"I don't." It was Norman's turn to interrupt. "I don't have any outstanding debts. Nothing that would cause someone to come looking for me with a gun, anyway."

"But it's not a debt you have now. Don't you see?" As if it might help, I set down my fork so I could concentrate on explaining things as clearly as possible. "The guy didn't know you as Jacques or Bill or Fred or by any of your other identities. He said *Norman*. He knew you back when you were the real you. And that means—"

"It might have something to do with one of the scams you ran back in the days when you were Norman." This came from Jim, and he so succinctly said what I'd been beating around the bush to explain, I could have kissed him. If I didn't have a mouth full of waffle. "This bloke, he must have had a grudge for a very long time."

"And we're back to square one." So that we could set the table for our breakfast, I'd taken the list of scams Norman had written out earlier and put it over near the sink. I retrieved it and put it on the table in front of Norman, then handed him the pen.

"Go ahead," I instructed him. "Put a check mark next to the scams you ran back when you were Norman."

WHAT WITH THE SURPRISE OF FINDING MONSIEUR (I was having a hard time getting used to thinking of him as Norman), the double surprise of Jim showing up at the shop, and the wine and the waffles and the stories we exchanged and the theories we tossed back and forth, we were all pretty exhausted by the time eight o'clock rolled around. Rather than beating our brains and wasting our time, we decided to meet again later that afternoon at Jim's, before the dinner hour at Bellywasher's.

We smuggled Monsieur . . . er, I mean, Norman . . . out of the shop wrapped in an oversized shawl Eve had once left there and wearing the straw gardening hat I kept in the backseat of my car on the off chance that one of these days, I might actually have a garden to wear it in. It was still early and most of the retail shops on the street weren't open yet. As far as we could see, the coast was clear; there was no one watching us or Très Bonne Cuisine. But even though he was confident they wouldn't be followed, Jim was no dummy. He drove the round-about way to his house in the Clarendon neighborhood of Arlington, bustled Norman inside, and settled him in the guest room with the miniblinds closed.

I had other plans. I made a call, and even before I told him he deserved his very own superhero outfit, Raymond agreed to forgo his Friday beauty nap and work the shop for me that day. And me? I went home and took a nice, long nap. Between that and a shower, I was rarin' to go by the time I got to Jim's for our powwow.

I, too, took the long way to Clarendon and maybe Norman's paranoia was getting to me, because in case someone was watching me, I offered to park a couple of blocks from Jim's house and walk the rest of the way. (Yes, I was imagining myself slipping in and out of the shadows in a very detectivelike way.)

Jim would have none of that. His place is on a too-close-to-seedy-for-comfort street, and he insisted I park in the driveway. He met me even before I got to the front door.

And I'm not complaining or anything. I mean, being welcomed to Jim's with a hug and a kiss was just about the best way I could think of to end twenty-four hours full of shocks and revelations. But what Jim didn't know was that usually when I get to his place, I take my time walking up the front steps and across the porch to his door.

Time to confess: I have some fantasies when it comes to Jim.

OK, that's not much of a confession. Anyone who knows me knows I'm nuts about Jim.

Truth is, though, I've also got some fantasies about his house, too.

Not that it's my kind of place. It's got too much gingerbread outside and, thanks to the old lady who sold it to him for a song, too many rooms inside papered in too many floral prints. His front porch is a riot of potted plants. Most of them are herbs he uses at the restaurant and I can understand the appeal. Really. But I always have to control the urge to straighten and sweep and get rid of maybe just a few of those overflowing pots. Just to make things a little more orderly.

Even with all that, I usually let my mind wander as I make my way up the front walk, and in those wanderings, I wonder what it would be like if the place was mine. Mine and Jim's.

Back in the day when I first met Jim, the very thought sent terror up my spine. I mean, the one man I'd sworn to love and cherish had gone and done me wrong, and after the disaster that was my marriage, I wasn't about to jump into another relationship where there was the teeniest chance of me getting my heart smashed (again) in a couple million pieces.

But that, as they say, is ancient history. And Jim isn't Peter.

It took a couple months for that truth to finally settle in, but now that it had, I was at peace with it. In fact, I liked imagining how Jim and I would spend our days together. And our nights.

"You're flushed." Jim touched a hand to my cheek. "You feeling all right?"

Since Norman was waiting inside and we had a mystery to solve, I thought it best not to confess what I was really thinking. At least not right then and there. Instead, I followed Jim into the house. It wasn't until after the front door was closed and locked behind us that Norman stepped out of the kitchen. Now that he'd slept in a real bed for the first time in a couple weeks and had a hot shower and lunch, he looked like a new man.

At least as new as any French chef could look now that he was just an ordinary guy dressed in a pair of Jim's flannel lounge pants (rolled at the hem) and a green and white soccer jersey that was way tighter around the middle than it was when Jim wore it.

Just to be sure we were safe, Jim checked the doors and windows—again—before we gathered around the table in the dining room with its fire engine red walls.

"So?" The look I gave Norman was expectant. "You were going to think about the scams you ran when you were Norman. Have you come up with anything that might help us figure out who's after you?"

Honestly, I was hoping for something a little more definitive than a shrug, but when he glanced at the written list on the table (I'd been bold enough to title it *Norman Scams*), a shrug was all I got from Norman. That and: "I'm drawing a blank. Honest, Annie, I've tried. I've spent all day thinking about it, and as far as I can remember, there isn't a person in the world who hates me enough to want to shoot me. There isn't anything at all I've ever done to anyone that would make them want to force me to talk. Talk? About what?"

"What do people ever want other people to talk about?" I was hoping for more, and I'm afraid my tone betrayed my disappointment. "Sex? Money? Secrets? Any of this ringing a bell?"

Another shrug from Norman. "Sorry to tell you, my love life has never been exciting enough for someone to want to hurt me because of it. Sure, I've had a few flings in my day, and a couple girlfriends here and there. Almost married one of them back when I was Fred Gardner. But hey, she was a real lady." The way Norman's eyes sparkled when he talked about her, I was sure she was. "A woman like that doesn't hold a grudge because a guy walked out on her. At least not for too long. And I hear she ended up doing pretty good for herself, anyway. She married an orthodontist and they've got five great kids."

"Then what about secrets?" Jim had gone into the kitchen and he pushed through the door, a pot of coffee in one hand and a plate of muffins in the other. I tried my best to stay out of Jim's and everyone else's kitchens, but just before the door swung closed, I saw a glimpse of the avocado green appliances and turquoise countertops that he swore he was going to swap out for something a little more twenty-first century one day soon.

There were cups on the table and Jim poured and handed them around. "You've told us already that you were in prison once. Maybe there's some other secret in your past—"

"Don't you think I would tell you if there was? I'd really like to get to the bottom of this. I swear, I wouldn't hold anything back." Norman's shoulders had only barely slumped when Jim passed a plate of freshly baked cranberry almond muffins under his nose. Norman took a whiff. His eyes lit up and he didn't look nearly as discouraged anymore.

I always knew he was a man after my own heart.

He had already taken a muffin, split it open, and buttered a portion of it before he said, "If only I could think of something."

"Money." It was the one thing we hadn't discussed. Since my mouth was full of muffin, too, and the word came out sounding more like "Mny," I swallowed and repeated.

"Money. The killer said it was payback time, and to me, that sounds like it has something to do with money. I've been to your home, Norman. It's nice. It's more than nice. You drive a Jag. You own a successful business.

Pardon me for not being politically correct, but that's not bad for an ex-con."

This time, Norman's shrug was more nonchalant. Like the one he'd used so often when he was Jacques Lavoie. "I'm not suffering, that's for sure, but I'm not loaded, either. I've worked hard for everything I've earned. I mean, lately." Obviously thinking we were going to call him on the being-honest vow he'd made, he cleared his throat. "Sure, I ran a bunch of scams back in the day, but they never earned me really big bucks. Now, Très Bonne Cuisine . . ." Even though he'd ditched the phony French accent, when he said the name of the store, he still added a bit of European pizzazz. "That place has made me a bundle. But hey, like I said, I've worked for it. Nobody can begrudge me that. Every penny of it's been honest. Well, except for the Vavoom!"

I thought about this while I nibbled on another piece of muffin. "So where did the money come from in the first place?" I asked, and I kept my eyes on Norman while I spoke. Promises or no promises, I wasn't ready to trust him implicitly. I needed to gauge his reactions and measure his answers. I needed to watch his eyes when I said, "I mean, the money you used to open the shop. Where did you get the initial capital to invest, anyway?"

A totally honest man would have answered without hesitation.

A liar would have, too.

Norman's response was somewhere right in the middle.

Carefully, he buttered half his muffin. "It was a card game," Norman finally admitted. "Just a friendly poker game. Nothing shady about that."

"You won enough money in a card game to open a store with a huge, expensive inventory?" I thought about the figures I'd heard thrown around, rent and utilities, salaries and taxes, and neighborhood retail association fees. Sure, Très Bonne Cuisine was successful, but with those kinds of expenditures, it was a wonder any business could stay afloat.

"Just to open the doors . . ." I was in the middle of a bite of muffin, so I swallowed before I continued. "It must have cost plenty to get the place decorated and stocked. I've been looking over packing lists and picking tickets. Even at wholesale, the merchandise you sell isn't cheap."

"It was kind of a high-stakes card game." Norman said this as if it was no big deal.

I thought otherwise.

I pinned him with a look. "How high were the stakes?"

He stalled by making a face.

"Norman!" The name came out as a warning, not from me, but from Jim. It was amazing how much whammy he could pack into rolling that *r* in Norman's name.

It was enough to make Norman's face pale. "I won three hundred thousand dollars," he mumbled.

"Three hundred—!" I could barely get the words out. Maybe that's because a piece of muffin was stuck in my throat. I washed it down with a gulp of coffee. "Norman, that means if you won big, somebody lost big."

"Yeah, I guess. But that doesn't have anything to do with what happened to Greg."

"And you know this, how?" Again, it was Jim's turn, and again, he put that Scottish burr of his to good use. When Jim is dead serious, it's hard to ignore that earnest rumble. It sounds a whole lot like thunder.

Norman got up from the table and did a turn around the room. "He's not that kind of guy," he said.

"He who?"

Jim and I managed that bit of mangled English at the same time and together, we waited for an answer. It didn't come until Norman dropped back into his chair at the dining room table.

"Victor Pasqual," he said.

OK, let me make something perfectly clear here: I know nothing (and I do mean nothing) about poker. I also know very little about popular culture. It's not that I'm not interested in those tell-all magazines at the grocery store checkout counter, it's just that I don't have the time to care. Besides, if anything really juicy is happening to any celebrity (the ones I've heard of and the ones I haven't), Eve is sure to fill me in.

In a nutshell, what this means is that my mind is a vast pop culture wasteland.

But even I had heard of Victor Pasqual.

"The billionaire recluse who owns that hotel in Atlantic City and never goes outside and the only time anyone sees him is during one of his card games?" I stared across the table at Norman, wondering how he managed to run in those circles. I couldn't hold my curiosity in for long. "How on earth did you manage to run in those circles?"

"It was a long time ago." He waved away the idea that he was anything even remotely like a celebrity hanger-on. "Vic, he wasn't quite as eccentric back then. I knew a guy who knew a guy who . . . well, you get the picture. I was invited to a game. I won."

"Three hundred thousand dollars." I was having a hard time getting past the figure. But then, I am a numbers person, and these numbers, they were enough to take my breath away. "You won three hundred thousand dollars from a notorious gambler in a poker game, and you don't think that's important? This Victor Pasqual is rich and, from everything I've heard about him, a little crazy, too. He sounds exactly like the kind of guy who might hold a grudge."

"Which means . . ." Jim said this, but I knew him

well enough to know he wasn't exactly anxious to hear my answer. He had that look on his face, the one that told me he saw the wheels in my head turning and he was afraid of where they might take me.

Which is why I answered as matter-of-factly as I was able. "We're going to need to talk to Victor Pasqual."

"The man never leaves the penthouse apartment at his hotel." This from Jim.

"Except to play poker," Norman added.

And they couldn't see where we were headed?

My muffin and coffee finished, I got up from the table, grabbed my purse, and headed for the door. "Then we're going to need to play poker with him," I said. "And I know exactly where I can learn to do that."

 THESE DAYS, IT DOESN'T TAKE A DETECTIVE TO FIND people.

I mean, really, all you need is the Internet and a few smarts.

I had both, and within an hour of leaving Jim's, I was parked in another part of town in front of a tiny brick house with a neat front walk and flower beds where marigolds bobbed their heads in the evening light.

It was the kind of house I'd always dreamed of owning.

The kind I'd been saving for.

The kind I'd had ripped out from under me when Peter left and took half our bank account (and half the down payment we'd saved over the years) with him.

It was the house Peter and Mindy/Mandy bought after they'd married.

I did my best to set aside the anger that assailed me when I considered this. After all, it wasn't why I was there.

I reminded myself of the fact as I rang the bell, then stepped back and waited.

Peter was the only person I knew who played poker.

I needed to learn to play poker.

So—

"Hi!" When the door was opened by a trim blonde in white shorts and a purple tank top, I tried to be as friendly as possible. As much as I'd heard about Mindy/Mandy (and believe me, I'd heard plenty) we'd never actually met face-to-face.

She was shorter than me. She was slimmer. And younger. Her hips weren't as round, her hair was cut short, and there wasn't an unruly curl in sight. She had a ring in her belly button.

"I'm Annie," I said, and I knew exactly when the pieces fell into place and she realized which Annie, exactly, I was. That would have been when she looked a little as if she'd bitten into a lemon. I looked past her into the house with its sleek, modern furniture and walls that were painted an especially appealing tone of beige (though truth be told, the shade was a little dark for my tastes).

"I hate to bother you, but I was wondering if I could talk to Peter for a minute."

Mindy/Mandy stepped onto the porch and closed the door behind her.

"You don't know."

My blank expression said it all.

Mindy/Mandy shrugged. Her tank top gaped and, like it or not, I saw that her breasts were round and firm and perky. As much as I hated to even think about it, I could see why Peter had been attracted. I wondered what she wore behind the counter at the dry cleaner's, and if the day Peter had first walked in there and been smitten on the spot, she was displaying her pierced belly button for the world to see.

"Peter, he said he'd seen you."

Mindy/Mandy's words snapped me out of my thoughts, and it was just as well.

"He stopped in," I said automatically. "To the restaurant where I work. And the gourmet shop where I work and . . ." No doubt that sounded as weird to her as it did to me so I simply added, "He just stopped in to say hello. To talk. That's all. I don't want you to think—"

Her laugh stopped me cold and Mindy/Mandy opened the door and stepped back inside. "I'm sorry I can't help. Peter isn't here. He doesn't live here anymore. In fact, we're getting a divorce."

Thirteen

✠

WAS I SURPRISED?
Not really.

Not by Mindy/Mandy, or by anything she'd told me.

Suddenly, the whole thing about Peter showing up again in my life was starting to make a whole lot of sense.

The real question was how I felt about it.

And the real answer to that question?

The next Monday night, I told myself I'd better figure it out, and I'd better figure it out fast. Peter was on his way over to Bellywasher's, and before our cooking students left and he showed up, I needed to have a plan.

As to how I'd found Peter in the first place after striking out at Mindy/Mandy's . . . well, like I said, these days, you don't need to be a great detective to track people down. Of course it helped that his soon-to-be-second ex-missus knew which extended-stay hotel Peter was staying at and didn't mind giving me the number.

Contacting Peter and asking him to give me some poker pointers was a better plan than dwelling on the fact that he was soon to be a free man, and I was the free woman who'd once dreamed that he'd see the light, walk away from Mindy/Mandy, and come crawling back to me.

It was also way better than brooding, and brooding was exactly what I did when I thought about how divorces worked. I certainly didn't know the ins and outs of Peter's relationship with his current wife, nor did I want to. But I guessed that Mindy/Mandy was soon to be the sole owner of the house that should have been mine.

"Annie!"

I shook myself out of my thoughts and found Jim watching me. A couple seconds ticked by before I realized where I was—in front of the cooking class—and what I was supposed to be doing—showing them how to use a variety of citrus juicers.

Considering that at the beginning of the evening I'd demonstrated a kitchen torch—with less than successful results—I had to give Jim a lot of credit. At least he was willing to give me a second chance. Apparently, he didn't hold a couple of singed aprons and a siren blast from the smoke alarm against me.

"Citrus juicers!" I beamed a smile at the students gathered around me and, call me paranoid, but I saw the way they backed away from the table when they realized I'd be the one doing the show-and-tell.

"You're safe. This one doesn't even plug in." I held up the brightly colored heavy die-cast aluminum juicer for the class to see. Because I couldn't decide, I'd brought them in all three colors: orange, yellow, and green. "You put a half of a citrus fruit in here." I demonstrated with a lime, setting it into the rounded end of the bright green juicer. "Squeeze the two handles together." I did. "And the halved fruit is turned inside out." I showed them, along with the nice bit of juice I squeezed into a glass.

"For bigger jobs . . ." I moved on to the electric juicer on the table. "This one even has a filter that separates juice and seeds." I had a halved orange nearby and made a glass of juice, lickety-split.

"Very nice. Thank you." Jim gave me a smile before he turned his attention back to the class. "Just a couple of the gadgets that can make your cooking life easier. I think Annie's got a few more she brought with her . . ." He glanced my way and I nodded. "So when we're done with this next bit of cooking, she'll show you how to make the perfect cup of coffee."

The next item on the menu was eggs Sardou and while our students got to work and with nothing to do for the moment, I stepped back and simply watched.

I don't know where Jim got the notion to do breakfast foods rather than more traditional pub fare for the night's class. It might have been because of those memorable waffles Norman had served us a couple of mornings before. Wherever the idea came from, our students were eating it up.

Literally.

They'd already made heart-shaped pancakes on the special griddle I'd brought from Très Bonne Cuisine, as well as soft-boiled eggs. I have to admit, I was pretty proud of myself as far as the eggs were concerned. Without any help at all from Raymond, I'd searched the shelves at the shop and found adorable egg cups made of wire and complete with little legs and chicken feet. As long as I was having a fit of culinary brilliance, I'd also brought along an ingenious little device that fits over the tops of the eggs and cuts off the rounded part of the shell, scissors-style.

Thanks to Raymond's patient tutoring, I was actually able to demonstrate without too much of a mess.

"You're doing fine." After he'd demonstrated that mind-boggling, one-handed method he uses to crack eggs, Jim zipped by and gave me a quick smile. "Everything ready for later?"

I knew he wasn't referring to the other gadgets I'd brought to demonstrate. "Eve's coming," I told him. "And Marc and Damien said that as long as we're going to play cards, they want to sit in, too. But, Jim—"

We heard a groan as a student cracked an egg and ended up with a mess of white, yolk, and shell. She called Jim over for advice.

And I cooled my heels, waiting for him to finish.

When he was done and while part of the class was busy slicing artichoke hearts and another part was making creamed spinach, I tried again.

Jim was on his way over to see how things were going with the students who were taking their first stab at making hollandaise sauce, and I stopped him, a hand on his sleeve. Ever since the night I talked to Peter and he agreed to stop at Bellywasher's to give us a poker lesson, I'd wondered how Jim felt about the whole thing. I practiced a thousand ways to explain and a thousand more to reassure him. None of which had ever come out quite right. Now, Peter would be there in less than an hour and I didn't have time for long-winded explanations. Or for beating around the bush.

Sure, I was uncertain about what I'd say to Peter now that I knew his current marriage was drifting oh-so-near the rocks that destroyed ours.

Yes, I kept picturing myself in those early days when I learned about Mindy/Mandy, watched my whole world fall apart, and told myself I'd do anything—anything— if only I could get Peter back again.

Absolutely, I was having a giant case of mixed emotions, what with Peter's sudden reappearance looking less accidental and more like he wanted to reconnect with the woman who would still be his woman if not for the woman he left her for.

But Jim didn't have to know any of that.

I cared too much about him to let that happen.

And he cared too much about his class for me to keep him standing there when his students needed his help. That's why I just blurted out, "You know this doesn't mean anything to me, don't you?"

"The hollandaise?" Jim is not one to be dense, and he sure isn't dumb. The fact that he was pretending to be clueless was my first hint that the whole Peter-showing-up thing actually might bother him more than he was willing to admit.

"Not the hollandaise." As if he needed me to point this out. "Peter. You know, Peter coming over here and—"

Jim was as matter-of-fact as he could be considering that he was keeping his voice down so our students wouldn't overhear. "I know that in order to help Norman, you need to talk to that Victor Pasqual fellow. I know you'll never be able to get close to Pasqual if you can't play poker, though how you're going to manage that even if you can play poker is a mystery to me and, I sus-pect, to you at this point. Nonetheless, I know you, and I know you want to be prepared. I know you don't know how to play poker, and, as I am more than willing to ad-mit, neither do I. What's that Eve read in that tabloid newspaper she's been carrying around with her? These days, Pasqual's obsessed with Texas Hold'em. I don't even know what that is. That means, if you're going to learn to play cards, you need to ask the advice of some-one who does know how. And since you're acquainted with him, I know it also makes perfect sense for that someone to be Peter."

"So . . ." OK, so it wasn't exactly subtle. At this point, it made more sense just to lay things on the line than it did to dillydally. "It doesn't bother you?"

When one of the hollandaise cooks screeched and pointed in a panic to the double boiler where the egg yolks, lemon juice, and water were supposed to be gently heating and instead were bubbling over like a volcano, Jim told her to turn off the stove, then held up one finger, asking for another moment before he turned his attention back to me. "When you first started investigating, I was opposed to it. You know that, Annie. I was worried for your safety. But now . . ." He grabbed a whisk to take over to the hollandaise makers, and continued:

"You've got a gift. And you're using it to make the world a better place. You need to do what you have to do. You need to do what makes you happy."

And with that, he was gone.

And I was left feeling more perplexed than ever.

I had to do what I had to do? I had to do what made me happy?

Was Jim telling me to get back together with Peter? Did he think I wanted to?

Would Jim be happier if I did?

He was already repairing the hollandaise disaster, so I had time to ponder all this. It was just as well that I heard a knock on the front door of the restaurant; all that pondering was getting me nowhere and making my head hurt, to boot.

Finding Peter at the front door didn't help. He was dressed in nicely worn jeans and the raspberry-colored golf shirt I'd given him for his birthday just a couple months before he met Mindy/Mandy. With his dark hair and eyes, Peter had always looked good in vivid colors. Some things never change.

Maybe he knew what I was thinking because he smiled. "You look terrific," he said with a quick glance at my yellow T-shirt, my black pants, and the white apron I wore over them both. "This cooking thing is good for you."

"You wouldn't say that if you ever saw me in the kitchen."

"Oh, I don't know." A tiny half smile playing around his lips, he cocked his head, and he looked so lost in some pleasant thought, I wondered if there had actually been a triumphant moment in my cooking life that I had blocked out.

Or not.

"We're not here to talk about my cooking," I reminded him. And myself. "We're here to learn how to play poker."

"And I've got everything you need. Right in here." He held up a paper shopping bag at the same time he glanced at the clock that hung above the bar. "Looks like we've got a few minutes before your class is over. Can I buy you a beer?"

I wasn't one for giving freebies but he was, after all, there to do us a favor. I poured a glass of the beer I knew was Peter's favorite and brought it over to the table we'd set up for our game, and when he reached for his wallet, I refused to even think about it. He took a sip of the beer, smiled his approval, and sat down. I would have, too, if I wasn't feeling as if my skin was crawling with electricity.

There was only one way to settle my nerves and I knew it.

I stood my ground and looked down at Peter. "You want to tell me what this is all about?"

"This?" He held the glass of beer up to the light and examined its amber color. "I'd say it's all about wheat and hops and the magic that is yeast. It's chemistry, you know. And that's something I know a lot about. But something tells me that's not what you're talking about."

"It's not." I dropped into the chair next to his. "This whole thing," I said. "You showing up here. What's it about, Peter?"

I suspected he looked at me the way he looked at the high school juniors who just didn't get the latest homework assignment. "I'm teaching you how to play Texas Hold'em. You did ask me to come by and do a quick poker clinic, right?"

"Not *that* 'this.' The *other* 'this.' " I shook my head, doing my best to order my thoughts. "You've been hanging around, Peter. Here and at Très Bonne Cuisine. And you and Mindy/Mandy are getting a—"

"You know about that, huh?" He didn't look sorry, just a little embarrassed. I guess I would have, too, considering it was time for him to fess up: He'd left the woman who was supposed to be the love of his life for the woman who was the new love of his life, only as it turned out, she apparently wasn't. "That's how you found me, right? I never did have a chance to ask you when you called the other night. I should have known you talked to M—"

"Yes. And she told me you're getting a divorce. I'm sorry." I really was. It was the first I realized it, and something about admitting the emotion—to him and to myself—opened the floodgate of my questions. "I don't want to know what went wrong. It's none of my business. But you do owe me the truth, Peter. Does your divorce have anything to do with the fact that you've been coming around to see me? Are you looking to—"

"Get back together?" Big points for him. He didn't try to pull the wool over my eyes and pretend this was the first he'd considered what I was thinking. But he did sound skeptical.

I was relieved.

And maybe a little disappointed.

And definitely confused.

"It's not easy for me to admit I made a mistake." Peter reached over and put one hand over mine. If he was a stranger, I would have told him to get lost and yanked it away. If he was a friend, I would have flipped my hand over so our fingers could entwine.

But Peter was something else. Something in between. Friend and enemy. Lover and stranger. The man I'd sworn to love, honor, and cherish all the days of my life.

Yeah, that one. The one who'd chosen a belly button ring over a wedding ring.

The one whose face I pictured when I used to dream about this moment. This was the crawling-back scene, live and in color.

I tensed, wondering how I'd respond when he finally said the words.

"I'm lonely." Not exactly the declaration I was waiting for, but that didn't keep his words from smacking me right between the heart and the stomach. We'd been apart for nearly two years. Still, thinking of him as sad and lonely had a way of tugging at heartstrings I didn't know were still attached to Peter.

He must have sensed my reaction, because he leaned a little nearer. "I'm not asking you to take me back, Annie," he said, and before I could decide if this was good or bad, he went on. "I thought we could just . . . I don't know . . ." He shrugged and pulled back, and when he removed his hand from mine, I sat back, too, and put my hands in my lap where they were safer. "I thought we could be friends. You know, like we used to be. I thought that maybe someday you'd understand."

"About those mistakes you talked about?"

"About everything." He scraped a hand through his hair. "I don't mean right now. Tonight. I just thought if we started out slow . . ." He shot a shy smile my way and I was instantly transported back to the day we'd met. That was the way Peter had smiled at me then, and that smile had led to what I'd always thought was my very own personal happily-ever-after. "I miss you." He looked relieved at having said the words. "I want you back in my life. That's why when you asked me to come over and talk to you about cards . . ." He reached into the shopping bag he'd brought with him and put two decks of cards on the table, then reached in again and brought out a container of plastic poker chips. "I never thought the way to a woman's heart was through Texas Hold'em. But hey, if that's what it takes!" Peter laughed and pulled one of the decks of cards from its box. He ruffled the cards through his fingers, shuffling them. "Only, when we talked, you never explained why you wanted to learn to play cards. You guys here at the restaurant having some sort of fund-raising Texas Hold'em tournament? It's the only thing I can really think of that would explain you wanting to gamble. Let's face it, you're not the type."

I wasn't, and I knew it. Which didn't prevent me from asking, "What type am I?"

"Safe. Dependable. Reliable." Believe me, Peter didn't say any of this like it was anything to be ashamed of. He was just stating facts, and even though I knew the facts were facts and I wasn't ashamed of them, either, I felt my spine stiffen. Just a little.

"Your personality doesn't exactly mesh with the daring sort of spirit a person needs to be a gambler," he pointed out. "Playing cards is like going on an adventure, see. Even the small-time kind of card games I get into. Each one is like a quest, a mission. And my job is to see if I can outwit the other guys at the table. Sometimes I do that by playing it safe. Other times I've got to bluff and take chances no sane person ever would. No offense, Annie, but you're not that type. You like the straight and narrow. The safe. The secure. So if you want to learn to play Texas Hold'em, it must because of—"

"Murder. I'm investigating a murder."

Peter lost his grip, and a few of the cards slipped out of his hand and landed on the floor. He bent to retrieve them and when he finally sat up and got settled, there was color in his cheeks. He whistled below his breath.

Believe me, I did not hold any of this against him. It isn't every day that someone reveals that she's looking into a murder. Especially someone who isn't with the police.

So Peter's surprise . . . well, I could understand that.

And I was prepared for his questions, too.

But when he came out with a skeptical, "You? Investigating a murder? You're kidding me, right?" I guess I sort of lost it.

"You think it's funny?" I asked him, even though he didn't say he did. "You think I'm not smart enough? That I don't have the nerve?"

"I didn't say that." He reached for his beer and took another drink, looking at me the same way the students back in class did when I reached for that first citrus juicer and they were afraid to see what might happen next. "I just never thought of you as the type."

"Which type is that? The type who has to make her own way in life after her husband walks out on her?"

He wasn't expecting that, but then, I guess I wasn't, either. Even so, after two years of holding in my anger, it felt good.

Peter discounting my feelings did not.

As if it was all nothing, he waved a hand in the air. "That was a long time ago, Annie."

"You think?"

"I think you're still angry. It makes me wonder why."

"Not for the reason you think." Of course, I didn't know exactly what he was thinking, but it sure felt good to pretend I did.

"You're serious." He gave me a sidelong look. "I mean about investigating murders. Like you're some kind of detective or something. It's—"

"Amazing?"

"I was going to say a little delusional."

"Because you don't think I'm capable."

"Because I don't think a bank teller who isn't a bank teller anymore knows anything about murder."

"Except I do. I've already solved three."

"You don't have to try and impress me."

"Is that what you think I'm trying to do?"

"I think what you should be trying to do is calm down and get a grip on reality. Nobody just investigates murders. Nobody like you, anyway. And I'm happy to teach you how to play poker. Honest, I am. But the least you can do is tell me why you want to learn, without making up fantastic stories."

"People don't investigate murders?"

"Not people like you."

It was as simple as that.

At least to Peter.

"So if I was using a cooking torch, and I almost started the kitchen on fire, you wouldn't let me use the cooking torch again?"

"We're talking about cooking torches?" When I didn't answer, he gritted his jaw. "No, of course I wouldn't let you use it again. If you're incapable—"

"And if I wanted to play cards with someone you thought it was next to impossible for me to play cards with, you'd tell me to get lost. Or would you tell me to learn anyway, because you knew I'd find a way to make things happen the way I wanted them to happen?"

"You're scaring me now." He pushed his chair away from the table—and from me. "You're not making any sense."

"And you're not giving me any answers."

"Because there's nothing to answer. If you wanted to play poker with someone you could never play poker against would I teach you to play poker? That's crazy talk, Annie. I think the fumes from the cooking oil around here are getting to your brain."

"And I think . . ." I pushed back from the table, too, and stood.

"Where are you going?" he asked.

"I'll be right back." It wasn't an answer. He didn't deserve one, and I didn't owe him one, either.

Instead, I strode into the kitchen and even though Jim was just about to plate up poached eggs on top of creamed spinach and artichoke hearts, I walked right up to him and gave him a big kiss.

Our students thought either it was cute or I was a lunatic. Uneasy and not sure how to respond, a couple applauded.

And Jim?

When I was done, he looked at me as if I was crazy. But there was a twinkle in his eyes.

"What's that for?" he asked.

"It's for you. You're the one who told me I have to do what makes me happy."

He caught his breath. "And . . . ?"

"And you, Jim MacDonald . . ." Just to be certain he knew I was serious, I gave him a quick kiss. "There isn't a shred of doubt in my mind, and there shouldn't be in yours. You are absolutely the one who makes me happy."

Fourteen

❖

HERE'S THE THING ABOUT ATLANTIC CITY: EVEN WITH the bumper-to-bumper traffic on I-95, it's less than a four-hour drive from Arlington. But it might as well be on another planet. Sure, the D.C. area has its share of nightlife, its movers and its shakers. But Atlantic City . . .

Where D.C. can be elegant and dignified, Atlantic City is bright and brash. They say the city is always turned on, and whoever *they* are, they're not kidding. As we drove into town a few nights after our Texas Hold'em clinic, the sky above the city glowed, as if the whole of A.C. (as the locals call it) wore a neon halo.

The Pasqual Palace was the brightest and brashest of them all—from its garishly spotlighted towers of guest rooms to a casino decorated in rich brocades, crystal chandeliers, and carpets so plush my sandals sank as we crossed to the bank of elevators that would take us up to the exclusive penthouse. The place was all about gaudy, flashy, and fancy.

Over on our right, the light atop a slot machine flashed

and swirled, and an upbeat electronic tune blared a song of gambling success. The granny sitting in front of the slot whooped and hollered while on the other side of the aisle, a scantily clad waitress called out, "Drinks, anyone?" and a roulette wheel whirred.

Truth be told, we hadn't even been in town for a couple hours and already I was desperate for a little peace, a little quiet, and a whole lot less sensory overload. Still, I could see the appeal. There were actually people who thrived in this kind of atmosphere. Or so I'd heard. And I've got to say, if they were looking for overstimulation, they'd come to the right place.

I wrapped an arm through Jim's, desperate to hang on to the calm center of sanity he represented in my life. When we passed a poker game in progress at one of the nearby tables and I thought of where we were headed and what we were there to accomplish, terror gripped the pit of my stomach. "Maybe we should have brought Peter with us after all," I said.

Eve was right behind us and she clicked her tongue. I wasn't sure if it was in response to what I'd said or to the way an elderly man ogled her in her white evening gown with its spaghetti straps and plunging neckline.

"Don't be silly." When she said this, I knew she was talking to me. Besides, she'd already warned the old guy to back off with a look that was at once friendly and standoffish. Beauty queens, apparently, are born knowing the fine art of rejecting a guy—and sending him away smiling. "We don't need Peter to tell us how to play cards. Or to play for us. You were there Monday night, Annie. You saw us. We were awesome!"

Had Eve not been so bedazzled by our surroundings and our impending meeting with Victor Pasqual himself, she might have been more accurate. *We* were not awesome at Peter's Texas Hold'em clinic on Monday night. In fact, *we* played pretty much like the amateurs we were. Eve, on the other hand, was awesome.

Who could have guessed that a li'l ol' beauty queen from the South would somehow instinctively know when to hold 'em, know when to fold 'em, know when to walk away, and know when to twinkle her way through bluffs so outrageous the players around her crumbled and she was left winning hands that she never should have played in the first place.

There was an attendant at the door of the private elevator to the far right, and after Eve showed him her invitation to the night's poker game, he called the elevator and we waited.

Eve is not one to get nervous. She never has been. I remember sitting in the audience while she was onstage at countless beauty pageants. My hands shook. My heart raced. My blood pressure climbed until it felt like my head was going to pop. And Eve? Then, like now, she was as icy cool as her brilliant white gown.

"Do I look OK?" she asked.

"Of course you do. You look better than OK." There was no denying that. Though Eve always dressed with care and a whole lot more pizzazz than I ever had or could ever hope to have, she'd pulled out all the stops that night. Besides her knock 'em dead gown, she was wearing diamonds that glittered on her ears and at her throat. They matched the sparkling rhinestone collar Doc was wearing and when I complimented her, Eve smiled down at the dog in her arms.

"You hear that, sweetie pie?" She rubbed noses with the dog. "Annie says I look good."

"You look cool and confident, too." She did. She was. At the same time I envied her the ability. I wondered and panicked and worried—just as I'd been wondering and panicking and worrying since the night of our poker clinic. What if we weren't doing the right thing?

I swallowed my misgivings along with the sour taste in my mouth and told Eve, "You're going to do great."

"I'd better." Eve handed the dog to Jim, who was too surprised to do anything but take Doc off her hands. Jim is not an unkind person by any means, and I know for a fact that he has a soft spot in his heart for animals. I've seen the way he greets every dog we meet when we walk in the park. But Jim is also not one to forget, and I don't think he'll ever forget the time Eve snuck Doc into the kitchen at Bellywasher's, or the digestive disaster that resulted when she fed the dog too many rich foods. Now Jim held the tiny dog a little uncertainly, as if he wasn't sure what it would do, or what he should do with it.

"I don't want Doc to know," Eve whispered, turning her back on Jim and the dog. "You know, about the c-o-l-l-a-r."

"Doc can't spell. And he doesn't know what you're talking about when you say collar, anyway." As if to contradict me, Doc yipped. I ignored him and went right on. "The dog isn't going to know that if you—"

"Lose tonight, I won't be able to get his diamond collar out of hock." Under the perfect coating of perfect pink blush that complimented her skin tone perfectly, Eve paled. "You hush, Annie. Don't say it. Don't even think such a thing. I pawned Doc's collar for a good cause, so we had the stake to get me in this game. But I am not going home empty-handed." She turned around and scooped the dog out of Jim's hands so she could give him a hug. The dog, not Jim. "I wouldn't do that to my sweet'ums."

And really, I might not see the need to spell in front of Doc, but I wasn't about to complain. That's how grateful I was. Without Eve's generous offer, we wouldn't be here in the first place, not after we found out that it cost twenty-five thousand dollars just to get into Victor Pasqual's Friday night Texas Hold'em game.

As to how it all happened in the first place . . .

I glanced to my left, and at the man in the tuxedo who waited for the elevator with us, and honest to gosh, if I didn't know it was Norman under that dark, shaggy wig and behind the bushy, glued-on mustache, I never would have suspected a thing. I never argued with Norman when he said he wanted to come along. After all, he had as much right to be there as we did. More, really, since this was his chance to check out Victor Pasqual after all these years and see if the millionaire gambler looked anything like the man who walked into Très Bonne Cuisine and shot Greg.

I never questioned Norman when he said he would feel safer wearing a disguise, either. I understood exactly why he wanted to keep a low profile. Especially after Norman had finally talked to Tyler, been officially eliminated as a suspect—and officially put on notice that the killer who was still out there somewhere was probably still looking for him.

Besides all that, if it wasn't for Norman, we wouldn't be there at all. It turned out that he still had a few connections from back in the day. He knew a guy who knew a guy who knew a guy who claimed he could get one of us into the game, and, true to his word (and after a goodly sum of money had exchanged hands thanks to Norman, who was more than willing to pay it), our invitation to the card game was couriered over the next day. Of course, all along, I had every intention of being the one who would sit in on the game. That way, I could get close to Victor Pasqual and make what Peter called "table talk," in an effort to find out what he knew about Norman Applebaum—and Greg's murder.

That was before reality sank in, and when it did, I saw the error of my ways. I was too conservative to win at poker. I was too hesitant, too cautious. Jim, on the other hand, was too emotional. It didn't take an expert to pick up on his not-so-subtle body language he started signaling the moment Peter had us together for our how-to class. When he held good cards, Jim's burr deepened almost beyond understanding. When his hand was bad, he had a way of tapping his fingers against the table, impatient to get things over with. He might as well have spelled out *loser* in Morse code. Over time, Peter assured him (and me, for that matter), there was a slim chance we both might actually turn into decent players.

But time was the one thing we didn't have.

Eve, on the other hand, was one thing we did.

"Peter could have played for us. If I drummed it into his head enough, he might have asked Pasqual the right questions." I kept my voice down when I said this to Jim and I didn't have to worry, Eve was busy cooing to Doc.

Jim, too, spoke quietly. "You losing your nerve?"

"No. Yes." I paced in front of the elevator. "This could be a disaster."

"Aye." When the elevator arrived and the doors swished open, Jim stepped aside so I could go first. "But think of how much more of a disaster it would be if you weren't investigating. We wouldn't know nearly as much as we do now, and Norman might not be safe. Plus—"

Just as the elevator doors closed, a man raced inside. "Investigating. Oh, I like the sound of that!"

"Peter?" I gave him a careful look because, let's face it, I figured I was hallucinating. "You're not supposed to be here. You're supposed to be back in Arlington."

"And miss all the fun?" Peter chafed his hands together. He looked Eve's way. "You might need some pointers. And besides, I always wondered what it might be like to be part of the Scooby Gang. You guys are as close as I'll ever get." Peter leaned nearer to me. "Who's the guy with the mustache?" he asked.

Luckily, I didn't have a chance to answer. After a

smooth, quick ride, the elevator doors opened and we found ourselves in a lobby even more sumptuous than the one downstairs. Walls of glass allowed us a bird's-eye look at the Boardwalk and the Atlantic Ocean beyond. Tiny lights twinkled on a terrace that overlooked the view. In front of us was another wall of glass and beyond that, we saw tuxedoed waiters and dealers getting ready for the game.

"It's like something out of a James Bond movie," Jim said, and I had to agree with him. The men around us were high rollers; I could tell by the way they were dressed and by the smell of their expensive cigars. Of course when Eve announced that she was there for the game, there were a couple of chuckles. And more than a couple of guys who couldn't keep their eyes off her.

She, though, is nothing if not single-minded. Especially when it comes to being the center of attention. Eve held back, and when an elevator across the lobby opened, and Victor Pasqual stepped out, she made her move, jockeying for position and making her way through the crowd of dour, serious gamblers as easily as Moses through the Red Sea.

I recognized Pasqual's face, of course, from seeing him on TV. He was a little older than middle-aged, a little shorter than average, and a little wider than large. He wasn't an attractive man, and in a loud orange and brown plaid sport coat and brown pants in a shade that didn't match, he certainly wasn't the best-dressed fellow in the room. What he was, though, was larger than life.

"Hi, fellas!" Pasqual's voice was a lot like Atlantic City, loud and brassy. He marched across the plush carpet like he owned the place and, since he did, I guess that was perfectly appropriate. He shook hands with a couple of the cigar-smoking men and stopped cold when he got to Eve.

"Well, good evening!" He grabbed her outstretched

hand and kissed it with more enthusiasm than style. "It's a little early for me to be dreaming. Don't tell me you're here for the card game, sweetie." He pressed a hand to his chest. "I don't think my old heart could take it!"

Eve knew just how to handle comments like that. "Why, Victor, honey!" Her accent was more Southern than magnolias. "Aren't you just the sweetest thing."

I left them at it, stepping into the hospitality room we'd been told was reserved for the guests of those playing in the game. As soon as we were out of earshot, I buttonholed Norman.

"Well?" I watched him watching Victor through the open doorway. "Is it him? Is that the man you saw walk into Très Bonne Cuisine and shoot Greg?"

Norman had to part the bangs on his dark wig for a better look. He squinted and stared. "I dunno."

Before I could let go the breath I was holding, Peter was at my side. "You think Pasqual is a murderer? That's what this is all about?" He was so hopped up on adrenaline and the excitement of being in the presence of a real poker hero, he could barely stand still. "You're crazy. You know that, don't you, Annie? No way Victor Pasqual would ever kill anybody."

I hissed to remind him to keep his voice down and, grabbing his arm, I dragged Peter closer to the windows and farther from anywhere anyone could hear us.

"He's a legend, Annie." At least Peter got the message. He whispered, just like I did. "And he's rich. Hey!" When he saw movement in the glass-enclosed room where the game would be played, Peter headed for the door. "They said we could watch from here if we weren't any distraction. Oh, man, this is the most exciting night of my life!"

That's funny, I thought the most exciting night of his life was—

Never mind.

As soon as Peter was gone, Jim came over and wrapped an arm around my shoulders.

"Everything all right?" he asked.

"It will be when we get out of here. And if . . ." I glanced toward the poker game. There were seats for nine, and Eve had taken the one on Victor's right. "If she can stay in the game long enough. And if she can get him to talk."

🍴 "I WISH WE COULD SEE THE CARDS EVERYONE WAS holding."

For about the hundredth time since the card play started, Peter stood in the doorway of the hospitality room and craned his neck for a better look into the card room. He moved to his left. He moved to his right. "If I knew what Pasqual's pocket cards were—"

"I'm sure that's why they have the rooms set up this way." I poked Peter in the ribs to stop him from dancing around and looking too anxious. "If we could see the cards, we might signal the players."

"I know, I know." He scraped a hand through his hair the way he always did when he was antsy. "But I can't stand the suspense. And Eve—!" When Eve tossed in another red chip, Peter groaned. I didn't know how much the red chips were worth. I didn't want to know. "She's not listening to anything I told her. She shouldn't be grinning and chatting and acting so girlie. She's giving too much away."

"Or not!" Eve reached to the middle of the table and scooped all the chips to her pile and I poked Peter in the ribs again, telling him without a word that he didn't know everything there was to know about Texas Hold'em. Apparently, a grinning, chatty, girlie girl could do pretty well at the game. "Look." I pointed when Pasqual stood up from the table. "They're taking a break."

Two of the card players who'd started the night had already run out of chips and when the door to the card room opened, one of the men stalked to the elevator and left. The other didn't look nearly as upset by his losses. He stuck around to say good-bye to his fellow players before he came into the hospitality room for a glass of Scotch.

When she sauntered out of the card room, I closed in on Eve.

"So?" I tried not to sound too anxious, but really, how could I help myself? "You're talking to Pasqual. I've seen you talking to him. Did you find out anything?"

How she managed, I don't know, but Eve looked as fresh and perky as she had when the night started. She looped an arm through mine and together we walked to the refreshment table. She pointed at a pricey bottle of sparkling water and a waiting server opened it for her and poured it into a crystal glass. "Vic's favorite color is blue," she said. "His favorite holiday is Christmas. He lives alone, but he talks to his mama every day. Isn't that nice? He's never been married and those tabloid stories we've read linking him to all those Hollywood starlets . . ." She tossed her head and laughed. "Why, don't you just know it, gossipmongers have a way of getting carried away. Is that what you were hoping to find out, Annie?"

It wasn't, and Eve knew it. Which was why she grinned when Pasqual approached the refreshment table.

"Vic, honey . . ." I didn't imagine many people were so forward as to grab Victor Pasqual's hand, but when Eve did, he sure didn't object. She piloted him my way. "This is my friend Annie. The one I told you I wanted you to meet. Annie is just the cleverest thing. She's a detective, you know."

"A detective!" Pasqual was anything but subtle. His words boomed through the room. He wiggled his eyebrows. "Holy smokes, little lady, you're not going to cuff me and drag me off somewhere private, are you?"

I smiled and pretended he was funny while I extended my hand. "It's nice to meet you, Mr. Pasqual."

As he'd done with Eve, he grabbed my hand and gave it a sloppy kiss. I resisted the urge to wipe my hand against my black skirt.

"So . . ." There was a crystal punch bowl nearby, filled with ice and brimming with bottles of a cheap, off-brand beer that was apparently Pasqual's favorite. When he looked that way, a waiter made a move to get him a bottle, but Victor was too quick. He grabbed a bottle, twisted off the cap, and took a glug. When the waiter looked disappointed at not being able to help, Pasqual handed the man a one-hundred-dollar bill. "Thanks for trying," he said, before he turned his attention back to me. "What do you detect?"

"Oh, this and that." I didn't do well at being coy, and I knew I wasn't there just to make small talk, but it was hard not to be at a loss for words. Did I say that Victor Pasqual was larger than life? I'm not sure even that hyperbole describes him. He was bigger than that. Louder. Merrier. He reminded me of a New Jersey Santa Claus. Well, except for the loud sport coat and the beer.

"One of the cases I'm working on now involves someone you might know," I said, finding my voice just as the dealer inside the card room called out that play would begin again in five minutes. I watched Pasqual carefully, gauging his reaction when I said, "Norman Applebaum."

"Who?" Pasqual finished the rest of his beer in one swallow and reached for another. "Never heard of the guy."

"I thought you might remember him, seeing that he won three hundred thousand dollars from you in a poker game."

"Three hundred thousand? Really?" Pasqual's eyes bulged, and he laughed. "Oh, heck. That's pocket change." He grabbed Eve's arm. "Come on, honey. Let's see if you can play the rest of the game as well as you played the start. You are going to sit right next to me again, aren't you?"

As he pulled her away, Eve looked over her shoulder at me and shrugged.

And me?

I watched and waited and wondered.

Could anyone pretend to be as clueless as Pasqual did when I mentioned Norman's name? And if he really didn't know Norman, did that mean he didn't hold a grudge against the man who'd won so much money from him?

Honestly, I didn't know. But I knew one thing for sure: If Victor Paqual was the killer we were looking for, he sure wasn't acting very guilty.

THE FIRST THING I DID WHEN EVE AND VICTOR LEFT the hospitality room was look toward Norman, who was squirreled away behind a potted palm.

"Well?" I mouthed the word, glancing toward Pasqual and raising my eyebrows as if to ask, *Is he the guy?*

Norman's only response was a shrug.

It was not what I was hoping for.

Discouraged, and wondering what on earth to do next, I dropped into a nearby armchair. Jim had been outside with Doc, and when the elevator across the lobby opened, he and the dog stepped out. He gave me a look. I answered with a shrug.

And we were right back where we started.

That's where we stayed, too, until the wee hours of the morning when—finally—the game was over.

As soon as I saw it was, I popped out of the chair where I'd spent part of the last hour dozing and the

other part worrying. I was waiting outside the card room
door when Eve walked out.

"Well?"

She ignored me. Which was just as well. I wasn't sure
if I was asking if she'd won enough to get Doc's collar
out of hock, or if she'd found out anything useful from
Victor Pasqual.

Eve, though, didn't miss a beat. I saw her glance
around just long enough to make sure Norman was within
earshot, then give Victor that teasing little half smile of
hers. The one that never fails to make the male of the
species melt into a pile of mush.

"It's payback time, Norman," Victor said.

And with that, he was gone, headed over toward his
private elevator.

It took me a moment to find my voice. "What . . . ?"
From the elevator, I saw Victor wave at Eve and Eve
wave back. "What was that all about?"

"Oh, that? That was me being brilliant!" She grinned
and called Norman over. "So . . . ?"

Norman shook his head. "It isn't him," he said. "Now
that I've heard him say that, I'm sure of it."

"But . . . ?" Eve was ready to walk over to where Jim
waited with Doc, so I grabbed her arm to stop her. "How
did you get him to say that?"

"That was easy. I told Vic I'd seen a movie once. And
in it, the hero and heroine, they had this sort of code
worked out. When one of them said, 'It's payback time,
Norman,' the other one knew it was time for . . . well,
you know, Annie . . . time for them to get intimate."

I couldn't catch my breath. "And you're going to . . .
get intimate . . . with Victor Pasqual?"

Eve laughed and reached for another bottle of sparkling
water. "Don't be silly, sugar. He thinks I'm coming up to
his private apartment, but that's not going to happen, girlfriend. I'll call him tomorrow before we check out and tell

him it broke my heart, but I was just too, too tuckered out to give him the kind of attention I know he needs. He'll understand."

"You are brilliant!" I pulled Eve into a brief hug before we walked over to the elevator that would take us back down to the main lobby of the hotel. Norman and Jim followed, and though we tried to outpace Peter, we weren't successful. The five of us waited together for the next elevator. "That was the perfect way to find out if Victor was the killer."

"Pish-tush!" The elevator arrived and we stepped inside. "I didn't need him to say it at all, I just thought it might help Norman here make up his mind." Eve was taller than Norman, and she ruffled a hand through his wig. "I knew Victor wasn't the killer hours ago. He couldn't have been. The night Greg was killed, Victor was on a cruise in the Mediterranean with his mama."

I was speechless. Truly. Thanks to Eve, we'd accomplished everything we'd set out to do. Sure, eliminating Victor Pasqual left us without a suspect in Greg's death, but it was still an important step forward. Now the only thing I had to worry about—

"There's my little sweet'ums." While I was busy thinking, Eve grabbed Doc out of Jim's arms and gave him a ferocious hug. "Good news, my little honey bunny," she cooed to the dog. "When we get home, we're going to get your collar out of that nasty pawnbroker's shop. And I think I won just enough . . ." By this time we were all staring at her, and Eve knew it. That's why she smiled at Doc. "I think I won enough to buy you a new outfit. And one for me, too."

Fifteen

✖

SURE, IT WAS DISAPPOINTING TO HAVE TO ELIMINATE Victor Pasqual as a suspect. After all, without him, we really didn't have any suspects.

But honestly, by that time, I'm not sure any of us cared.

We liked Victor Pasqual, and besides, we were all so relieved that Eve hadn't lost her money, there was nothing that could have destroyed our good mood.

Well, almost nothing.

Down in the lobby, we decided to go out to breakfast before we began the long drive back to Arlington. We even included Peter (like I said, we were in good moods) on the sole condition that he stop calling us the Scooby Gang, and never breathe a word—to anyone—about the fact that for a brief moment in time, Victor Pasqual was a murder suspect.

But no sooner had we stepped out of the Pasqual Palace, onto the street, and out of the neon aura that surrounded the hotel than a curious thing happened.

I heard a car door slam and I was so wrapped up in

getting all the details of the card game from Eve, I didn't pay any attention.

I should have.

Then I would have noticed the dark sedan parked nearby, and the man wearing a ski mask who jumped out of it, darted forward, and grabbed Norman.

"Back off."

The voice wasn't familiar to me, but I knew in an instant that Norman recognized it. His mouth dropped open and even the green neon glow from down the street couldn't add color to his cheeks.

Jim shot forward, but the man in the ski mask wasn't taking chances. There was a knife tucked into his belt and he grabbed it and waved it at us. Jim was closest to the flashing blade; he had to lean back to stay out of harm's way. My stomach went cold.

"I said, back off," the masked man grumbled, and he tightened his hold on Norman and yanked him toward the waiting car.

Honest to gosh, I don't know what possessed me. I knew it wasn't wise to try to fight off a man with a weapon. I knew it was smarter just to let the man take Norman, to commit the license plate of the dark sedan to memory, and to wait about half a nanosecond once they were gone and then call the police.

But I've got to say, one look at that masked man holding on to our friend . . .

One thought about the way that knife had come too close to Jim for comfort . . .

Well, truth be told, I snapped.

Eve was standing next to me so I barely needed to move at all to give Doc just a little pinch on the butt.

Predictably, the dog wasn't happy.

Doc doesn't bark. Not exactly. The sound that comes out of that tiny body of his is more of a yap. A loud, interminable, annoying-as-not-much-else-can-be yap.

Just for good measure, Doc threw in a snarl and lunge, too.

At the same time Eve struggled to keep the dog in her arms, Jim grabbed Norman and pulled him—hard—out of the masked man's grip.

And me? Taking my cue from Doc, I let out a scream that shook the windows of the buildings around us.

I kept right on screaming, too, until the front doors of the Pasqual Palace swung open and a couple of valets and a bellhop ran outside to see what was happening.

The masked man took one look at the commotion and ran back to his car.

And me? I was still screaming when he started up the engine and peeled rubber down the street.

"Ya pure mad dafty!"

I was pretty sure I'd just been insulted, but since Jim raced forward then hugged me tight when he said it, I didn't hold it against him. "You could have been hurt."

"You could have been hurt." I pulled away long enough to look into his eyes. But only until I realized I'd missed another opportunity. By the time I untangled myself from Jim's arms and raced to the street, the black sedan—and its license plates—were long gone.

"Wow."

During the confrontation, I had lost track of Peter. Now he stepped out of the shadows where he'd apparently (and very wisely) scooted to stay out of harm's way. He was slack-jawed and winded when he looked from Jim and me to where Eve was consoling Doc and Norman at the same time. "You guys . . . I thought you were kidding when you said you . . . I mean, I didn't think you were serious when you told me . . . You really are investigating a murder, aren't you?"

Call it the fallout of a shock; I started to laugh. So did everyone else but Peter. Oh, and Doc.

Doc just kept on yapping.

* * *

MY SIGH WAS AN EXACT ECHO OF EVE'S, AND THE sounds overlapped and rippled the air. It was the first noise any of us had made since we sat down to consider the current status of our case, and I looked from Jim, sitting on my right, to Norman, and from Norman to Eve, and from Eve to (believe it or not) Tyler. Notice I do not mention Peter. We hadn't breathed a word of this meeting to him and, though it made me feel a little guilty, I knew it was the right thing to do. A man who hid in the shadows while his friends fought off a kidnapper was not good under pressure.

Because we were being careful, we'd decided to mix things up and meet at my apartment rather than at Jim's house, and we were crammed around my kitchen table. I'd poured iced tea the minute everybody got there, and there was an open bag of thick, salty pretzels on the table. No one was eating them.

But then, kidnap attempts can have that sort of effect on people.

It was Saturday, and after driving through what was left of the night to get back from A.C., Jim had already worked the lunch crowd at Bellywasher's and was getting ready to head back for the dinner rush. He hadn't said a word in protest when I suggested this meeting, but I knew he was exhausted. The fact that he was such a good sport and such a good friend to Norman meant more than I can say. Not that I didn't want to say it. But every time I thought about what a great guy Jim was, and how much he supported me and believed in me, I got all choked up.

As for Norman himself, he wasn't saying anything—not out loud, anyway—but I could tell he was disappointed as well as worried. He'd pinned his hopes on finding out something useful from Victor Pasqual.

When that portion of our investigation went bust, and now that we knew the killer was hot on our trail, Norman's hopes of ever living a worry-free life again had vanished.

Norman was edgy and out of sorts. He didn't speak a word all the way back from New Jersey, and now he drummed his fingers against my oak table, tapped his foot against the linoleum, and kept looking over his shoulder to my one and only kitchen window. Seeing as how we were on the fourth floor, I'm not sure what—or who—he was keeping an eye out for; I only knew that when he didn't see anything or anyone, he looked relieved. At least for a second or two. Then the drumming and the tapping and the looking over his shoulder started all over again.

As for Eve and Tyler . . . well, it should come as no surprise that I was not enamored of the idea of inviting Tyler to our little meeting, but I wasn't (as Jim had so eloquently put it) *pure mad dafty*, either. It was obvious that whoever the man in the mask was, he'd been following me. First to Fredericksburg, then all the way to Atlantic City.

It was just as obvious that I'd led him right to Norman.

We weren't taking any more chances. We had called in Tyler for muscle.

Did I feel better or worse having him there? I couldn't deny that I felt more secure. Now if only he'd offer a little professional advice. If he had any to offer. So far, that hadn't happened, and the only thing he'd done was plunk himself down next to Eve and pat Doc (who was sitting in her lap) in a halfhearted way I suspected was designed to win Eve over.

It was apparently working. When I got up to get the pretzels, I noticed that they were holding hands under the table.

"Not a good idea." I was talking about Eve and Tyler, and I was talking to myself. It came out louder than I expected.

Maybe it was just as well; at least my comment pulled everyone out of the doldrums.

Doc's ears perked up. Eve's eyes glistened. Jim turned my way. And Norman stopped the drumming and the tapping and the looking. Thank goodness! I hadn't realized how annoying all that noise was until it was quiet.

"If you mean traipsing all the way to Atlantic City for nothing, you can say that again."

The comment came from Tyler and since he was the one I was thinking about in the first place (and since what I was thinking wasn't very charitable), I wasn't exactly pleased. I didn't need him to remind me of the shortcomings of my investigation. I grabbed a pretzel just as Tyler did. Across the table, we stared each other down and chomped.

"You should have called me," he said.

He was probably right. Which didn't stop me from saying, "And told you what?" It was hard to talk with a mouthful of pretzel, so I chewed and swallowed. "That we had a suspect who maybe wasn't a suspect so maybe we should talk to him?"

"Or I could have. Talked to him, that is." Tyler brushed crumbs from the front of his button-front plaid shirt. Since it was the weekend, he was officially off the time clock, and he wasn't wearing an impeccably tailored suit like usual. Or one of the dress shirts that are just a teensy bit too small so they show off the breadth of his chest.

Tyler was not the jeans and plaid shirt type.

He was still plenty intimidating.

But let me make one thing perfectly clear: that is not why I dropped my head on the table. I dropped my head on the table because I felt the weight of the investigation

on my shoulders and it was too much for me. I dropped
my head on the table because I was worried about Norman, and sorry about Greg. I dropped my head on the
table because I saw Eve scoot her chair just a little
closer to Tyler's, and there was something in that one
little movement—something so intimate—that I knew
once and for all that my best friend had lost her mind.
Again.

Oh, yeah, I dropped my head on the table because I
knew there was trouble coming.

And I knew there was nothing I could do about it.

"We should have called you," I groaned, agreeing with
Tyler in what was probably a world's first. "You could
have saved us the cost of gas to New Jersey and then Eve
wouldn't have had to risk the money she got from pawn-
ing Doc's collar and—"

"Oh, honey!" I looked up long enough to see Eve
wave a dismissive hand in my direction. How she'd had
time for a fresh manicure since we got back from New
Jersey was anybody's guess. "It's the least I could do
and you know it. Besides . . ." No one preens like Eve.
She beamed a smile at all of us that rested just a bit
longer on Tyler. "I did great at that card game. That Victor Pasqual, he's a darned nice guy."

"Which doesn't mean he isn't the killer." Tyler's gaze
swung to me as he said this, and the message was clear.
If I was running this investigation, I was doing a mighty
poor job of it.

My spine stiffened and I sat up. While I was at it, I
grabbed another pretzel.

"Victor Pasqual doesn't care about money. We all
saw that." I glanced around, taking in Norman and Jim
and Eve, who I knew would back me up if I needed it. At
least about this. "He tipped the waiter with a hundred-
dollar bill."

"So . . ." Tyler snaffled another pretzel. "That means he can't be a killer?"

"It means he doesn't have the motivation. If money doesn't mean anything to him—"

"You mean if one hundred dollars doesn't mean anything to him. That's a far cry from three hundred thousand dollars. For three hundred thousand dollars . . . well, there's no telling what a man might do for that kind of money."

I bit my pretzel. "You weren't there. You didn't see him. Victor Pasqual is a really nice man."

Tyler's top lip curled. It made it easier for him to trade me crunch for crunch. "Nobody that rich is ever a really nice man. How do you think he got that rich in the first place?"

"And what difference does that make?" It was Jim's turn to get in on the action. He did it with his usual level-headed thoughtfulness. "What matters is that the man has an alibi for the night of the murder. He was out of the country. Surely the police can check that, right? You can tell if his passport was used."

"And that's important." It was, too, which was why I shot a smile Jim's way to thank him for pointing it out. "But what's more important is that Norman didn't recognize his voice. And he did recognize the voice of the guy in the black sedan. Victor Pasqual is not the guy."

"But he could have sent the guy who was the guy. You know, a hired killer. That would explain why the guy back in Atlantic City was so persistent. A hired killer," he pointed out, as if we all didn't all watch our share of B movies and cop shows on TV, "is not going to quit. He's going to try again. As soon as he can."

Of course we'd all thought of this. But none of us had been callous enough to say it.

Norman's eyes went wide. His face went pale. The

drumming and the tapping and the looking over his shoulder started again.

If my legs were long enough, I would have kicked Tyler under the table.

"This is getting us nowhere." Once again, Jim was the calm, rational one, and I was grateful. It's hard to be the voice of reason when you have a mouthful of pretzel. "You've told us, Tyler, all the things we shouldn't have done. But what we really need to know is what we should do now. This maniac is still after Norman and—"

"We'll take care of it." Tyler said this like he knew what he was talking about, but I don't think one of us there around the table believed it. Not even Tyler. So far, the police had zilch. Just like we did. "We're following leads, we're questioning people. We're—"

"What leads? What people?" I had swallowed my mouthful, so I was prepared to speak again. "How can you have any leads, Tyler, when we don't know any more now than we did the night Greg was killed? Or have you been holding out on us?" Call me naive, but I hadn't thought of this before and, just so the notion couldn't choke me, I grabbed another pretzel. I pointed across the table at Tyler with it. "Is there something you haven't told us?"

"Something like mind your own business?" Tyler reached for a pretzel, too. He bit it in half. "You've been going around in circles, chasing your tails," Tyler said. "You haven't accomplished a thing. Except . . ." I've never seen a glacier. I mean not out in nature. But I know that sometimes because of the way the light hits the ice crystals, glaciers look blue.

Tyler's eyes are that color.

They're just as warm.

His frosty gaze swiveled to Norman. "Except to find out your friend here is a petty criminal."

"The statute of limitations has run out on all that

stuff," I reminded him. Though I didn't realize I'd done it, I found myself on my feet, staring Tyler down. "None of what Norman did justifies anyone wanting to kill him. So we'd better figure out what's going on."

"No. What *you'd* better do is back off and let the professionals do what they're supposed to do," Tyler shot back.

"He's right, honey." Eve didn't look any happier supporting Tyler than I did hearing her do it. "We're getting nowhere and—"

"All we need to do," Jim interrupted her, "is give Annie a chance. She'll find the answers. She always does."

"No, what we really need to do is just forget the whole thing."

This comment came from Norman, and it was so unexpected, and spoken so quietly, it got all our attention. His shoulders rose and fell before he pushed back his chair and got to his feet.

"None of this is worth watching you guys tear at each other," he said. "It won't bring Greg back, and it won't keep me safe. Don't you see? You can't do that. None of you. If someone's out to get me . . . well, maybe next time I won't be so lucky and get away."

"We're not going to let that happen."

Tyler and I answered together and when our gazes snapped and met, there was one second of unspoken challenge between us. That was right before we realized we were on the same page. If we could agree about this, maybe we could find common ground on finding Greg's killer, too.

Big points for Tyler, he let me be the one who delivered the message. I lifted my chin and fisted my hands at my sides. "We're going to find the guy," I told Norman. My steely demeanor may have been more convincing if pretzel crumbs didn't dot my black T-shirt. I didn't brush them away. "Really, Norman. We're close. I know we are.

I've done this sort of thing before. Tyler's done this sort of thing before. Plenty more times than I have." As a sort of conciliatory gesture, I glanced Tyler's way. "All we need to do is reason our way through things. You know, look at everything we've already discovered. Think about things in a new way, from new angles."

Tyler slapped a hand against the table. "Exactly."

"So where do we begin?" Norman asked.

That, of course, was the hard part. But I wasn't about to let Norman know that. Instead, I collected myself and sat back down, and, hey, if I sounded far more confident than I felt . . . well, Norman didn't need to know that.

My voice cool and steady, I walked us through all we'd recently found out. "Victor Pasqual has a motive, and no opportunity, and he's a nice guy. Three hundred thousand dollars is chump change for him. We were lucky we even got that close to him and we wouldn't have if not for the fact that Eve pawned Doc's collar and—"

A thought hit, and honest to goodness, I don't know how long I sat there, my mouth agape and my mind racing. It was, apparently, long enough to worry Jim. He put a hand on my arm and leaned over so he could stare me in the face. "Annie? Are ye all right?"

I rewound my thinking process and went over it in my head again before I dared to speak, and when I did, my voice was breathy. Then again, I had a good excuse: My heart was pounding like a jackhammer. "Norman, you won three hundred thousand dollars in a card game with Victor Pasqual."

Norman nodded.

"It cost us twenty-five thousand dollars to get in Pasqual's game, and the biggest winner of the night came away with . . ." I looked at Eve.

She shrugged. "It wasn't me. I got all my money back and then some, but I think that li'l ol' fellow across the table—the skinny little guy from Texas?—I think he was the big winner. At the end of the evening, he said something about his take being somewhere around fifty thousand."

"He put in twenty-five and he left with fifty." So far, so good. The facts were lining up with my new theory. "So when you played, Norman . . . back when you won the money to open Très Bonne Cuisine . . . how much did you have to have for a stake?"

Norman still wasn't following, but I could tell Jim and Tyler already saw where I was headed. They leaned forward, their gazes trained on Norman.

And I did, too. Which was why I noticed that he didn't have to think about it. Not at all.

"One hundred and fifty thousand," Norman said.

"And where—" I could tell Tyler was about to interrupt so I shot him a look. This was my thought, my theory. I got to ask the question. "Norman, you sure didn't make that kind of money putting dishwashing soap in a bottle and calling it a miracle cleaner. Where did you get the one hundred and fifty thousand dollars?"

"Oh." The truth dawned, and, slowly, Norman sank back into his chair. Just like that, though, he discounted everything I'd said. "No way." He shook his head. "That has nothing to do with what happened to Greg. It couldn't."

"Because . . . ?"

I allowed Tyler this bit of a question before I took over again.

"Why, Norman? Why can't it? Where did you get the money in the first place?"

While Norman gathered his thoughts, I reached for the legal pad and pen I had left near at hand, and when he started to talk, I took notes.

"It was back in prison," Norman said. "You know, in Nevada. I told you all about that." He looked around the table, confirming that we all knew the story. "My cell-mate was a guy named Howard. Howard Fish. He was a crusty old goat. A small-time con who'd been in and out of the system all his life. We didn't get along well at first. I mean, Howard, didn't appreciate having to share his space with a first-timer like me. But after a couple months . . . well, Howard, he found out he had lung can-cer, and I guess that sort of softened him up. He talked, I listened." Norman shrugged. "You know how it is with older people. They like telling stories."

"And this Howard, he told you how you could steal a hundred thousand dollars?"

I took offense at Tyler's question. Norman didn't.

"It was nothing like that," Norman said. "It was legit. Really. One day they decided Howard would be better off in the prison infirmary. He was pretty weak by then. In fact, he died just a couple days later. But right before they came for him, he told me how much he appreciated having me around when he was sick. Then he started talking about a cabin he owned up near Pyramid Lake, and Howard—he said when I got out, I should go up there and look under the loose floorboard near the fire-place. I mean, it sounded like something out of a movie, right?" Norman laughed, ill at ease. "But hey, once I was out, I wasn't sure where to go or what I was going to do. I remembered what Howard said, and I went up to Pyra-mid Lake. There was the cabin, just like Howard said. And the key was under a big chunk of granite near the front door. He told me that, too. So if all that was right, I figured what he said about the floorboard was, too. I pried it up. That's where I found the hundred and fifty thousand dollars."

We all sat quietly, thinking of the implications, but I was the one who asked, "That was before you ran all those other scams, as Fred and Bill and all those other folks, right?"

"Well, I knew a hundred fifty thousand wouldn't last forever, and a man's got to make a living. I invested the money," Norman explained. "Because I knew I wanted to do something with food. A restaurant, a gourmet shop . . . I was looking around, considering my options. But the money, it wasn't adding up fast enough. So when I met some people who knew Victor and they said they could get me into a game . . ."

In a not-so-good imitation of a Vulcan mind meld, I stared at Norman, and when he still didn't get it, I laid it on the line.

"The hundred and fifty thousand, Norman. Have you ever wondered where Howard got it?"

He shrugged. "Don't ask, don't tell. Nobody else knew the money was there and I figured someday, somebody might buy that cabin and find it. Or somebody might buy the land and knock the cabin down and find it. Either way, I had as much right to that money as they did. More, seeing as how Howard told me I could have it."

"Yeah, but don't you get it?" Tyler had kept silent as long as he was able. "If Howard got that money illegally—"

The truth was dawning. I could tell because Norman's face went from pale to ashen. Because I couldn't stand to watch him suffer, I leaped out of my chair, checking the clock above the kitchen sink as I did. "I've got just enough time to hit the library before it closes," I said. "I'll meet you all at Bellywasher's this evening."

"But, honey . . ." I was already at the front door when Eve found her voice and called after me. "What on earth are you looking for?"

Jim knew. I could tell from the look he gave me when I turned around. Of course, Tyler did, too. Norman would figure it out himself eventually. So I told Eve, "I'm going to find out where a small-time con like Howard Fish got a hundred and fifty thousand dollars."

* * *

THE NEAREST BRANCH OF THE ARLINGTON PUBLIC LI-
brary closes at five on Saturdays so I didn't have
much time. I raced through my research, then raced over
to Bellywasher's, copies of the microfiche pages I'd discovered in hand.

By the time I got there, though, Saturday evening
dinner pandemonium had started, and I had to squeeze
my way through the line outside the door. Jim was behind the bar mixing martinis. Eve was busy making sure
a table of eight near the window was happy and comfortable. Tyler was nowhere to be seen.

Neither was Norman.

I pushed through the swinging doors that led into the
kitchen and found Marc and Damien slammed with or-
ders and Heidi, our one and only waitress, busy loading
plates onto trays. She was frazzled and I instantly felt
obligated, so I stowed my notepad and microfiche copies
in the storage room where we kept the clean linens and
did the only thing I could do—I pitched in and helped.

By the time there was enough of a lull for me to ask
about Norman, my T-shirt was dotted with marinara and
so were my hands. I grabbed a towel to wipe them clean,
retrieved the papers from the storage closet, and headed
out to the alley behind the restaurant where (Marc and
Damien assured me) they'd last seen Norman.

Sure enough, there he was, sitting on an overturned
fruit crate and admiring Jim's motorcycle.

I didn't waste any time.

"Who was the other guy?" I asked Norman.

I was hoping for more in return than a blank look, but
since a blank look was all I got, I had no choice but to
work with it.

I waved the copies under his nose. "I found an article

about Howard Fish. When you knew him, he was in prison for a bank robbery."

That got Norman's attention. He looked a little green around the gills. "Does that mean I'll have to pay the money back?" he asked.

"That's the least of your worries." I slapped the copies down on the lid of a nearby trash can and paged through them until I found what I was looking for. "One guy— Howard—went to prison for the robbery," I told Norman. "But see here . . ." I pointed, but I never gave him time to look before I forged on ahead. "Two guys. Two guys, Norman." I stabbed a finger at the article. "Two guys were accused of the robbery. That means—"

All the green drained from Norman's face. "I never knew," he breathed. "That means there's another guy out there."

"Yeah, and something tells me he's looking for his money. I don't know what the cops are going to say about you paying back this money, but I know one thing. That guy who was Howard's accomplice, he's convinced it's payback time, Norman."

Sixteen

✖

OF COURSE THE BIG QUESTION WAS WHAT WE WERE going to do about all this.

It says a great deal about how baffled I was (not to mention how worried I was for Norman's safety and how much I wanted to see justice done for Greg), that I realized beyond the shadow of a doubt that at this stage of the game, there was only one person who had the answer.

But when I left Norman in the alley and went into my office, I didn't expect to find him sitting in my desk chair.

I closed the door, blocking out the hum of voices from the restaurant, and turned to where Tyler sat. "Howard Fish had an accomplice," I told him.

He didn't look surprised. Honestly, did I expect him to?

Tyler leaned back and made himself comfortable. "I know that. Guy by the name of Matt O'Hara. I went back to the station and made some calls after we left your place. That's how I know. And before you can ask, no, I don't know where this O'Hara character is. He's had a couple run-ins with the law, I do know that. He's got a record in Arizona and Texas and a couple other states. He just got released from prison in Alabama. I'm having some files faxed over and with any luck, Norman will recognize his picture. O'Hara might be the guy we're looking for."

"So the question now is—"

"You might as well know this right away, I'm not here to talk to you about Norman." Tyler's a well-chiseled kind of guy. Angular face. Angular body. He folded his arms across his broad chest and stared at me the way I imagined he'd stared at hundreds of perps over the years. I knew how they felt, too. Just looking into Tyler's icy blue eyes made my stomach jump and my blood whoosh inside my ears. "You don't like me, Annie."

I was prepared to talk about the case, and what we should do, and how we could assure Norman's safety. I was not prepared for a heart-to-heart. When it comes to Tyler, I don't think I'll ever be.

I wasn't prepared to get too close to him, either, which was why I stayed put near the door instead of sitting down in my desk chair. I eyed him up, and I suppose I was trying to gauge his mood as well as his sincerity. I should have known better. Cops—especially cops like Tyler— don't give away their thoughts. Not easily. And not to just anyone.

But remember, I'd known Tyler for a long time. I also knew he was the kind of cop—and the kind of man— who appreciated hearing the truth. The simplest course of action seemed to be to cut to the chase.

"You broke Eve's heart." I shouldn't have had to point this out, but since guys can sometimes be unconscious when it comes to emotions, I figured it wouldn't hurt. "You called off your engagement to her. Now you show up and—"

"You think I'm going to do it again."

"I think a guy who's already engaged should remember he's already engaged and not hang around the woman who he used to be engaged to before he got engaged again."

The fact that he followed my logic says something about Tyler. I'm not sure what, but something.

"Kaitlin and I . . . we've called off the wedding."

This was news to me, and I suspect Eve didn't know it either. Not yet, anyway. If she did, I would have heard all about it. I thought through the implications. "You called off your wedding because you're seeing Eve?"

"Kaitlin and I called off the wedding because we don't want to get married. We should have realized it before, but, well . . ." His shrug spoke volumes. So did the level look he aimed my way. "You know how it is, Annie. Sometimes these relationship things, they get out of hand. Then things just don't work out."

At least he didn't say Peter's name. Then again, Tyler was more subtle than that. Just so he knew that I knew it, I looked at him as carefully as he was studying me. "Are you going to ask Eve to marry you again?"

He didn't answer right away. I would have felt better if he did. *Yes or no, get it over with and let me deal. Don't leave me wondering—and worrying.* He knew it drove me crazy. Which was exactly why he was doing it, and why he sat back and stretched out his long legs. "Me and Eve, we're not anywhere near that stage in our relationship."

"Which means you're going to string her along for a while before you break her heart again."

"You think?" He stood, and suddenly my small office felt even smaller.

Like a best friend would let something like a little unspoken coercion stop her?

I raised my chin and, though I was tempted to take a

step back, I stood my ground. "I can't stand by and watch you hurt Eve again," I told Tyler.

"Admirable." The expression that sped across his face might have been mistaken for a smile by someone who didn't know him. "But I have no intention of hurting Eve."

"Yeah, I remember. Just like last time. Let's see . . ." I pretended to think about it, but let's face it, I didn't really have to. Just like a best friend stands up for her best friend, a best friend never forgets. "That time when you didn't hurt her, that's when you made her feel inferior, right? You said she wasn't smart. And that she wasn't career-minded so she couldn't possibly understand how important your job is to you. You told her that she wasn't successful enough to satisfy your perverse need to have a woman on your arm who can impress your friends by more than just her looks. You were cruel to her, Tyler. You hurt her. Bad."

"I know." Something very much like regret softened his expression, but I wasn't about to be fooled. Remember, I said I'd known Tyler a long time. "I've told Eve I was wrong," he said. "I've told her I'm sorry."

A better woman would have taken the comment at face value, and maybe even softened a little. I wasn't about to let Tyler off the hook so easily.

Even though there wasn't much room to move, I took a step forward, just so he'd know I wasn't going to fold like an origami stork. "So that apology of yours . . . you telling Eve you're sorry . . . that's supposed to make everything all better?"

"No. But it's supposed to start to make everything better."

I had another opportunity to be charitable. I chose not to take it.

"So Eve is just supposed to forgive and forget, that's what you're telling me?" The very notion offended me so deeply, I nearly choked on my words. "You can't just break a woman's heart into a couple million pieces and then show up again and expect her to pretend it never happened. You hurt her too deeply. You disappointed her. She trusted you. She depended on you. She thought you'd be there for her and—"

"We're talking about me and Eve, Annie. Not about you and Peter. What he did to you, don't take that out on me."

Tyler's words hit like a slap, and I found myself staring at him, wishing I could find a way to tell him he was wrong, and knowing it was impossible. See, for the first time in his hard-nosed, strong-armed, one-upmanship life, Tyler Cooper was absolutely, one hundred percent right.

"I'm sorry." OK, so it wasn't the most eloquent way to let him know, but it was sincere, and, for all his faults, I think Tyler appreciates sincerity. My laugh was both embarrassed and uneasy. "I guess that's what some shrink would call transference. You're hanging around. Peter's hanging around. And I'm just sort of taking what I feel about him and piling it onto you." I took a step away from Tyler, a symbolic way of letting him know that if he was genuine, I was willing to back off. "What Eve and you do, it's none of my business."

Like I said, he's subtle. At least he didn't come right out and call me an idiot. Instead, he rolled his eyes. "Of course it's your business. You and Eve are best friends. But Annie . . ." Tyler reached for my hand and gave it a squeeze. Just as quickly, he knew he'd gone too far in exposing his softer side and he dropped my hand like a hot potato. "I don't know if we'll work it out," he told me. "But I do know I'm going to try. It would be easier if I didn't find you gunning for me around every corner."

"It's that obvious, huh?" I tried for a smile.

So did Tyler. "Look, if you see me stepping out of

line . . . well, I guess if you see me stepping out of line, I can be pretty sure you'll call me on it."

"I will." My nod reinforced my answer. "And if you see me sticking my nose where it doesn't belong—"

"I'll tell you that, too. And you won't listen."

I might have taken offense if Tyler didn't grin.

And if it wasn't true.

"Speaking of that . . ." We weren't, but this seemed as good a time as any to talk to Tyler about what I wanted to talk to him about in the first place. When I sat down near my desk, he took the guest chair. "What *are* we going to do about Norman?"

Tyler scrubbed his hands over his face. "Wish I knew," he said, and I realized that, like Tyler, I appreciated the truth. Even when I didn't want to hear it. "Seems like all we can do is wait for the killer to come after him again."

A shiver snaked up my back. Telling Norman he could start leading a normal life again, then hanging him out to dry, didn't seem like a kindness. "There's got to be a better way. A way to bring the guy out in the open and still maintain some control," I said. "You know, a way for Norman to expose himself—you know what I mean," I added when I saw a smirk on Tyler's face. "A way for him to come out in public and for you to be there to make sure he's all right."

"You mean like using him as a decoy."

It wasn't what I meant when I said it, but now that Tyler mentioned it . . .

My computer was on so I clicked on the Internet and from there to the information about the food show where Norman—or at least his alter ego, Jacques Lavoie—was supposed to do a cooking demonstration.

"It's tomorrow," I said, pointing to the screen so Tyler knew what I was talking about. "I'll bet Norman hasn't officially canceled. I'm sure he forgot all about it. What if he did it, Tyler? What if he went to the food show and did that cooking demonstration? There probably wouldn't be an immediate threat. I mean, the guy wants to talk to Norman, right? Not kill him. If it really is this O'Hara fellow, he wants to find out what happened to the money from the bank robbery, and he wants the money back. He wouldn't risk hurting Norman before he can find out what's going on. And you, you could be there—"

"For protection." Tyler's gaze was steely. "It might work. Could you convince him?"

I wasn't sure. Until I thought that a man who rebottles dishwashing soap and sells it as a miracle cleaner . . . well, deep down inside, a man like that has to have a lot of nerve.

THE RONALD REAGAN BUILDING AND INTERNATIONAL Trade Center has an amphitheater that seats six hundred and twenty-five. A half hour before Jacques Lavoie was set to step out onstage and demonstrate an array of French foods and cooking techniques, the place was just about packed.

And any one of those six hundred and twenty-five people could have been Greg's killer.

I looked over the crowd, checking faces against what I remembered of the man who'd tried to snatch Norman off the street in Atlantic City. Needless to say, I got nowhere fast, and honestly, I should have known this from the start. I'd tangled with a couple of killers in my day, and none of them were what I expected. Now the only thing I had to go on was that the person who'd shot Greg and the person who'd darted out of that black sedan back in A.C. was a man.

A couple hundred of the people in the audience were men.

Was I going to lose heart? Not by a long shot. I scanned the crowd one more time, looking for Tyler and the other detectives who were there to assure Norman's safety, and confident we were doing the right thing in the right way, I wiped any residual worry from my expression and turned toward where Norman was waiting in the wings.

In khakis, a blue shirt, and a crisp Très Bonne Cuisine apron, he looked the part of the French chef so many knew and loved.

The only question now was, could he pull it off?

"You ready?" I gave him a quick hug. "You've got a lot of fans out there waiting for you."

"I do?" It was Norman's voice, Norman's nervous gaze that traveled to the stage and beyond, as if he could see the audience gathering on the other side of the curtain. We heard the murmur of the crowd and, like me, I had no doubt he was thinking that one of those voices might sound awfully familiar if it said, "It's payback time, Norman."

Unlike me, Norman wasn't very good about hiding his jitteriness. (At least I thought I was doing a pretty good job of it.) He ran his tongue over his lips. He shifted from foot to foot. Even though we needed special passes to get backstage and that should have assured us that everyone there really belonged, his gaze darted over his shoulder and, from there, up to the catwalk that crossed the stage high above our heads.

Norman's voice was as fidgety as his movements. "I dunno, Annie. I'm not sure I can do this. What if . . . what if he's out there waiting?"

"That's exactly what we want to happen." I put a hand on Norman's shoulder and leaned in closer so that none of the stagehands working around us could hear. "You're going to be fine. There are plenty of cops out there and a couple more stationed here backstage. Nobody's going to get anywhere near you. Not before they get the guy first. You remember what we said last night."

"It's the best way. It's the only way." Norman was talking the talk, but if his breathlessness meant anything, it meant he wasn't anywhere near ready to walk the walk.

This time, I gave his shoulder a pat. "Jim's here." I looked over to where Jim was chopping and dicing and slicing the food Norman—er, Jacques—would be using for his demonstration. "You don't think he's going to let anything happen to you, do you?"

Norman tried for a smile. "Jim's a real friend. After he found out everything he found out about me . . . after you all did . . . you all could have walked away."

"That's not what friends do."

Another smile. This one lasted a millisecond longer. "You think Jim's a good enough friend to do the demo for me?"

Since I suspected Norman wasn't kidding, I didn't answer.

Instead, I smoothed a hand over the place near the neckline of his apron where *Très Bonne Cuisine* was embroidered in minty letters the exact color of the store's shopping bags. I could practically feel the hum of nervousness that coursed through Norman's body.

"You look handsome," I said.

He made a face. "Folks aren't going to think I'm so handsome when this story comes out. What's going to happen, Annie? I mean, even if the cops get this guy? Word's going to get out that I'm an ex-con, that I learned to cook in prison. My career is going to tank, the shop is going to fold, my reputation—"

"Hey!" I am usually not so rude as to interrupt someone, but it was either that or watch Norman dissolve with a case of the screaming meemies. I looked him in the eye. "You've got to stay focused and alert."

"I know that."

I would have felt more confident if he sounded like he meant it.

"You've got to remember that there are lots of people out there who are looking forward to seeing you, and lots of people on the sidelines who are here specifically to make sure you're safe."

This time, he didn't even try to talk, he just nodded.

"You can do this, N—" I swallowed what I was going to say. "You can do this, Jacques. You have to. For Greg."

"Yes." As if in response to his affirmative answer, the technicians tested the lighting, and at that very moment, a spotlight came on and illuminated the cooking demonstration area with its gleaming pots and pans and its pristine cooking surfaces. Norman stood a little taller. His smile inched up. There was suddenly a Pepé Le Pew swagger in his step and a very Gallic tilt to his chin. "It is *très bien*, yes?" Jacques Lavoie smiled back at me. "We will have a wonderful time showing these lovely people the quiche and the soup and the crêpes suzette. It will be—"

"Jacques!" We'd brought Raymond along to the show, partly because we knew he'd be a great help, but mostly because as soon as he heard that his culinary hero was back and doing a cooking demonstration at the region's premier food show, there was no way we could convince him to stay in Arlington. Jim was officially in charge of the food. Raymond's job was to take care of the supplies, and when he raced over to where we stood I saw clear proof that Raymond did not share Jacques' love of the spotlight and the kind of preshow pandemonium I'd seen even before our classes at Bellywasher's.

Raymond's eyes were bright. The collar of his oxford shirt was damp. When he got close enough, I saw that his hands were shaking. "We don't have a mandoline!" he wailed.

I was tempted to ask if we were playing music, but
have no fear. A couple weeks behind the front counter
of Très Bonne Cuisine, and I was prepared. "I know I
brought it," I said, thinking back to the night before
and our frantic trip to the shop to pack everything
Jacques would need. "It was in the box with the salad
spinner."

"The big brown box with the red logo on it?" I would
have felt more confident if Raymond didn't swallow hard
when he asked this. Muscular hulk or not, he deflated in
front of our eyes. "I threw it out. I thought it was empty. It
went into the big Dumpster behind the building."

The thought of Dumpster diving did not appeal to
me. I checked my watch. "There's no time to go back to
the shop to get another one."

"And not one thing to worry about!" Jacques' smile
was as bright as the stage lights. "We are at a food show,
ne sommes-nous pas? Annie, you will go see my good
friend Claude Brooking. He has a booth here somewhere. He will gladly let us use a mandoline. And Raymond, *mon ami . . .*" Jacques wound an arm through
Raymond's and walked him back onto the stage. "We
must check the crêpe pans, *n'est pas?*"

I left them at it, skirting a couple of technicians who
were doing a last-minute sound check and heading out
through the wings and to the auditorium. I knew Eve
was somewhere in the back of the house with Tyler and
I had an eye out for her.

Which was why I didn't see Peter until he stepped
right in front of me.

"Whoa!" I pulled up short and caught my breath.
"What are you—?"

"I saw the ad in the newspaper. You know . . ." Peter
looked around to make sure no one was paying any attention to us. "About your friend Jacques . . . I figured

this had something to do with our case so I knew you'd need my help."

"That's really nice." It was, in a twisted sort of way, so I didn't feel guilty saying it. "But Peter . . ." A group of elderly ladies headed past us and toward the senior seating that had been reserved in the front of the auditorium, and I pulled Peter aside. "It's not that I don't appreciate your help . . ." I was at a crossroads here, and I sucked in a long breath. But honestly, I didn't have to think about what to say.

"I don't want to see you anymore, Peter."

I guess the message didn't sink in. He stared at me.

"Peter?" I was tempted to grab his arm, but I thought it best to avoid personal contact. "You heard me, right? I appreciate your wanting to help with our case. I do. But Peter, you're hanging around because you're lonely, and, Peter . . ." I really didn't have time for this sort of melodrama so I just blurted it out. "I'm over you, Peter. Totally, completely, one hundred percent over you. So if you want to establish some sort of wonderful, lasting relationship, you should know that you're going to need to do it with someone else. I'm in love with Jim."

"The cook?" It was the first thing that penetrated his shock, and Peter blinked at me in wonder. "You and a cook?"

"Me and a fantastic, supportive guy. He's got a great sense of humor. He's got terrific plans for the future of his business. He's caring and he's dependable."

"And I'm not."

I had been forced to be brutally honest, but that didn't mean I was heartless. I gave Peter a quick kiss on the cheek.

"I think you could be," I said. "And I think you will be. Once you find the right woman. I hope you do, Peter. I truly do. I wish you every happiness in the world."

And because the clock was ticking and I was on the hunt for a mandoline, I didn't wait and I didn't say another word. I raced up the aisle toward where I saw Eve standing with Tyler.

And when I did?

When I did, I had a smile on my face.

But then, that's what always happens when I know in my heart that I just did the right thing.

Seventeen

NORMAN . . . ER, JACQUES . . . DID SAY CLAUDE BROOK-
ing was a friend, so I assumed they might have
some things in common.

Like charming little gourmet shops.

Or cute French accents (even if they weren't real).

What Eve and I discovered—after we wasted precious
minutes searching for Claude in the maze of booths selling everything from cookware to cookie mixes to knife
sharpeners—was a mishmash of tables piled with every
cheap kitchen gadget imaginable. (Yes, I know, this makes
me sound like a cooking snob, and honestly, it's not like
me, but a couple weeks at Très Bonne Cuisine is bound to
do that to a person).

Claude's merchandise was displayed around a huge RV
that had been pulled right onto the site. Just in case that
wasn't conspicuous enough, the RV had a yellow banner
draped across the side of it that proclaimed *Brooking
Cooking* in huge red letters.

And Claude Brooking?

I didn't even have to ask. Claude Brooking had to be

the guy in the blue, yellow, and orange Hawaiian shirt who was doing his best to schmooze a couple of ladies into buying colorful little plastic cups that clipped over the side of a pot.

"You've never seen anything like these," he said, and forget the French accent. Claude and Norman must have known each other back in New Jersey. "Look at this, sweetie. You put your egg in here, see. Then you hang this contraption onto your pot and boil your egg. Then . . ." He slipped the plastic holder off the pot with a motion that said *voilà*, even if Claude didn't. "You can serve the egg right from this thing. Is that wonderful, or what? And the price? For anybody else, these are four for twenty dollars. But today only as a show special . . ." Claude gave the women a wink. "Today only and only for you two, you get all four of them and a set of matching measuring spoons for a mere twenty dollars. It's once in a lifetime. I'm a crazy man even to offer you this kind of deal. What do you say, ladies? Can I wrap up a set for each of you?"

They were all too eager, and I checked my watch—again—and waited as patiently as I could while Claude rang up the sale.

When he was done, I stepped forward.

"For you, little lady . . ." Claude wiggled his eyebrows at me, then slid his gaze to Eve, who was standing at my side. "Today only and only for you two, I'm willing to deal. What will it be?" He gestured toward the hodgepodge that was his on-the-road showroom. "Anything at all. Including me, if you'll take me home."

I would have laughed, just to be polite. If I had time. "Jacques Lavoie," I said instead. "He's a friend of yours, right? He's doing a cooking demonstration and—"

"He's back?" Claude's hair was way too dark for a man of his middle years. So were his eyebrows. They shot up his forehead. "I called him a couple times and left messages. He never called back."

"He's been busy. So are we." I scanned the tables, searching for a mandoline. When I didn't see one, I had no choice but to throw myself on Claude's mercy. "His demonstration is about to start and—"

"Really? That's so cool!" Claude reached under the table, produced a sign that said *Out to Lunch, Be Right Back,* and balanced it on a pile of tea infusers. "You going back to the amphitheater?" he asked. "I'll walk with you."

"That's fine. Really." The only way to stop him was to put a hand on his arm. "But Jacques needs a mandoline."

"Going to play music, is he?" A few weeks before, I might have laughed at the joke. Now I knew how lame it was and Eve didn't get it at all, seeing as how she didn't know about the musical instrument or the kitchen gadget. Claude was the only one who chuckled before he asked, "Jacques, he needs it now?"

I checked my watch again and gauged the time remaining against how far we had to walk back to the amphitheater. "He needs it right now."

Claude nodded his understanding and started looking. He looked on the table where the tea infusers were stacked, and on another table dotted with precarious piles of strawberry hullers, cherry pitters, and cheese graters. Failing there, he moved on to a third table, this one filled with staggering heaps of folding chopsticks (I know, I'd never heard of them, either), can openers, and oven mitts that could supposedly withstand temperatures of up to five hundred degrees.

"I know I've got a mandoline here somewhere," Claude said along with something else, but by this time he was down on his hands and knees, searching through the boxes stowed under the tables and it was hard to hear him. "If you can just be patient . . ."

"I'm trying," I said from between my gritted teeth,

and because she understood, Eve gave me a pat on the back.

When Claude popped back up from the nether reaches of his stock supply, I breathed a sigh of relief—until I noticed he was empty-handed.

"Might be in the RV," he said, poking a thumb over his shoulder. "Give me a minute, will you? I'll just go inside for a quick look-see."

He did, and when he did, I dropped my head into my hands.

"I wanted everything to go smoothly," I grumbled. "You know, just to make this easier for Norman."

"He's nervous, but he shouldn't be." At my side, Eve didn't look nearly as edgy as I felt. "Tyler's got everything under control," she said. "There are cops stationed at all the doors. There are cops backstage and in the sound booth of the amphitheater, and even in the audience. Nobody is going to get close enough to Norman to kidnap him. Nothing's going to happen to him."

"Nothing's going to happen to his cooking, either, not if we don't get that mandoline so he can slice the onions for the French onion soup." I glanced over my shoulder toward the RV. There was no sign of Claude. "You don't suppose the inside of that place looks anything like the outside here, do you?" The very thought was enough to offend my sense of order, and I shivered. "How's he ever going to find that mandoline in time?" I scanned the booths nearest to us. If one of them had a mandoline, believe me, I would have bought it with my own hard-earned money and headed straight for the amphitheater with it. The way it was, there was a super-duper cleanup mop being sold at the booth to our right, and all-organic potato chips on our left. There wasn't a mandoline in sight.

There was no sign of Claude, either, and because the precious minutes were ticking away, I stepped around the tables that bordered his space and headed up the stairs and into the RV, with Eve right behind me.

My intuition was right on: The inside of Claude's RV looked a whole lot like the outside space where he did business. There were boxes piled on the floor and on the table behind the driver's seat and the built-in bench behind it. There were boxes stacked three high to our left, all along the hallwaylike space that led to a room where I could see a couple of built-in bunk beds that were stacked with boxes. I could see open packages of gadgets scattered about, and charge receipts (both new and used). I could see plastic carry bags that said *Brooking Cooking* on the side, and ripped-open cartons that had at one time contained everything from measuring cups to salt shakers.

I could see everything and anything—but Claude.

"Claude?" Over my shoulder, I gave Eve an "I don't know what's going on" sort of look and, leading the way, I sidled toward the bedroom, my back pressed to the wall of boxes. "Claude, are you all right? Did you find the mandoline? We don't have a lot of time and—" My gasp drowned out the rest of my words.

That's because I found Claude lying facedown on the bedroom floor. There was a quickly growing pool of blood around the gash at the back of his head.

"Oh, my gosh!" Behind me, I felt, rather than saw, Eve pull back. She never did do well with blood and gore.

I can't say I did, either, but I knew an emergency when I saw one. I dropped down on the floor beside Claude and felt for a pulse and when I didn't find one, I grabbed my cell phone out of my pocket. I guess I was so busy pressing the buttons on it and hoping for a cell signal that never materialized, I didn't hear the door of the RV slam shut.

I didn't realize Eve was gasping to find words to

warn me, either. Not until I finally looked up, frustrated by my phone, and found her with one arm yanked behind her back and a knife to her throat.

I was on my feet in a flash, but I knew better than to make another move. Not when that blade was right up against Eve's windpipe.

"Who . . . what?" I looked past Eve to the man who stood behind her. He was a little older than middle-aged, and bald. He looked vaguely familiar, though I couldn't sort through my panic and fear to figure out why. I didn't have to ask, either, but I was so taken aback and so terrified, I couldn't keep my words to myself. "What on earth are you doing? What do you want?"

The man laughed. It wasn't a pleasant sound.

"I want what I've always wanted," he said. "I want what's mine. I thought I had to go to Norman to get it, but you ladies, you're the answer to my prayers."

"We don't know anything." That was Eve talking, and I had to give her credit, what with her being able to do that while there was a gleaming knife blade pressing into the delicate flesh of her throat. "We don't know anything about Norman, or the money, or the bank robbery or—"

My grimace came too late for her to take back her words.

"Look . . ." I tried to sound calm. Big points for me since by this time, I was so afraid of what might happen to Eve, so worried about Claude, and so claustrophobic, I would have leaped out the window near the bunk beds—if there weren't boxes piled high in front of it. "Look . . ." I tried again. "I think you've got us mixed up with someone else. Eve's right. We really don't know anything."

"I don't care if you do." The man had a handkerchief in his pocket and when he pulled it out, a strong chemical odor filled the room. He pressed the cloth to Eve's nose and mouth, and a second later her eyes closed and she sank to the floor. "Your turn." He stepped over her and toward me, and because of the clutter, I had nowhere to go. Because of the knife, I couldn't fight back.

He yanked the cell phone out of my hand and tossed it over his shoulder. I saw it land in an open packing box. Then I saw the handkerchief heading for my face.

"Finally, I've got what I need," I heard the man say just as the handkerchief smothered my face. My head buzzed. My vision blurred. His voice came from a million miles away. "Norman will listen now. He has to. You're his friends. And now, you're my hostages."

I DREAMED I WAS WORKING AT TRÈS BONNE CUISINE, helping a man in a black and white golf shirt who was walking down the aisles, browsing. We stopped near the soup mixes and he adjusted his thick glasses on the bridge of his nose and smiled when he found what he was looking for on a nearby shelf.

"Finally," he said, "I've got what I need," and he handed me a bottle of chloroform.

Like an icy wave, the memory washed over me and I jerked awake and gasped for breath. My eyes flew open and in that one moment, I realized why the man who'd kidnapped us looked so familiar: He was a Très Bonne Cuisine customer I'd waited on just after Greg's murder.

Which meant all those days ago, he was hot on Norman's trail. He'd been following me all along—and I'd led him straight to Norman in Atlantic City and, from there, straight here to the food show.

The enormity of the realization flashed through my bloodstream and for I don't know how long, I lay on the built-in bench in what passed for the dining area of the RV, trying to make sense of it all. It might have been easier if my mouth wasn't fuzzy and my head didn't pound. It might have been a whole lot more comfortable if my wrists and my ankles weren't duct-taped.

Carefully, I shifted my weight. Since my hands were behind my back, I wobbled a bit, but I managed to sit up so I could see to my right, into the driver's area of the RV (it was empty) and to my left and back to the bedroom (from this angle, all I could see were boxes in the hallway and what looked to be the entire contents of the display we'd seen outside the RV; there were kitchen gadgets everywhere, as if our abductor had simply opened the door and shoveled them in). Eve was similarly bound and slumped on the bench across from me. I didn't like the pallor of her skin.

"Eve!" I realized the moment I called out to her that I was alerting our kidnapper to the fact that I was awake and that it might have been smarter not to, but I was beyond caring. How could I when Eve looked so fragile and pale? "Eve, wake up. Answer me. Are you all right?"

When she shifted and groaned, her head rolled forward. I let go a sigh of relief.

"You're OK?"

Her eyes fluttered open. "Annie? What . . . what happened?"

I didn't bother to tell her that at this point, that wasn't the question. The only question that mattered was, what were we going to do now?

From where I was sitting, I could see the big-as-a-picture-window windshield at the front of the RV. Beyond it, there were few lights left on in the exposition center and, as far as I could see, no people around, either.

"It must be late," I said and by this time I'd pulled myself together enough to keep my voice down. "The show must be over. There's nobody out in the hall."

Eve had to look over her shoulder to see what I could

see. When she did, tears filled her eyes. "What's going to happen?" she asked. "What does he want? Is he going to hurt us?"

I thought about Claude and wondered if his body was still back in the bedroom where we'd last seen it. "If he wanted to hurt us, he would have done it by now," I told her. She looked relieved to hear it so I guess in the great scheme of things, I could justify the little white lie. "I think he wants to use us to get at Norman, to get his money back."

A single tear slipped down Eve's cheek. Only she could make crying look attractive. If I let myself go (and believe me, I was close enough to panic that it just might happen), my nose would get red, my eyes would puff, and my skin would get blotchy. Eve cried like the heroine in a romantic blockbuster. She sniffed decorously, too. "What are we going to do, Annie?"

I didn't have the heart to tell her that I didn't have a clue.

Maybe it was just as well. Before I could open my mouth, we heard the sounds of a key turning in the door. The next thing we knew, the man who must have been Matt O'Hara hoisted himself up into the RV.

"Well, lookee who's awake." He beamed a smile at us. It made my blood run cold. "Just in time, too. I was just about to make a call to your friend Norman."

"We can't help you." My words scraped out of my parched mouth. "We don't know where Norman is."

He barely gave me a look. "Shut up. And don't lie to me. It won't do you any good. I know he was here doing a cooking demonstration today. I sat right there in the auditorium and watched it. Sorry you had to miss it, ladies. You would have loved the drama. Especially when a little kid in the audience popped a paper bag. I swear, Norman just about fainted, right there onstage. That's how much of a scared little girl he is."

I took offense at him making fun of Norman. I took more offense at him assuming that little girls are always scared. He might have noticed my scowl if he'd bothered to look.

Instead, O'Hara shifted his gaze to Eve, who wilted beneath it. "You said you knew about the bank robbery. What else do you two know?"

There didn't seem to be any point in trying to fake our way through this so I simply told the truth. "We know that you and Howard Fish robbed a bank back in Nevada. He was holding the money for you, right? What, were you set to meet somewhere so you could split it? Is that when the cops caught up to you?"

"The cops caught up to that idiot, Howard." O'Hara spat the words. "The rat bastard squealed on me, so eventually, yeah, they caught up to me, too."

"But Howard was convicted, and you were cut loose. After that, he wouldn't tell you where he stashed the money, would he?"

O'Hara slammed a fist against the nearest cardboard box. "Said he was doing the time, so he should take all the profits. I never could get him to tell me. Then Howard died, and I couldn't find out anything about anything. Until a friend on the inside told me about some dope named Norman Applebaum. Said he'd been Howard's cellmate for a while, that he'd been Howard's friend."

"And you put two and two together." This made sense and I know it sounds crazy, but at a time like that, logic was exactly what I needed. My emotions were too brittle. They couldn't be trusted. Logic was the only thing that was going to save us. "Why did it take you so long to find Norman?"

"Why do you care?" O'Hara reached into his pocket, and for a second I was afraid he'd pull out the chloroform-soaked hankie again. Lucky for us, he was looking for a piece of paper. He unfolded it, and, peering through the gathering gloom, I recognized the phone number of Très Bonne Cuisine.

"Been in prison," he said. I guess that was the answer to my question. "Took me a while to find your friend Norman. He likes to change his name. But now that I have found him . . ." O'Hara waved the piece of paper in front of my eyes. "As soon as we get out of here and I can get a cell signal, you're going to make a phone call for me."

"You won't get that far."

I signaled Eve to keep quiet, but it was too late. She was upset and when Eve is upset . . .

There was nothing I could do but sit back and pray that she'd come to her senses.

"There are cops all over this place," Eve said. "They'll stop us before you can drive this thing out of here. They'll find us."

"They must be looking." I said this to myself more than to anyone else. Again, I was sticking with rational thought, and this was as rational as thoughts came. Jim and Norman knew I'd been on my way to find Eve and go to Claude Brooking's booth for a mandoline. When we didn't return in time for the cooking demonstration, they must have been worried. They must have come looking for us.

"Of course they did." O'Hara saw the wheels were turning inside my head. "Why do you think I had to make sure you two wouldn't make a sound? They came looking, all right. But that Scottish guy, and that other one, the guy in the suit—he must be a cop, I can tell them a mile away—neither one of them knew that Brooking guy. I told them I was him and they bought right into it. Didn't recognize me from any of my mug shots. Good thing I shaved my head since my last prison picture was taken, lost some weight, too. That cop, he never suspected a thing. I told them I sent you away with whatever it was you'd come for.

And they headed off again, looking for you." He glanced at his watch. "That was hours ago. Think they're nice and worried by now?"

I pictured Jim and Tyler searching the building. I imagined how frantic Jim would be when he couldn't find me.

I told myself not to go there or my panic would swallow me whole.

"So what's your plan?"

I don't think O'Hara expected me to be so objective about the whole thing. Which didn't oblige him to answer. He kicked his way through the gadgets that littered the floor, climbed into the driver's seat, and turned the key in the ignition.

"We're going to head outside," he said, carefully pulling the RV toward the garage-sized doors I saw across the now-empty exhibition floor. "And when we stop to check out, if one of you makes even so much as one little bit of a noise . . ." He took his knife out of his pocket and left it on the front seat next to him. "One of you makes a noise and I cut the other one. That's a promise."

We were quiet when he pulled out of the hall, and we were quiet while he drove along the D.C. streets looking for a place to pull over and make his phone call. He finally found it across Woodrow Wilson Plaza in the Federal Triangle Metro parking lot.

O'Hara turned off the RV, punched the numbers on his cell phone, and held it up to my ear. I wasn't surprised when Jim answered the Très Bonne Cuisine phone.

"Jim?" My voice was tinged with tears and I knew that would get me nowhere. And it would worry Jim. I swallowed my emotions. "Jim, it's Annie."

"Annie, darlin'. Are you—"

"I'm fine, Jim. Eve is fine. We're with Matt O'Hara."

I heard Jim repeat this news to whoever was in the room with him, and I wasn't surprised to hear Tyler asking for details.

I didn't have a chance to provide any before O'Hara took the phone away.

"Now you see I'm not playing games," he said, and I don't know if Jim was on the phone, or if he was talking to Tyler. "You tell your friend Norman I want my money, and I want it now."

Whoever he was talking to repeated the message, and replied, and O'Hara scowled. "Tomorrow morning's too late." He listened for a moment. "Yeah, yeah. I know. It's not easy to get your hands on that much cash. OK. Tomorrow. Six a.m. and not a moment later. Put the money in a brown paper sack and put the sack in the trash can nearest to the entrance of the Washington Monument. Oh, and if you're not there . . ." I didn't like the smile that pulled at the corners of O'Hara's mouth. "If the money's not there and if the cops are, your two lady friends here are going to be dead."

Eighteen

❖

MATT O'HARA WAS SMART ENOUGH TO KNOW THAT if he parked at the Metro station all night, either the Metro Transit Police or an officer from the D.C. Metropolitan force would come a-knockin' to see what the RV was doing there.

Too bad.

I would have welcomed a hero, no matter what the uniform. The way it was, by the time the sun was down and the city was quiet, my wrists ached from being taped and I was pretty sure my feet and ankles weren't getting nearly enough blood flow. I was thirsty. I was hungry. I was exhausted. Oh, yeah, I was scared to death, too.

We left the Metro station and drove through the city, and though the boxes piled in front of the windows on the sides of the RV made it impossible to see in that direction, if I twisted just enough, I could see out the front windshield. My neck muscles ached and my insides were flopping around as if they were filled with nervous butterflies. Still, I couldn't pull my gaze away. I watched familiar scenery shoot past: the White House, the Lincoln Memorial, the Washington Monument. At night with its monuments bathed in light, Washington, D.C., is especially beautiful, and seeing the sights I'd seen so many times before and always taken for granted, realizing I might not ever seen them again, tears stung my eyes. After a couple hours of driving around in what seemed an aimless pattern, O'Hara pulled into a no-tell motel somewhere near Sterling, jumped out, and left us on our own.

"Now's our chance," I hissed at Eve, checking out the window to see what O'Hara was up to. I watched him go inside a door marked *Registration* and for the first time since our ordeal began, some of the tension drained from my body. Even a couple moments out of O'Hara's sight—and away from that menacing knife he was always flashing—was a welcome relief. "We've got to make a move, Eve. We've got to try and escape."

"And we're going to do this how?" Eve is not usually this sarcastic, but I suppose I couldn't blame her. We were under some major stress here. Good thing she didn't realize that she'd bitten off all her lipstick. If she had any idea how pale she looked without it (or how her hair stuck up at a funny angle over her left ear) she would have been even more upset. She squirmed. "I can't move my hands. I can't even feel my feet. Annie, what are we going to do? You don't suppose he's—"

She didn't have a chance to finish. The door snapped open and Matt O'Hara clomped back onto the RV, kicking his way through discarded kitchen gadgets from the door over to where we sat.

"Can't expect me to stay in his hellhole all night," he said, though one glance out the window at the motel with its peeling paint and a parking lot that was largely empty and pocked with potholes made me wonder if he was talking about the RV or the motel. "But I'm not stupid, neither." He yanked at my hands, just to make sure they were bound good and tight, and when he was sure, he checked my legs, then Eve's legs and hands. "My room is right over there." He poked his chin toward the window of the nearest room. "And I'm a light sleeper. One peep out of either of you two and . . ." In what had become a cliché that would have been laughable if it wasn't so darned terrifying, he pulled out his knife and held it up and into a pool of neon orange light thrown by the motel's sign. Thanks to the piled boxes and the way he'd parked under a broken light, the rest of the RV was a mishmash of shadows. "You're going to stay here locked up good and tight."

"We're hungry." I tried to appeal to his humanity. "We're thirsty and—"

"Shut up." So much for humanity. "When I have my money, then you'll eat. And if I don't get my money . . ." I didn't like the way he smiled. He'd already opened the door of the RV and had started down the steps when he turned to us one last time. "By the way, I told the desk clerk inside that I was on my way to a dog show. That I was transportin' a couple pit bulls that were as ornery as a son of a bitch. You'd like the guy." There was that smile again, the one that made my skin crawl. "Keeps a pistol behind the counter. You know, just in case. I told him if he hears any noise from this here RV or sees the door open . . . well, I explained how these dogs of mine can sometimes get a little testy. I told him if he sees anything—anything at all—he should just start shootin'. Paid him fifty bucks to make sure he stays awake all night and watches, too." O'Hara tipped his head. "Good night, ladies. Enjoy every minute of it, because if your friend Norman don't have that money for me tomorrow bright and early . . . well, I wasn't bullshittin' when I told that fella on the phone that it just might be your last night on earth."

It wasn't until I heard the key turn in the door lock that I dared to breathe again.

"We've got to do something, Eve. And we've got to do it now."

"I dunno." Her eyes were round, and even in the semidarkness I could tell they were bright with unshed tears. "You heard what he said, Annie. If we make any noise, that clerk, he's going to—"

"Then we're going to have to make sure we're really quiet, aren't we?" Again, I tested the strength of the tape around my wrists. It didn't give an inch. "O'Hara, when he took my cell phone away, he threw it into a box in the bedroom," I reminded Eve. "If we can get to it . . ."

"How?" Eve's voice was clogged, and I knew it wouldn't take much for the dam to burst. I tried not to notice. If I did, I'd give in to my fear, too. "Annie, I can't move an inch. How are we going to—"

"But we can move an inch." To prove it, I scooted across the bench where I sat trussed like a Thanksgiving turkey. "Our hands are bound and so are our legs, but we can move a little. Maybe if we can just get to—"

I scooted again. Too far. I landed on my butt on the floor and in a heap of kitchen gadgets.

"Shh!" Her eyes wide, Eve darted a look at the door. "What if that clerk thinks we're pit bulls?"

"I didn't make that much noise," I muttered, and rightfully so. I couldn't have caused too much of a ruckus considering I landed on a pile of strawberry hullers. They were not the most comfortable cushion in the world and I wriggled off them and immediately sat on a corkscrew. I will not report what I said. What I said after I was done saying what I said was, "That's it! We can get out of here, Eve. I know we can."

She did not look convinced. "You gonna scoot your way to the door?" she asked. Her accent made her sound every inch the Southern belle. The sarcasm did not. I might have pointed this out if she didn't breeze right on. "And what are you going to do then? Kick at the door? What if that clerk with the gun—"

"He wouldn't shoot. Even if he thought there were dogs in here." This is what I wanted to believe so I made sure I packed enough oomph into the statement to convince us both. "People don't just go around shooting dogs. People like dogs."

I knew I'd made a mistake the moment the words were past my lips, but by that time, it was too late. I heard Eve swig her nose in unladylike fashion. "I miss Doc," she said. Her words were nearly drowned by her tears. "What if I never see him again? What if they don't find us right away and he's home for days and days by himself and—"

"No way am I going to let you go there." I said this with oomph, too. Eve needed oomph (or at least the good impression of it I was trying my darnedest to convey) to keep from being swallowed whole by her worries. "And besides, nothing's going to happen to Doc. Jim and Norman and Tyler already know we're missing. You don't think they're going to leave Doc alone, do you?" I knew in my heart this was true. For all his issues with Doc, Jim is not mean. He'd never abandon the little guy. "Doc is in good hands."

"I know." If only Eve sounded more convinced! "It's just that—"

"I know." I cut her off because I didn't need her to start a laundry list of her fears. My own list was already plenty long, and I couldn't risk adding to it. With that in mind, I felt around behind me and got poked with the business end of the corkscrew. My fingers were stiff and unresponsive, so it took a while, but I managed to hang on to that corkscrew long enough to prop it against the nearest cardboard box. I scuttled back against it.

"Annie, what in the world—"

I didn't bother trying to explain. Instead, I concentrated on using the corkscrew to poke holes in the duct tape. When I heard the first hole pop, I congratulated myself, but I didn't stop trying. If I could make holes all along the tape that bound my wrists . . .

An hour later—after knocking over and picking up the corkscrew a couple of dozen times—I had made a total of three small holes. My wrists were as confined as ever.

"At this rate, we're going to be here until next week," I grumbled, and peered through the dark to see if I could find anything that might be more useful.

I saw a mallet (not so good for slicing tape), an herb mincer (great for cutting, but these small, round gadgets use rollers to cut herbs into tiny pieces, and since I couldn't hold it and roll it across the tape, it wouldn't do me a bit of good), a pizza cutter (same problem as with the herb mincer), and—

"An oyster knife!" My fingers closed around the knife and I nearly choked on my tears of joy. "Stainless steal blade," I told Eve, "Santoprene handle. Santoprene is a thermoplastic compound. It's processed like any other plastic, but it's very durable. It can withstand hot and cold and—"

"Annie, this proves it. You have worked at Très Bonne Cuisine too long."

Eve was right, but I was too jazzed by my discovery to care. As I did with the corkscrew, I fumbled behind my back to wedge the knife between the floor and the nearest packing box. Then I got to work. I stabbed myself a couple of times, I broke two fingernails, and I sliced into my index finger. By the time another hour had passed, my fingers were slick with my own blood, but the tape on my wrists felt looser.

"You've got to hurry, Annie."

I didn't need the reminder. In the dark, it was hard to

say how long we'd been there or what time it might be, but I wasn't going to take any chances. The sooner I had my hands on my cell phone and called Jim, the happier I'd be.

"Annie!" Eve's warning stopped me cold. Her harsh whisper sent chills up my spine.

She craned her neck to see out the windshield. "The door of the office is opening, Annie. Somebody's coming out. Oh, Annie! It's a man. He's coming . . . he's coming this way!"

For a second, I thought about screaming and, really, I suppose it might have been the best option. But I thought about Claude Brooking, too, before I thought about that motel desk clerk. I thought about Matt O'Hara in his room, and I thought about that big ol' knife of his. If the desk clerk heard us and tried to help, he might suffer the same fate as Claude.

That, I couldn't even bring myself to think about.

"Shh." I signaled Eve to keep quiet. "What's he doing?" I whispered.

Leaning forward, Eve grunted. "Lighting a cigarette. Smoking a cigarette. Do you think he has his gun?"

"I think his gun is the least of our worries." Because I knew I could do it silently, I worked on the duct tape some more. "What time do you suppose it is?"

Through the gloom, I saw Eve shrug. "It must be late. Tyler, he must be real worried."

Kidnapping or no kidnapping, it was the perfect opening, and, Eve being the best friend a girl could ever have, I was duty bound to take it. It was hardly the time for girl talk, but spilling my guts (figuratively only) beat giving in to the panic that coursed through my veins, pumping my blood and making the cuts and nicks on my hands bleed even more.

"I talked to Tyler," I said, my voice far more casual than the situation warranted. "I don't know if you know this, Eve. I mean, I think if you did, you might have mentioned it. Or at least hinted at how you felt about it. Tyler, he told me that his engagement to Kaitlin—"

"It's been called off. I know that, Annie."

I turned as much as I was able so that I could watch her carefully without losing my vantage point in regard to the oyster knife. "You don't sound—"

"Happy?" Eve's laugh was watery. "It's kind of hard to be happy when we've been kidnapped and there's a vicious killer right outside our door who's standing there oh so casually smoking a cigarette and is probably thinking about blowing us away and—"

"He's a motel clerk." I couldn't afford for her to get even more agitated, and honestly, at this point, I wasn't sure what might send her over the edge. I balanced my tone somewhere between logic and giving Eve the equivalent of a verbal slap. "He's not a killer, Eve. He's not going to hurt us. He doesn't even know we're here."

"He's—" Eve hiccuped over her words. I saw her shoulders rise and freeze before they fell again. "Oh, thank goodness! He's going back inside."

Relieved, I sawed at the tape some more, but like the corkscrew had done so many times, the knife kept falling over. Grappling for it, positioning it, and getting it wedged against the box again took more time than we had. The precious minutes ticking away and my fingers trembling, I prayed the knife would stay in place this time, and got back to work. "I wasn't talking about you being happy about our situation, Eve. Of course you're not happy. Who could be happy about this?"

Stress or no stress, when it comes to love, Eve is cool under pressure. At least on the outside. She pretended she didn't know what I was talking about so I had no choice but to set her straight.

"I was talking about Tyler. I was talking about Tyler and Kaitlin's engagement. You don't sound happy about them calling it off. Not as happy as I thought you'd be. I figured you couldn't wait until—"

"Oh, Annie, have you completely lost your mind?" Eve squealed before she realized her mistake. If she could have used her hands, she would have slapped them over her mouth. Instinctively, she slouched further into her seat and stared at the windshield. When the clerk didn't come out of his office again and there was no sign of life from O'Hara's room, her sigh and mine overlapped.

"Have you completely lost your mind?" she hissed. "You can't really think—"

"Well, what else am I supposed to think? You and Tyler have been talking on the phone, and seeing each other, and who knows what else!"

"We haven't done that." I couldn't tell if Eve was disappointed by this or not. She shook her head. "Are you worried that I'm going to get back together with Tyler? Or are you worried that I won't?"

Interesting questions, and unusually insightful considering they came from Eve. I paused for a moment, thinking. "I'm worried that you'll get hurt again," I said, truthful because at this point there didn't seem to be any reason not to be. "He broke your heart."

"And he's said he's sorry."

"He said you weren't smart."

"He's apologized for that."

"He walked out on you."

"And he knows it was a mistake."

"You're going to get engaged again, aren't you?"

Even through the gloom, I saw Eve throw back her shoulders. "When I do," she said, "you will—as always—be the first to know."

"And if you do—"

"Annie, honey!" Eve's voice teetered on the brink of laughter as much as anyone's could, considering the circumstances. "You are getting way ahead of yourself. Right now, I'm just having a good time with the boy. Isn't that enough?"

"It never has been before. You always get engaged."

"Well, maybe I've learned my lesson." Even with the cover of darkness, I saw Eve glance away. "Maybe you have, too, recently, right?"

"You mean about Peter?" I would have laughed if it was funny. Nothing about what we were going through was funny. Including this new wrinkle in our conversation. "I told Peter to get lost," I said, then instantly felt guilty for taking so much poetic license, so I amended it. "Well, not in so many words. I wasn't mean or anything. But I did tell him that there was no reason for him to be hanging around. I told him I loved Jim."

I saw the flash of Eve's whiter-than-white teeth. "It's about time you realized it," she said.

"It's also about time for us to get out of here." I sawed at the tape some more. "Now that we know who's after Norman, we can help Tyler capture Matt O'Hara. We can give him a description and tell him about the RV he's driving. And we can tell him about Claude, too. Poor Claude." I shook off the thought. It was that or dissolve into a puddle of terrified mush. "Tyler will have everything he needs to find and arrest O'Hara. Then Norman will be safe."

Even as I said it, the last of the duct tape snapped. I can't begin to describe how good it felt, or how grateful I was to finally stretch my arms after so many hours. I shook out my hands, getting rid of the pins and needles, and I was just about to grab the oyster knife to get to work on the tape around my ankles, when I heard a sound outside the door.

"Annie!" Because she didn't know if I heard it, Eve whispered a desperate warning. I was way ahead of her. Moving awkwardly thanks to the tape around my ankles,

I pushed myself up, scrambling (well, it was more like waddling) to get back onto the bench across from Eve.

I made it just in time. When Matt O'Hara opened the door and a thin stream of anemic morning light made its way into the RV, I was right back where he'd last seen me, my now-free hands firmly behind my back.

"Thought you two would be sleeping." He made his way toward the driver's seat, kicking through the gadgets and debris. It was all I could do not to gasp when one kick sent a rolling pin wheeling across the floor. It knocked against the cardboard box where I'd just been sitting and I watched my oyster knife fall and carom off into the darkness.

"Then again, I guess I shouldn't be surprised." I'd been so busy watching my knife—and my hope of freedom—disappear, I reminded myself I couldn't afford to give the man cause for suspicion. I gulped and turned my attention back to O'Hara, who continued, "If I were you, I'd want to be awake for what just could be the last couple hours of my life, too."

Chuckling, he slid into the driver's seat. I closed my eyes, whispered a prayer of thanksgiving that he hadn't thought to check our hands again, and sat stiff and unmoving as we made our way to the Washington Monument.

It was early; the parking lot was deserted. As far as I could see, there was no sign of Jim, Tyler, Norman—or the money O'Hara was waiting for.

"You'd better hope your friend Norman's got a watch that isn't running slow." O'Hara checked his own watch. "He's got twelve minutes. No, wait. Eleven. He's got eleven minutes." O'Hara hauled himself out of the driver's seat and went to the door. "And so do you."

With that, he was gone. And I knew I had eleven minutes . . . well, less than eleven minutes, to finish freeing myself.

I was on the floor again in a flash and, using my hands to keep me upright, I did a sort of shuffling/ kneeling/scudding along the floor, desperately looking for the oyster knife.

No luck.

But I did find a cheese grater.

"Eighteen/ten stainless steel," I told Eve, grabbing for the grater and holding it up so she could see it. "Photo-etched blades, easy cleaning, large handle. Ultra coarse, coarse and fine grating surfaces, and—"

"Give it up, girlfriend!" One look at the cheese grater and Eve felt the same wallop of relief I did. I could tell because her words shimmered with hope. "Let's just get the hell out of here!"

I didn't need to be told twice. My stiff fingers working as furiously as they were able, I scraped the grater over the tape on my ankles and watched as duct tape shards floated to the floor like shiny snowflakes. Within a couple minutes, I was free.

I controlled a hoot of joy and jumped to my feet.

A second later, I was back down on the floor, rubbing my legs. "They're asleep," I moaned. "My legs aren't working." I didn't let that stop me. Ignoring the pain, I made my way over to Eve and got to work on the tape around her ankles and wrists.

We were sore, we were frightened out of our minds, we were barely able to move, but within minutes, we were poised at the door, ready to make a run for it.

I took one last look out the windows of the RV. I would have felt more confident if I could see Matt O'Hara. If I knew where he was and what he was doing. If he was too close to the RV . . .

I told myself not to go there and told Eve I'd count to three. By the time I got to two, my nervous energy got the best of me. I slammed open the door and, half running, half falling, I made it to the bottom of the steps. I waited there for Eve, who was no more steady on her feet than I was. I wished we could have taken longer to get our circulation moving, but at the first noise of the door opening, Matt O'Hara came running from around the other side of the RV.

One look at him—and the knife in his hand—and I didn't wait another instant.

"Go. Now." I yanked Eve down the steps and gave her a push in the direction of the monument. I followed right behind, running as fast as I could.

It wasn't fast enough.

My legs cramped, and I buckled.

"Don't stop!" When it looked as if Eve was going to come back to help me, I waved her on. "Go. Get help," I screamed, but as it turned out, I really didn't have to. No sooner were we out of the RV than I saw Jim sprinting in our direction. Tyler was right behind him and if I wasn't so busy running for my life (OK, it wasn't actually running, it was more like crawling quickly), I actually might have been amused by the look on his face. It was obvious both he and Jim were supposed to be lying low, waiting for the money drop to be completed. And just as obvious (at least to me) that there was no way on earth Jim was going to wait now that he saw me.

I pivoted and pulled myself to my feet so I could race toward him.

I would have made it, too, if Matt O'Hara's arm didn't snake around my waist. He jerked me off my feet.

"One step closer and she's dead." I couldn't see O'Hara, he was behind me, but I had no doubt he was flashing his knife. Jim screeched to a stop and I saw his face go pale. I also saw that Eve was safe with a uniformed police officer who'd come out from behind the monument where he'd been concealed. I told myself that was good. I told myself we'd celebrate both our escapes later. I told myself not to panic.

That was before I felt O'Hara's blade nick the skin of my throat.

"You're not going to arrest me," O'Hara growled. "I'm not going back to prison."

"No one is going to arrest you." Tyler had caught up to Jim, and he took a careful step forward, his hands out in the universal gesture that said *Take it slow, take it easy.* "You can leave, O'Hara. I'll let you leave. But only if Annie stays behind."

O'Hara dragged me back. "She's coming with me."

When he took another slow step toward us, my eyes were on Tyler, and when I slid my gaze to the side toward Jim, I saw that he was gone. Even my pumping adrenaline wasn't enough to fool me. This was a curious turn of events. So was the look that flashed across Tyler's face. One that told me in no uncertain terms that he was pissed.

That was right before I felt something slam into O'Hara.

He loosened his hold and I spun around.

The something in question was Jim, who'd outflanked O'Hara and tackled him from behind. O'Hara's knife flashed and I stifled a scream. It was all I had time to do before another uniformed cop put an arm around me and Tyler jumped into the fray. A gun beats a knife any day and no sooner had Tyler pointed his at O'Hara than he gave up.

"Drop the knife," Tyler instructed, and as soon as O'Hara had, Jim raced forward and took me into his arms.

"Ye're safe. Ye're all right. I've been so worried!"

Over Jim's shoulder, I watched Tyler slap the cuffs on Matt O'Hara. I saw Norman come around from the back of the RV, looking just as relieved as I felt. Eve was still a little unsteady on her feet, but she was walking over on the arm of a police officer.

Everyone I loved and cared about was safe; the mystery was solved.

Thank goodness! I could go back to where I started. Today *was* the first day of the rest of my life.

Nineteen

✖

BY THE NEXT WEEKEND, MOST OF THE EXCITEMENT had died down. Most of it.

There was still the whole issue of Norman paying back Howard Fish's ill-gotten money.

Not to worry, Norman could afford it and the high-priced attorneys he paid to handle his case were bound and determined to make the process as painless as possible.

As a matter of fact, in spite of the impending loss of a hundred and fifty thousand of his hard-earned dollars, things were actually looking up for Norman.

Remember how he was worried that his past might come back to haunt him, I mean the whole thing about him not being a French chef, but being a convicted criminal instead?

As fate would have it, once the newspapers got ahold of the kidnapping story and the truth was revealed about Norman's past, word raced through the D.C. cooking community and beyond. It was only the following Saturday and already Norman had been interviewed by a couple of major newspapers, two weekly magazines, and producers for a segment on *Dateline*. Big time. And getting bigger. Just that afternoon, a producer had called from the Food Network. There was talk of creating a show called *The Cooking Con*, and they wanted Norman to star.

Thankfully, all was well that ended well, and keeping that in mind, along with the fact that I could finally get back to work doing what I was supposed to be doing instead of either running a gourmet shop or working on a murder investigation, I flicked on the computer in my office at Bellywasher's and got down to business. There were plenty of invoices to enter into my QuickBooks program and plenty of financial details to catch up with.

I was already deep into it when my office door opened.

"There you are!" Jim stepped inside and closed the door. But not before he set something down on the floor behind him. I cursed myself for being so caught up in the minutiae of our checking account, I hadn't been paying more attention. Whatever the something was, it was something big. Like the size of a gallon of milk.

It also was supposed to be a surprise. At least that's what I figured, considering that Jim went out of his way to make sure he stood dead in front of it so I couldn't see it.

I wheeled my desk chair a little to the right.

He moved to his left to block my line of sight.

"What's going on?"

It was a logical question so he shouldn't have just shrugged.

I'd been in such a good mood since the day I thought I was going to die and didn't, I didn't even mind this little bit of teasing. But turnabout is fair play, right? I got up and strolled over to where Jim stood, hoping to distract him, but he was too quick for me. Just when I was about to take a look at what was on the floor behind him, he swiveled to block me.

I had no choice but to pull out all the stops.

I tipped my head and gave him a tiny smile. "I thought you were happy I wasn't hurt by Matt O'Hara."

"As happy as any man can be."

"I thought you were grateful that Norman is fine and back working at Très Bonne Cuisine. I thought you were thrilled to have me back here at the restaurant."

"Truer words were never spoken." Jim's smile was bright, but I couldn't help but notice it wavered a bit around the edges. As if he were nervous.

More curious than ever, I linked my hands around his waist and gave him a hug. There are few things I like better than hugging Jim. The fact that while I was doing it, I also got to take a peek behind his back was something of a bonus.

"A paint can!" As quickly as I hugged Jim, I pulled away. "You're being all mysterious about a paint can?"

"It's not just any paint can." To prove it, Jim reached down and picked up the gallon can of name-brand paint.

It looked like just any paint can to me.

"You see . . ." The can was heavy. He set it back down. "I've been doing my best to scrape the money together, but ye know how it is around here, Annie. There's always something that needs fixing, something that needs taking care of. So the paint . . . it doesn't really take the place of what I've been wanting to buy, but it conveys my message, you see."

"I don't."

He was exasperated with himself for not explaining things more clearly. "What I'm saying . . ." Again he lifted the paint can, and this time, he turned it around so I could see the front. He pointed.

I read. "Simplicity Beige." I thought the look I gave him spoke volumes about how I had not a clue what he was getting at. When he didn't respond to it, I forged ahead. "Nice choice of color. What are you painting?"

"What are you painting?" Jim held the can out to me.

I had never been given a can of paint before. I accepted it as graciously as I could, lifting it with both hands and holding it close to my body.

I looked from the can to Jim. "I'm painting . . . ?"

"The living room. The dining room. Our bedroom. Whatever you like. They have lots of different shades of beige. I thought we'd start with the more basic one and, from there, you could just let yourself go wild."

"Wild?" I'm not usually slow on the uptake but right about then, I was feeling as if my intellect was mired in quicksand. I stuck with the tried and true. "My landlord takes care of the painting. Besides, they don't allow renters to paint."

"So it's a good thing you won't be renting anymore."

By this time, I'd about had it. I set the paint can on the floor so I could prop my fists on my hips. "Would you mind telling me what you're talking about?"

"It isn't a ring, Annie. And I will buy you a ring. I swear. As soon as I'm able. But it is a promise that I'll love you forever. And it is a way to show I love you, and—"

The truth dawned and my words stuck in my throat. "Are you . . . are you asking me . . . ?"

"To decide how you want to paint every single room of my house, yes. To live there with me, yes. To love me forever, yes, yes, yes. Because that's how long I'll be lovin' you, Annie, darling. I'm asking ye to marry me. Will you?"

I couldn't get my answer out fast enough.

But then I guess I didn't have to.

My kiss was the only answer Jim needed.

RECIPES

✦

**Cranberry Almond Muffins
Perfect for Brainstorming
Sessions**

**Bellywasher's Tuesday Special
Fried Ravioli**

**Using a Zester Broiled Lamb Chops
with Lemon Caper Sauce**

**Cooking Class Jamaican
Sorrell Rum Punch**

**Raymond's Baked Bananas
and Blueberries**

**Norman's Apple(baum) Slices
with Maple Glaze**

**Jim's Celebration Tennessee
Whiskey Cake**

**Annie's Beige Icing—
to Celebrate a Very Special,
Very Beige Occasion**

**Middle of the Night
Chocolate Mousse**

Cranberry Almond Muffins
Perfect for Brainstorming Sessions
Makes 6 large

1½ cups all-purpose flour
½ cup sugar
1 teaspoon baking powder
¼ teaspoon baking soda
¼ teaspoon salt
2 large eggs

¼ cup melted butter
½ cup sour cream
½ teaspoon almond extract
¾ cup sliced almonds
½ cup cranberry sauce

Preheat oven to 375°. Line muffin pans with paper cups, or spray with cooking spray. Mix flour, sugar, baking powder, baking soda, and salt in a large bowl. Break eggs into another bowl. Whisk in butter, sour cream, and almond extract. When blended, stir in ½ cup almonds. Pour egg mixture over dry ingredients and fold in just until dry ingredients are moistened. Spoon 2 tablespoons of batter into each muffin cup. Top with 1 tablespoon of cranberry sauce, then with remaining batter. Sprinkle with almonds. Bake 30–35 minutes or until brown. Cool 20 minutes before removing from pans.

CRANBERRY SAUCE

1 bag fresh cranberries
1 cup sugar
1 cup port wine

Combine all ingredients and cook on medium heat until thickened. (You won't need it all for the recipe. Refrigerate leftovers and serve with dinner.)

Bellywasher's Tuesday Special Fried Ravioli

Note: to save time, you can use store-bought cheese ravioli. The frying process is the same. (Jim would never dream of cutting corners like this.)

1 package of wonton wrappers
½ cup mascarpone cheese (about 4 ounces)
¼ cup goat cheese (2 ounces)
Chives, about half a bunch, chopped
Salt and pepper to taste
Olive oil, for frying (Don't waste your expensive extra virgin olive oil here, the taste will be lost in the heat. Light olive oil is perfect, and it doesn't smoke as quickly.)
2 eggs, lightly beaten
2 cups Italian-style bread crumbs
¼ cup freshly grated Parmesan cheese
Marinara sauce, for dipping (store-bought or homemade)

TO MAKE THE RAVIOLI:

Wonton wrappers will dry out, so keep a damp paper towel over the open package as you work.

Mix the mascarpone, goat cheese, chives, salt, and pepper together in a bowl.

Take one wonton wrapper and with a pastry brush, brush water along the edges.

Place a small dollop of the cheese mixture in the center; be sure not to overfill, or your ravioli will burst in the hot water.

Place another wonton wrapper on top, and then press the edges together to form the ravioli. The water should act like glue and seal the edges. Be sure there are no holes, so that your cheese doesn't leak out during cooking.

Place finished ravioli aside and continue until you have used all the wonton wrappers.

Cook ravioli in batches. In boiling, lightly salted water, cook the ravioli for about a minute or two. When the ravioli rise to the surface and the wonton wrappers have become translucent, they're done!

TO FRY THE RAVIOLI:

Pour olive oil into large fry pan, about 2 inches. Heat over medium heat for about 5 minutes, or until a thermometer reaches 352°F.

Put the eggs and the bread crumbs in separate bowls. Working in batches, dip ravioli in egg to coat completely, allowing excess to drip back into the bowl. Dredge ravioli in the bread crumbs, and shake off the extra. Place the ravioli aside, and continue until all your ravioli are coated.

Fry the ravioli in batches, turning occasionally, about 3 minutes. You want them to be a golden brown. Transfer to a paper towel and continue until all the ravioli are done.

Top the fried ravioli with Parmesan and serve with marinara sauce for dipping.

Using a Zester Broiled Lamb Chops with Lemon Caper Sauce
Serves 2

two 1½-inch-thick loin lamb chops

Salt and pepper

1 tablespoon unsalted butter

1 teaspoon freshly grated lemon zest

1 teaspoon drained bottled capers

1 tablespoon fresh lemon juice

Pat the lamb chops dry and sprinkle them with salt and pepper to taste. Broil them on the rack of a broiler pan under a preheated broiler about 4 inches from the heat for 6 minutes. Turn the chops, broil them for 4–8 minutes more. Turn off heat and let chops stand for 5 minutes. While the chops are standing, in a small saucepan melt the butter and stir in the zest, the capers, the lemon juice, and salt and pepper to taste. Transfer chops to 2 plates and pour sauce over them.

Cooking Class Jamaican Sorrell Rum Punch

Makes about 8 cups

2 ounces (about 1½ cups) dried sorrel calyxes (also called jamaica or hibiscus)

Two 1-inch cubes of peeled fresh ginger, chopped fine

3 whole cloves

5¾ cups water

¾ cup sugar

1½ cups amber rum

2 cups ice cubes, or to taste

Lime and orange slices for garnish

In a heat-proof bowl combine the sorrel, ginger, and cloves. In a saucepan bring 5 cups of the water to a boil. Then pour water over the sorrel mixture, and let the mixture steep for 4 hours or overnight. While the mixture is steeping, in a small saucepan bring the remaining ¾ cup water and the sugar to a boil, stirring until the sugar is dissolved. Let the syrup cool. Strain the sorrel liquid into a pitcher, discarding the solids, stir in the sugar syrup, the rum, and the ice cubes, and garnish the punch with the lime and orange slices.

Raymond's Baked Bananas and Blueberries

6 bananas, peeled and sliced lengthwise
1 cup fresh blueberries (though you can also use frozen)
1 cup pecans, chopped
½ cup brown sugar
1 cup orange juice
Butter, sliced into small pieces
Whipped cream, for topping (if desired)

Place the bananas in a buttered dish. Sprinkle with blueberries and chopped pecans, then brown sugar. Pour the orange juice over top. Dot with butter. Bake in a 350° oven for 20 minutes. Serve hot, topped with whipped cream if desired.

Norman's Apple(baum) Slices with Maple Glaze
Serves 6

4 Golden Delicious apples (about 1½ pounds)

2 tablespoons unsalted butter

3 tablespoons Grade B maple syrup (or Grade A maple syrup flavored with 1 drop maple extract, or to taste)

1 tablespoon water

1 teaspoon fresh lemon juice

¼ teaspoon cinnamon

Salt

Peel and core apples and cut into ¼-inch-thick slices. In a 12-inch heavy skillet heat butter over moderately high heat until foam subsides and sauté apples, turning them, until golden and tender. Stir in maple syrup, water, lemon juice, cinnamon, and a pinch of salt and cook, stirring, until apples are glazed.

Jim's Celebration Tennessee Whiskey Cake

2 cups all-purpose flour
½ teaspoon nutmeg
6 eggs, separated
1 cup butter, softened
2 cups sugar
½ cup Jack Daniel's whiskey
2½ cups raisins
1½ cups pecans, chopped

Place flour in dry skillet. Cook over medium heat while stirring until it is pale brown in color. Stir in nutmeg and set aside. In small bowl beat egg whites until stiff. Set aside. In large mixing bowl cream butter and sugar until light and fluffy. Add egg yolks and beat well. Add whiskey and stir to blend. Beat in flour, then fold in egg whites, raisins, and pecans. Pour into greased and floured 9-inch tube pan. Bake at 300° for 2½ hours, or until toothpick inserted in center comes out clean.

Annie's Beige Icing—
To Celebrate a Very Special, Very Beige Occasion

1 cup brown sugar

½ cup water

2 beaten egg whites

1 teaspoon vanilla

¼ teaspoon cream of tartar

Boil sugar and water until it spins into a thread. In the meantime, beat egg whites until they're frothy. Pour hot syrup over beaten egg whites and ¼ teaspoon cream of tartar. Add vanilla. Beat until it holds a peak. Frost a cake and celebrate a very special occasion.

Middle of the Night Chocolate Mousse
Serves 8

2 cups chilled heavy cream
4 large egg yolks
3 tablespoons sugar
1 teaspoon vanilla
7 oz fine-quality bittersweet chocolate (not unsweetened), chopped

Garnish: lightly sweetened whipped cream
Special equipment: an instant-read thermometer

Heat ¾ cup cream in a 1-quart heavy saucepan until hot. Whisk together yolks, sugar, and a pinch of salt in a metal bowl until combined well, then add hot cream in a slow stream, whisking until combined. Transfer mixture to saucepan and cook over moderately low heat, stirring constantly, until it registers 160°F on thermometer. Pour custard through a fine-mesh sieve into a bowl and stir in vanilla.

Melt chocolate in a double boiler or a metal bowl set over a pan of simmering water (or in a glass bowl in a microwave at 50 percent power 3 to 5 minutes), stirring frequently. Whisk custard into chocolate until smooth, then cool.

Beat remaining 1¼ cups cream in a bowl with an electric mixer until it just holds stiff peaks. Whisk ¼ of cream into chocolate custard to lighten, then fold in remaining cream gently but thoroughly.

Spoon mousse into 8 (6-ounce) stemmed glasses or ramekins and chill, covered, at least 6 hours. Let stand at room temperature about 20 minutes before serving.

COOKS' NOTES:
• Mousse can be chilled up to 1 day.
• Many of the fine-quality bittersweet chocolates sold at supermarkets typically contain 50 to 60 percent cocoa solids. If you choose chocolate with a higher percentage, your mousse may be slightly denser.